I0817792

PIERCING MAYBE

ALSO BY DAN CRAY

Mother Tongue

Friends From 4 A.M.
(Short Stories)

Soaring Stones
(Nonfiction)

PIERCING MAYBE

DAN CRAY

Published by Third Quandary Books
An imprint of Delcominy Creations, LLC
531 Main St., Ste. 231
El Segundo, CA 90245

Publisher's Note: This is a work of fiction. Names, characters, places, and incidents are a product of the author's imagination. Locales and public names are sometimes used for atmospheric purposes. Any resemblance to actual people, living or dead, or to businesses, companies, events, institutions, or locales is completely coincidental.

Cover by Carl Graves, Extended Imagery
Concept edits: David Bjerklie

Piercing Maybe/ Dan Cray -- 1st ed.
Library of Congress Control Number: 2018908986
ISBN 978-1-940317-13-7 (hardback) | 978-1-940317-12-0 (ebook)

For Jane

PIERCING MAYBE

PART ONE

PROXY

ONE

Lanai

Conception took place in a hammock.

Andra Barger kept herself unseen, trying not to watch as the couple finished, calmed, cuddled. After three years on the job she thought she'd pretty much seen it all, but this insatiable pair almost made her wish she was still interested in dating.

Almost.

She adjusted her sarong and inhaled some Kauai, awaiting confirmation. Palm silhouettes swayed and she swayed with them. Ocean currents massaged the shore near the couple's lanai, she mimicked them with a tilt of her head and a rush of her cascading, coconut hair, wondering why this was the first time she'd noticed that her training had become rote response. The North Shore breeze felt balmy so she responded, curtailing sweat, hormones, scent. Even at 2 a.m., with the world near-dormant, Andra maintained her defenses.

A striped band, one of two stacked above her right ankle, emitted a pale white glow. *Conception confirmed.*

She glanced at the couple, still entwined in the now-motionless hammock. Slipping out of her flip-flops, she stepped from the shadows.

Even on the open lanai, under moonlight with her bare legs extending from the sarong, Andra remained near-invisible. She strode to the hammock, her leg movements confined to knees-and-down, graceful footfalls silent atop the wood deck. The patio reeked of alcohol, and worse, as she approached. The couple were inebriated, spent, half asleep, in their own world. The woman's left hand dangled over the hammock's edge—how easy could it get? Hot air balloons, pools, backseats, those were the difficult jobs. Here, out in the open—easy pickins. She wondered whether her own mother had made things so convenient for whoever diminished her.

The thought made Andra hesitate. *This is wrong, this is wrong, this is wrong.* She swallowed, hard, while mashing her thumb against the jagged setting on her pearl ring, trying to regain focus. There was a time for regrets; looming over the target was not it.

She extended her left index finger. One dab of glittering gel, one brief smear against the woman's dangling palm, and it was over. The gel turned gold, then sunk into the woman's skin as if the palm was quicksand. Andra nudged a tiny flip-cap on her ring, sealing the gel supply, and returned to the shadows.

The ankle bracelet no longer glowed.

Her chest felt hollow and her eyes close to tears, same as at the end of every job. She placed a hand below her belly button, massaging, wondering... questioning. *It's okay, the woman's baby won't die.* Still, a zygote could develop into much more... so very much more. Now the woman's child would just be... well, the same as everyone else. Sure, diminishing served a purpose, but did that really justify...

A series of thudding sounds made her look up in surprise. Footsteps, she realized... heavy, commanding footsteps, coming up the stairs on the lanai's far end. *Now?* she thought. *At 2 am?*

Then she saw who it was and knew the couple in the hammock weren't the only ones who had gotten lucky that night. She pulled her sarong close around her shoulders and vanished into the shadows, knowing she hadn't just finished her job.

She'd finished it just in time.

Boots banged against the deck, knocks on a nonexistent door.

"Clear."

A man's voice, firm but uncertain.

The hammock stirred, but only the woman pushed herself up far enough to peek out. She had narrow shoulders and lean arms. Her auburn hair hung to one side, tangled and mashed like a spider's broken web. The edges of her lips flaked and her tongue looked pasty as she tried licking them, falling back into the hammock as she did. Bleary eyed, she squinted at the three tall silhouettes on her lanai. The first stepped forward, stubbled male cheeks and narrow green eyes materializing in dappled moonlight.

He ignored the woman, his eyes searching the shadows.

"No... I don't think we're clear at all," he said, his voice in the tractor-scraping-asphalt realm.

He nudged the woman back into the hammock, caressed her softly, and waited as alcohol, passion's glow, and 2 a.m. exhaustion worked their magic. Then he looked up.

"Somewhere within fifty yards," he said.

The silhouetted figures with him fanned out, one down the steps, the other over the lanai's forward rail, neither with silence or grace. Floodlight beams burst from their positions, illuminating palms and the sandy shoreline. The beams became a motion sickness test, wobbly from their user's movements, fuzzy from surf spray.

The stubbled man didn't move. He stood, studied, felt. Stepping further into the moonlight he scratched at his whiskers then smoothed his tattered Henley shirt. His hair seemed stringy in the moonlight, matching a beard textured like late-season pumpkin vines. A pocketed cell phone vibrated but he didn't reach for it. He looked thick with clothes, especially for Kauai, and they were as dark and leathered as his skin. A Buddha belly jiggled as he deliberately scuffed his boots on the wooden lanai.

After fidgeting with everything from his buttons to his earlobes, he pulled a matchbox from his khakis, removed a match, lit it, then tossed it down. The flame flared against the wooden deck but a boot-stomp kept it from catching. A second flame, flare, and stomp followed, then a third. The stubbled man made it seem absentminded. He opened and shut his mouth repeatedly, sometimes at weird angles, even though he wasn't saying anything.

By the tenth match several minutes had passed. Floodlights still danced across the beach, the planters, the lanai's underbelly, seemingly passing across every shadow.

Andra swayed with the palms, mimicked the sounds, muted the scents. She was good but floodlights were floodlights. She cringed as the beams flashed above her, then to one side, then off to the other. The searchers were becoming familiar with the area, recognizing the dense shadows from the palms, the surf from the sky. Night was no longer a single shade, the search no longer haphazard. The men knew if they aimed at a particular shadow just right...

A beam hit the darkened base of a fern next to Andra, illuminating her foot amid the root tangle. She slowed her jumping heart, but to her it still seemed so loud she was certain the entire island must hear the beating.

The search stopped, the men scrutinizing the palms, the roots, her half-concealed foot.

Then the beam moved on, away from Andra. She exhaled softly, but knew the beams were still active and the men were approaching her position, using their lights to scan the area as they advanced. She glanced around, searching for better concealment, or a weapon, or better yet a hidden path that could lead her away.

Nothing.

She considered her situation: a slender woman with no fighting skills, no weapon, no jagged finger rings, no shoes, and no clothes aside from her breezy sarong and the underlying swimsuit. Her knack for remaining calm was a point of pride, but hiding from a Mechen Klav security detail was very different from the occasional angry couple discovering her in the act of diminishing.

And if the rumors are true, the Klav want to find me right away. Not because I've done anything wrong, but because they're worried I might.

A beating wasn't going to stop that. Mutilation, dismemberment, rape... she clenched her teeth, terrified yet furious, determined not to let any such horrific assaults sway her convictions, or her opportunities for making some changes. Of course, the Mechen Klav officers would know that as well. Would they dispense with the horrors and simply kill her?

Highly possible, she decided, leaving her only one choice.

One I hate using.

Another beam flashed, this one on a coconut hanging some ten feet above her head. She felt exposed, her head and shoulders no longer in the pitch dark, still sheltered beneath fronds but likely visible to sharp eyes.

There weren't any sharp eyes on the beach. The beam moved on.

Again Andra exhaled. She heard the men approaching now, maybe twenty feet from her position. Right arm raised to shoulder height, fingers extended in the defensive position her grandmother had taught her so many years ago, she held her breath, waiting.

The light beams never came close. The men trudged past.

Then something dropped into the fronds next to her, snapping them with a huge crack. The subsequent crash, as the object hit the dried scrub below, seemed louder than the ocean waves. Whatever it was, it was large... bowling ball large, or so it seemed in the darkness.

The beams whirled. Just like that, Andra was floodlit... as was the fallen coconut near her feet.

The two men bounded over, objects—guns maybe?—in each hand. They shouted orders, hands-behind-head-type instructions, but she knew they weren't cops. She rose from her crouch, sarong draped loosely, right hand still positioned where her hair met her left shoulder.

I hate this, I hate this, I hate this.

Whatever the men were expecting, they seemed surprised to find her... probably an advantage, she supposed. They instructed her to walk forward, she did. They told her to remain still, she did. But her hands never went behind her head, and she never turned around. They noticed, and ordered her to comply.

Instead she let her mind glaze over, tilted her head, and made eye contact. Her irises felt strained as she flexed her eyelids the way her grandmother trained her, manipulating her eyes, expanding and contracting her pupils imperceptibly fast, dozens of times per second, so rapid she felt air stirring against her eyelashes.

The Mechen Klav officers stood motionless, transfixed.

Disgusted with herself, Andra walked right between them, pausing only as they lowered their floodlights and angled their bodies to let her pass. She hated them, not only for coming after her like this but for placing her in a position where she had to rely on skills best left forgotten, methods that only existed so one set of people could wield power over another. *Techniques created to help diminish pregnant mothers*, she thought, appalled.

She scanned her surroundings, searching for shrubs, hoping to find better density amid the palm trunks. Moments later she was in deep shadow, re-hidden among an adjacent grove.

The men still hadn't moved.

They'd come around any second now, most likely with mild headaches. *Because of the eye flicker*, Andra knew. *Because of the meditative alpha state it induced...*

one of the same repulsive, Old World tricks that make me a good diminisher.

Atop the lanai, the stubbled man couldn't see what had happened but apparently knew something wasn't right. Andra watched as he lit and stomped several matches, deep in thought. Eventually he lit yet another match but held it for a moment before letting it drop a couple feet from the hammock.

"This one doesn't get smashed," he called out.

Andra knew the statement was meant for her, not his men. She watched as he dropped another match, lit a few more, dropped them alongside one another. They flared atop the wood. Several fizzled.

"Plenty more," the man said.

His companions shook off their trance and returned to the deck, their body movements slumped, light beams bobbing atop their toes. Their stubbled leader shook his head. A few matches later, the deck finally caught fire. The flames were small, illuminating the man's boot, but licked at the surrounding wood, spreading in slow, quarter-inch segments.

"Lot of humidity," the man called. "But the hammock isn't too far away. You gonna' let the nice couple burn?"

He dropped a couple more matches, watching them ignite within the deck-top flames. As the pyre reached campfire level, deck boards spraying sparks and paint shriveling back along the corners, he backed away. The other two men were already down the steps, pulling back.

"Point of no return, lady," the man shouted, over the crackling flames. "Patience and shadows is a nice mantra, but another minute or so and you won't—"

Gushing water hit him in the face, knocking him over, then redirected to the base of the flames. The facsimile hiss of a thousand snakes erupted then died away. Flames and embers disappeared, steam in their place.

"Not the way to roll, Sandoval."

The arriving voice was male and commanding, yet had a slight drawl. Andra suppressed an involuntary heartbeat increase as recognition hit.

Sandoval, confused at hearing a man's voice from somewhere behind the steam and the spraying water, wiped the drips from his stubbled cheeks.

"Wade? What the hell, man? I was this close to—"

"To what, frying up a couple lovebirds?"

The water dropped away. Thick steam still rose from the charred beams but gaps had formed, exposing two bare forearms supporting a hose. As the steam thinned a man's angular face appeared, soot gathered in a cleft near his chin. He was everything high fashion wasn't: shell necklace over a black tee, fingerless biker gloves, patterned jeans and canvas shoes. Cop-walking across the deck, elbows held wide, he tossed the hose down and offered Sandoval a gloved hand.

Sandoval ignored it and pushed himself up, his hair and clothes soaked.

"Now listen, Wade," he said, shaking the water from his arms. "She already jacked the woman, hear? So there wasn't no danger of the job going south. But if we don't apply some pressure, let her know the council's got chops, she's gonna' screw everything up."

Wade stuck a toothpick between his teeth and began chewing. "Thought the Cinüe don't knock heads," he said, his mild southern drawl more obvious this time.

Sandoval spat.

"We do when there's a wildcard," he said. "And I don't need to tell you she's about to become one big-ass wildcard. But I guess maybe you're a wildcard too, huh."

Wade chewed his toothpick.

"You *know* what that woman just did," Sandoval said. "People won't accept anything less than her continuing to do the same thing, year after year, no questions asked—and making sure the laws mandating it remain in place. It's the only thing keeping this world in one piece. Now, does she understand that or not?"

Wade continued chewing. "This one don't need your message," he said. "This one knows what's at stake."

"Yeah? Well if she knows, why'd she ignore the rules and do her own sweet thing last year? Why'd the council order us to keep tabs on her? Hell, why does she make so much effort to dodge us?"

Sandoval stomped down the three lanai steps, pausing for a long glare at Wade on each one. "I thought you understood keeping peace means setting some examples," he said. "You really this clueless?"

The toothpick cracked. Wade flicked it onto the deck.

"Don't need clues," he said. "Just facts."

Sandoval scoffed. "You didn't see me here," he said.

"Back atcha."

Sandoval shook his head, then gestured to his companions. The three men tromped into the Kauai dark. Wade watched the men leave, then rolled up the hose and spent the next half hour doing what he could to clean the deck. The couple in the hammock never stirred.

"You're clear, they're out cold," he said, to the darkness off the lanai's edge.

Emotion welled in Andra's chest, but she resisted.

"Yoo hoo—mail's here," Wade tried.

He searched the shadows.

"It's important," he added. "But you already know that, right? You've heard the rumors."

I'm not here, Andra answered, to herself.

"Would it help if I buy you a shave ice?" Wade called. "Pineapple-mango, ice cream at the bottom?"

Andra swayed with the palms, mimicked the sounds, muted the scents.

"C'mon, I can't be spotted with you so time's running out," Wade said, his shell necklace clinking as he walked from one rail to the next, peering into the darkness. "You need to grab this mail now."

She let the palms, ocean, and balmy breeze serve as his answer.

"I mean it, Andra, this one's urgent. But hey, don't let me risking life and limb to deliver the most important mail of your life affect your decision or anything."

One palm silhouette went still.

Wade sighed. "Annie, please... no judgments, no baggage. Just the mail, I promise."

A silent moment passed. Andra collected herself. *Why not*, she decided, and stepped onto the lanai. Her sarong was island-thin but she didn't care. She lost her modesty when she lost her twenties.

"Jeez, Wade, helluva time," she said, readjusting the garment.

Wade shrugged. "Not really a nine-to-five guy, darlin.' "

An understatement, Andra thought, looking him over. His appearance personified the local "hang loose" attitude, even though he wasn't an islander: hair a perfect mess, chiseled cheeks an anime artist's dream. He chain-chewed toothpicks, which she hated, and acted as if the world operated on his schedule, which she hated even more. If not for his confidence, and the way he could say in two words what took others twenty...

She reined her thoughts. *One disaster with Wade was enough,* she reminded herself. *Never again.*

"Another one bites the dust, huh," he said, gesturing to woman in the hammock.

"Excuse me: you said no judgments."

He winked. "Just facts. Nice eyelash move with the beach boys. Haven't seen you work that one for awhile."

Andra angled her head, annoyed. "Can we get this done, please? I don't see an envelope. What kind of mail is this?"

Wade studied her, his eyes saying far more than his mouth.

"The kind we've wanted for years," he said. "But you already knew the invite was coming, and the uproar it's caused. Who tipped you about the Klav's plan to play hardball? Not your bro, he'd be thrilled."

"None of your business."

"Ah. Your mother, then. Figures."

He looked around, as if Sandoval might still be watching, then reached into his coat pocket and removed a slender object.

"Not out here," he told her, keeping the object covered. "Inside."

She glanced at the motionless hammock, shrugged, and followed Wade through an open doorway. The living room was lit by nightlight, enough to see the worn sofa and stained chairs of a rental home, but not much else. Wade stopped her before she could flip a light switch.

"Won't need it for *this* mail," he said, showing her the object.

She leaned in close. "A candlestick? You call that mail?"

He scratched his chin while nodding. "Light it. Probably been awhile since you've had a candlelit conversation."

Andra looked at him, irritated.

"Wrong time, wrong woman," she said, pushing his hand—candle still inside—against his gut.

Wade seemed amused. He reached inside his coat, fumbling for something.

"Never a wrong time," he said, flicking a lighter, igniting the candlewick. He shoved the candle at Andra, who took it in her hand without really knowing why.

"My job's done," Wade said. "What you do with the results, up to you. Though you know where I stand on all this... and where *you* stand, if you'll ever stop listening to your mother and move forward."

He returned the lighter to his jacket and brought forth a finger-sized, T-shaped object that he held to his lips like a whistle. Andra didn't hear a sound other than her own bristling emotions.

"After everything we went through, you still don't understand that I *have* moved forward?" she said. "That I can never, ever risk another pregnancy again?"

Wade walked back onto the lanai and started to say something, then stopped short.

"Can't comment," he finally said. "Not without breaking my promise."

She scoffed. "Wouldn't be a first."

He nodded. "Or a last."

A rumble erupted from the darkness just off the lanai, some sort of animal noise. Whatever it was sounded beefy yet smooth, a baritone velvet with a chest-reverberating purr at the finish. Andra couldn't place the sound to the specific Cinüe animal, but she knew enough to understand it meant Wade had broken another rule.

"Those aren't allowed," she muttered.

Wade flashed a devilish smile.

"Depends on who's doing the allowing," he said, winking. "You ever need to drop a note to anyone, you give me a call." He swung his legs over the lanai's rail and disappeared into the darkness, the baritone velvet purr fading along with him.

Andra was about to snuff the candle when its fragrance reached her nostrils. Unseen hands gripped her skull, passed through, squeezed her brain. Staggering, she screamed, certain her head was about to be crushed to bits.

TWO

Rupture

It's like having drain cleaner in my nasal passages.

Andra swallowed hard then gulped air, desperate to overcome the sensation of hands squeezing her head, trying but failing to keep herself from throwing up. With the crook of one arm covering her nose, she reached out with the other, holding the candle as far away as possible. The very ordinary looking, creme-colored wax produced an acidic, rotted, burned fragrance so repugnant she could barely focus on where she was, or why.

She vomited again then staggered onto the beach, trying to get as far as she could from the lanai and any of the nearby homes. Finally she dropped to her knees and jabbed the candle, wick-first, into the sand, extinguishing it.

Ten minutes later, the odor long removed by the island winds, she was still trying to clear the smell from her head.

What the hell did Wade bring me?

But she already knew the answer. This was a *necrospondence*—a message sent from the very heart of existence. Other diminishers received them too... rarely, but it was known to happen in urgent circumstances. She shuddered, remembering their stories, knowing that despite Wade suggesting this was the kind of mail she had always wanted it was nothing of the sort.

And the smell is only the beginning.

For a moment, a long moment, she considered ignoring the candle. But that wasn't really an option, not in her line of work. So she slowly rose to her feet, taking deep breaths, the unlit candle still in her right hand. Closer inspection revealed two additional matches stuck to the side, half-buried in the wax.

"Guess I'm not the only one who needs more than one shot at this," she said, to herself.

She looked up at the stars, crisp against the cosmic shroud, then down at the knee-printed sand a few inches from her toes. The message, she knew, could be from above or below, or from just about anywhere—not the kind of message that the human body absorbs easily.

The lanai was still only a few yards away so she moved further up the beach, away from the homes and into a breezy, palm-lined cove where waves lapped at eroding, volcanic rock. The area was sheltered, not only from view but from scent, possibly even from sound. The cove would help contain it... a thought that made her more nervous than she already felt.

Taking a deep breath, she removed a match, struck it, and held it to the wick.

Maybe there's too much wind for it to catch.

But the breeze acted more like fuel, and the wick seemed eager. It ignited like a small torch, finger-long with a loud rip, melting the creme-colored wax into puddles. The horrific odor erupted, overwhelming Andra, knocking her straight back into the sand. She gasped and cried out, loudly this time, as she felt the fumes overwhelm her nose, throat, chest. Her lungs ached; she wasn't so much breathing as choking, gulping pockets of stagnant air then expelling them in disgust. Her head swam, her brain pounded as bad as her lungs, even her toes throbbed.

Cursing, she forced herself into a sitting position, determined to get the message and be done. But the odor was too overwhelming, the pounding in her lungs too much. Raising the candle above her, she readied a throw, imagining how nice it would feel to toss the candle into the sea and extinguish it forever.

Then she looked into the flame and stopped. Her reeling mind slowed. The scent—though still repugnant—faded into the background. She stared, transfixed, as the flame's rising heat waves rippled the air, making the moonlit ocean shimmer even more than before. The hot air currents above the candle weren't just lifting, they were... digging, she decided... etching into the oxygen, into the tranquil vista, forming a small, convex gap. The ripples widened as she watched, parting the scene into a pearlescent, crescent-shaped rupture.

And there's something moving inside.

Her burning lungs no longer mattered. This, she guessed, was a look into something else... some *thing*, or some place, that she might never see again. Curious, she brought the candle closer, right up to her nose, peering inside the convex rupture just above the flame.

It was like peeking inside a Faberge egg, only the "egg" could spy upon another place. Pearl colorations clumped at the edges, then gave way to the streaks and squiggles of a dense forest, shy in depth but borderless to an unseen left and right. Artificial sunset streamed through the woods like angled girders, anchoring countless, canopied redwood trunks to shadowed, boulder-strewn terrain.

This time, no sign of movement.

Andra kept staring, convinced she had seen something shuffle past—a human silhouette maybe?—but the gap remained empty.

Seconds passed, still nothing... except intense pain in her right hand, she suddenly realized. Looking down, she saw the candle was half its original size, its fiery wax melting over the top of her hand, covering it. She tried dropping the candle or throwing it down, but couldn't. A portion of the wax had already hardened, somehow bonding it to her hand despite her best effort to break away. She clawed at it with fingernails and pounded at it with knuckles, no luck.

The rupture remained stationed above the flame regardless of her movements, dragged this way and that as she tried ditching the candle. Desperate, she blew at the flame but watched in horror as it re-flared each time it went out, like a birthday gag candle gone terribly wrong. She stuck the candle against the volcanic rock, then into sand, again with no results. The wax seemed to get hotter as it layered, sealing the inner heat from any exposure to cool air. Horrified, Andra ran toward the ocean, candle and rupture moving right along with her as her hand burned beneath the wax, her own charring flesh adding to the already sickening aroma.

Then she caught herself mid-yell as she again saw something move within the rupture.

It's... a limb, she realized. *An unnaturally long, narrow, reddish arm, just hovering in the woods.* Horrified, she noticed the arm's glowing, wax-covered, enflamed hand... a hand that looked exactly like... *like my own hand?*

Her legs came to an unconscious halt as the ramifications hit home. The red limb, and the hand, began dancing about the rupture's woodland interior in wild fashion... and Andra's arm responded, mirroring the movements as if locked in a muscular twitch. She tried holding her arm but couldn't stop the movement, not even with her left hand clamped to the right for extra support. She yelled in frustration, and pain, agonized as her right hand burned, and danced, the fingers angling into different positions with each movement.

All motion suddenly stopped. The red limb and hand went still, her forearm and hand too. Then it began again. Andra yelled out, pain-wracked and frustrated. Her hand and arm mimicked their eerie counterparts, bobbing and dancing, fiery hot wax notwithstanding.

Through the pain she saw the candle was now a stub, close to burning out... but she also saw something else: the hands, her own and the one within the rupture, were not only moving in a pattern but in the same pattern as before.

The motion stopped, then restarted once more. Again, same finger and arm movement patterns... something familiar. Something she learned during diminisher training...

It's sign language! The movements are the message!

She gritted her teeth, steeling herself to the pain of her own hand burning beneath the fiery wax, trying to memorize the finger motions, the patterns, assembling them together.

Sugar Dandruff Council convening in three days for renewal vote. You'll be my proxy. – Asantha Cooray VIII

Andra gasped; the rumors were true. But why on Earth would Asantha Cooray, the Cinüe's moldy oldie leader, want *her* to serve as proxy? *That makes no sense—I'm not even a natural Cinüe,* she thought. *And on the Sugar Dandruff Council, no less?* The council was the Cinüe mechanism for determining whether the diminishing program is renewed or suspended. She couldn't think of any reason why Cooray, the so-called "mother of diminishing," would appoint a troublemaker and noted dissenter to a council that only meets once every fifty years... and where a vote in favor was, unofficially, required.

The messaged "played" again, painfully so. Finally Andra couldn't bear it any more. She yelled out in agony, wringing her hand, hoping to fling the candle away. After three tries the candle, now just a stub, burned out, sending one final wisp of the ghastly smoke into Kauai's air. The heat ripples thinned, then faded. Andra didn't see any sign of the limb within the rupture, which was already narrowing. As the hot air dissipated the rupture vanished altogether.

Andra, gasping for fresh air and still in agony from the hot wax burning her hand, dashed for the ocean. She plunged her arm into the waves, and sighed as she at last felt relief from the heat.

Still dizzied and now exhausted, she tried standing but collapsed face-first into the temperate water. Her hand cooled but was still burned and throbbing. She tried pushing herself from the surf but couldn't, her left hand sinking into the sediment as a riptide hit, pulling her down as the overall current nudged her farther from shore.

Salt water hit her fume-scalded lungs, burning them even further. The sensation sent her thrashing, but another riptide nullified her effort. Fading, coughing, burning, she made one final attempt to escape... but instead pushed herself further into the ocean, unable to distinguish up from down as her body spun, helpless, in the darkened sea.

Limp and exhausted, Andra felt herself adrift, so lost to a web of pain, spasms, and darkness that she hardly noticed the arm wrapping around her waist. Eventually, amid dreamy, blurred candles and swirling red limbs, a funny smell—acrid, yet more pleasant than the necrospondence—focused her thoughts.

Rubbing alcohol, she decided, blinking herself awake.

Matted, pearlescent hues greeted her. *Wait—am I inside the rupture?* As her eyes and her foggy head cleared, sterility replaced fantasy. A bed's chrome handles gated her from a bland collection of white walls, curtains, and equipment. Confused, she recounted her crazy experiences and realized she was now at a hospital, meaning someone had helped her... probably saved her life.

She sat up, felt queasy, and thrust herself back down, allowing herself fifteen minutes to recover. *No more, though.*

The curtains surrounding her bed whipped open and a nurse with Annie-red curls peeked in, writing notes on a pad as she scrutinized Andra.

"Good to see you with us, Ms. Barger," she said, in a tone suggesting she might have said the same thing to thirty other people since beginning her shift. "How's the hand?"

Andra sat up again, this time noticing her right hand was bandaged.

"Still hurts," she said, "but not as bad."

The nurse maintained her indifference.

"Burns hurt," she said. "You're lucky you still have a hand. No burn specialists on the North Shore right now so you're in Poipu."

Poipu? Andra hadn't planned on visiting Kauai's largest town, even though it was only about thirty miles from where she was staying.

"How long since I was brought in here?"

The nurse checked the log.

"Seventeen hours ago," she said. "You're very fortunate, the candle wax that burned you had aloe and other ingredients that are helping to heal you. Doctor Binwadi says he's never seen anything like it. If you're wondering who brought you in, he was—"

Andra twisted, ignoring sore muscles she didn't even know she had, then slid herself off the bed until she felt feet and floor connect. "I'm not wondering," she said as the nurse went into a tizzy. "And I'm not staying."

She dressed in ten minutes, no easy task given her wrapped, aching hand and a resistant nursing staff. The hospital cafeteria was easier to work with—they had a pineapple-mango shave ice ready for her in less than a minute—but the discharge was taking forever. Since she didn't much care whether it was official she gave the staff thirty minutes to come up with the necessary paperwork, making it clear she would leave at that time regardless.

Her twin ankle bands flared yellow and vibrated.

She finished her shave ice, not the best she'd ever had but decent, then found a quiet hallway to remove and unroll the second ankle band. The job wasn't easy one-handed, but she managed to spread the band into a hair-thin, camel-colored note sheet. Shimmering, crimson words formed as she glanced over the sheet, appearing and disappearing in conjunction with the speed of her eye movements.

"Really? Here at the hospital?" she exclaimed aloud as she read the message.

She couldn't remember ever receiving a Summons to a location where she was already on-site. *Must be a mistake. Maybe I'll skip it. Be nice to finally have a legitimate excuse for skipping a diminishing assignment.* She read the message again then let go of the fragile sheet, which re-rolled into an ankle band. *Or maybe it's a setup. The Sugar Dandruff Council probably heard I slipped past the Klav, so they're steering me straight to them.*

But that didn't pass the gut test, especially since the Klav generally operated independent of the council and the ankle bands were always spot-on about conceptions, diminishing assignments, the whole thing. Andra watched the bands flare and vibrate again a minute later, wishing her colleagues would explain how they worked... or how the diminishing gel worked, for that matter.

Instead all I get for an answer is 'arcane tech.'

Arcane tech was a frustrating catchall term for any eye-popping capabilities the Cinüe didn't want to explain... and there were lots of them.

Again the bands flared and vibrated.

Too strange, she decided. *This is the reason they tell us to have a secondary receiver.*

She took out her phone and selected a number from the address book, placing the band back on her ankle while waiting for it to connect.

"Hey, been awhile," she said when she saw her mother's face appear on the screen.

Some daughters looked nothing like their mother, but Andra so closely resembled Maribel Barger that she worried she might someday inherit the tart personality too. Maribel's coconut hair had a few grays, the tanned skin a few wrinkles, but overall talking with her mom by phone always seemed like looking into a magic mirror that displayed her future self... though perhaps a funhouse magic mirror, given the way Maribel's chin was distorted by camera proximity.

Andra saw her mom hesitate before answering.

"This can't be good," Maribel said. "I told you never to call when you're on a job."

"Yeah, well... I had a little hospital time so I'm bending the rules."

"Hospital? How'd you get hurt this time?"

"I didn't. Listen, I'm just double-checking that my new assignment's in the same building where I already am."

"Sounds to me like you've misread something. I'll check."

She saw her mother lean to one side, out of frame, and heard her typing on a tablet. "The Summons is for... some nurse at your present location. That *is* unusual."

Okay, coincidence, Andra told herself.

"Just take care of it, no complaints or rebellions," her mother said. "We need everything flowing smoothly, now more than ever."

"Why? Is there a new problem?"

Maribel reappeared on-screen, wearing a stern look. "They're telling me Jackson's meds might not arrive like usual."

"What? I thought the council said we wouldn't have to worry as long as I cooperate."

Her mother scowled. "I can only guess you've done something to upset them... again."

Andra furrowed her brows. Her brother's cancer meds hadn't been an issue for more than a year. *Why would this come up now? That was the whole point of me filling in for him as a dimin—*

"What about the gel refills?" she said, interrupting her own disconcerting thought. "Are they still showing up?"

"Every week, like clockwork. This has nothing to do with the refill capsules for your ring, only the meds."

Andra flashed to the Mechen Klav... to what Sandoval had said. *Is this another way of bullying me*?

"You don't have to worry," she told her mother. "Nothing's changed."

Her mother wasn't buying it.

"Well something's changed," Maribel said. "Probably because of that mess last year, after what you did with your pregnancy. Someone threatening the meds has me worried. He won't make it long without them."

Andra nodded. "Mother, this whole thing's a mess. They hold us to their rules even though we're not Cinüe, but as soon as we ask a few questions about the tech or the leadership they clam up. We're only equal when they want something from us. Otherwise it's always 'sorry, you're human, not Cinüe.' Aren't you fed up with it? Because I am."

Maribel's scowl grew even deeper. "We've been through this before," she said. "It's not a boat we can rock with Jackson in the shape he's in. Understood?"

Andra rolled her eyes. "Not entirely," she said.

"Well that's just too bad. We have obligations, dear, whether we like them or not. The Cinüe are going to treat us exactly as you've described because these people are descended from a very long, very insular line... and we aren't."

"Aren't we? If you're technically second generation then Jackson and I are third, since Grandmother was adopted by—"

"Drop it, dear," Maribel said. "You've messed up enough already."

"Seriously Mother, how long does it take for them to treat us as one of them?

"I said, drop it."

Andra had no intention of dropping it... but she could live with putting the matter on hold for a few hours. "Let me see Jackson," she said. "Just for a second."

"Yeah, yeah, hold on."

Her mom's face blurred and bounced as she walked with the phone, an older model without an image stabilizer.

"He's probably asleep," she whispered. "But looking better than usual today."

Her face gave way to a small room with a home hospital bed. The man in bed looked a shadow of the strong, kindred spirit Andra knew while growing up. Skin covered his face the way sheets covered a laundry line, draped bone-to bone. His narrow eyebrows and pencil-thin mustache reached out in multiple directions, as if the hairs were looking for an escape route. His lips looked as pale as his skin, and he had dark spots beneath his closed eyes.

Andra clenched her bottom lip between her teeth before speaking.

"Has he been up at all?" she asked.

"Oh, maybe an hour today, about the same yesterday. Better than over the weekend, much better. But you know, it cycles."

Andra couldn't stop thinking about the boy who spent hours on his tire swing, the adolescent who dominated rugby, the man who won two marathons. *He was probably twice the diminisher I am.* Their family's diminishing commitment fell to the eldest child and Jackson, unlike his baby sister, was excited by the twist of fate that allowed a "lowly" human to try his hand at it.

His eyes fluttered, then opened halfway. A smile tugged at the corners of his lips as he spotted Andra's face on their mother's phone screen, but he didn't say anything.

"Get some rest," she whispered to him.

His mouth moved, but no sound came out. Then he tried again, this time with more success.

"It's... no different.. from... circumcision," he said, his voice soft but smooth.

Andra grinned, recognizing the usual launch point of their repeated debates.

"Circumcision's primarily cosmetic," she said, still in a whisper. "Diminishing makes biochemical changes."

He smiled, a full one this time, recognizing and enjoying her familiar answer. Andra missed their debates and figured this might be his way of saying he missed them too. She wished she could give him a full barrage, remind him that he'd never been pregnant, never faced the prospect of seeing his child intentionally... damaged. Maybe even explain to him how the view was different with your body surrounding a child, obligated to nurture, to protect... not to diminish.

But those debates were over, at least between the two of them.

I stepped in for him when he got sick, mimicking Cinüe custom to the letter, she thought, looking at Jackson. *So why would the council threaten his meds?*

Her mother was right. It had to be a message.

Are they using my brother's cancer to threaten me? And if the Sugar Dandruff Council is so worried about my vote, why would Asantha Cooray select me, of all people, as her proxy?

“Thanks Sis,” Jackson mumbled.

His eyelids closed again, but his breathing remained steady—better than Andra had seen him on other days. She closed her eyes too, said a silent prayer, then reopened them.

“You can get back on the phone, Mother,” she mumbled.

Her mother's face replaced Jackson's then bounced again, until she reached another room and sat down. She and Andra exchanged pleasantries for a few minutes, but Andra could tell that both her mind and her mother's hadn't left the subject of Jackson's meds.

“You know, Mom, there *is* one thing that's different,” she said, steering them back to something pertinent. “I just got a necrospondence. The rumors you heard were true. I'm a proxy. *Her* proxy.”

She saw her mother gasp.

“Yeah,” Andra said. “Surprised the hell out of me too.”

“It must be a mistake,” Maribel babbled. “Only direct descendants of the original Edenshire natives are allowed inside that council chamber, much less given a chance to vote.”

“Yeah, but Mother... Asantha was the one who adopted Grandmother, so maybe she decided—”

"Yes, yes, it doesn't matter. With your history and your bias against diminishing, no one will trust you to maintain the status quo. Hell, *I* don't trust you to ratify diminishing. That places a big target on your back. Do like I instructed when the rumor came up. Tell the council you're respectfully declining."

"Really? You're the one who's always pushing me to appease the council."

"To meet our family's traditional obligations, but this is no tradition. It's unusual, it's dangerous, and it sounds like a setup. If anything happens to you, I lose both my daughter *and* my son. No... decline it and move on."

"But—"

"No 'buts.' First it was Jackson pulled into diminishing, now they're pulling you into a very serious council session. Unless they tell you why they suddenly like our family, you're declining."

Andra hadn't seen her mother so upset in ages. "Mother, settle down... I'm not sure I can go through with it anyway."

The objections became silence. A long silence.

"Well of course you can't," Maribel finally said. "Lord knows you proved you have trouble making good decisions by running off with Wade last year, and we both saw how well *that* turned out, now, didn't we? That pregnancy mess alone should have been enough to disqualify you from a council that approves diminishing."

"*Votes*, Mother," she said, ignoring the jab at her time with Wade. "They *vote* on diminishing."

Her mother seemed apprehensive. "I know you're not that naïve," she said.

"But..."

"You need to decline regardless, but if you can't supply the vote you've been entrusted with then it's a done deal: you can't go," Maribel said. "It'd be a death sentence. I've heard too many stories over the years... stories that scare me, about things that I'd never want to have happen to you."

Andra felt her head throbbing as badly as her injured hand.

"I'll take care of things, Mother. I always have."

"Yes, well... for your brother's sake, see to it that doesn't change."

They said their goodbyes, but Andra dwelled on the conversation long after the phone call ended. Her mother never liked the Cinüe yet insisted Jackson and Andra follow their traditions to the letter, a mixed message she refused to explain. Still, this time something she said stood out: "Unless they tell you why they suddenly like our family, you're declining." She seemed to imply an extensive history with the council. *Maybe she was just referring to my pregnancy ruckus last year*, Andra thought. Then again... maybe not. She wished her grandmother was around to shed some light on the matter, but Dvora Lansky had passed away when Andra was just a girl. Since her grandfather died before she was born and her father was never part of her life, she couldn't think of anyone else who might be able to help.

She took the elevator upstairs and found the nurse listed in the Summons, entwined with a hospital administrator inside a utility closet. She gelled the nurse while giving her best sorry-I'm-a-lost-patient routine, waving her expired patient ID before the irritated, panicked couple. Her twin ankle bands turned a pale, "sugar dandruff" color.

Another damned diminishing on my ledger, she thought. *And this time I didn't even need to hide my identity.*

Which was ironic since, more than ever, she felt like going into hiding. She left the couple to their closet, but before she could walk away the administrator jumped up, stark naked, and slammed the door shut in front of her.

"Matthew, what are you—?" the confused nurse shouted.

Matthew ignored the nurse, grabbing Andra by the shoulders and shoving her against a mesh of mops, pails and broomsticks stacked next to the doorway.

"If you vote against diminishing, you'll answer for it," he said.

Andra shoved him away, uncertain whether his rancid breath or the proximity of his repulsive, unclothed genitals bothered her more.

"You're not Mechen Klav—who are you?" she said.

"Someone you need to listen to."

"You knocked someone up just to give me a message?" she said, incredulous.

He shrugged.

"There are worse ways," he said.

Now the nurse looked like she wanted to give Matthew a shove too.

Andra's mind reeled, aghast at what this man had just done. A diminished child would arrive in nine months, conceived for no other reason than to serve as bait, so someone could draw Andra close without suspicion.

"You're sick," she said, reopening the door. "All of you people, running this baby show of yours. You make me sick."

And you make me determined. Decline a chance at finally having a say in whether diminishing goes forward? Not a chance, she knew. This was too vital—much more important than her brother, her mother, or herself. She'd find a way to have her say and help her family. Somehow, she'd find a way. But it wasn't about them, not any more. Now, it was about doing what was best for everyone.

"Tell your friends: I'll be there whether they like it or not," she said, stepping through the closet's doorway. "I'll be Asantha Cooray's proxy on the Sugar Dandruff Council, and whatever happens, I *will* have a say. Good luck trying to stop me."

As she walked out she noticed Matthew close on her heels, so she slammed the door behind her. The man uttered the wail of someone with an appendage stuck in a closing door... and from the intensity of his scream, Andra could tell it wasn't a finger that got caught.

THREE

Thefts

The hospital's glass doors slid shut behind Andra, closing a chapter of her life... or at least that's how she preferred looking at it. She paused amid the facility's palm-lined foyer, still wearing the sarong, but now over a tank top and a set of shorts from the lobby store rather than her swimsuit. Her hand was wrapped, and would need dressings, treatments, maybe cosmetic surgery. The doctors prescribed painkillers, but she knew she couldn't take them with only two days left before the Sugar Dandruff Council.

Not that she'd have taken them anyway. *Yay for my stubborn streak*, she thought, though she knew it wasn't necessarily something to applaud. Now a cab to her hotel, another good shave ice, and some online air reservations were the only thing standing between her and—

"Ann! Over here!"

She saw the smile that always eased worries. Cristina Kuroda, former roommate, fellow diminisher, and forever-friend, ran the length of the foyer and looked like she'd have flown if she could have. She wrapped Andra in a bear hug, her compact frame radiating energy.

"How did you find me?" Andra said.

"Are you kidding?" Cristina said, lifting a pair of jeweled sunglasses. "If I can find someone preggers on an obscure peak in Tibet, I can find you lounging on Kauai."

Cristina had a habit of projecting every word like she was upstage, even if it was a grocery list. The two hugged again, then Andra stood back and admired. Though Cristina was Asian, her clothes and jewelry were a cultural hodgepodge; her turquoise chiffon blouse had the cuts and jags of a Paris runway, a polished, stone necklace hailed Indian craftsmanship, and six gaudy finger rings cherished Chinese. Her ankle bracelet and pumps, on the other hand: Italian... and not cheap Italian. None of that seemed as striking as her hair, which was mostly black but had luminescent silver and gold highlights.

"You know you don't need to wear all that fluff here on the islands, right?" Andra said.

"So I see," she said, gesturing at her friend's wardrobe. "Having fun with your beach time?"

"Yeah... not so much."

She followed Cristina to a rental car. The two spent a couple hours navigating traffic along the two-lane, shrub-and palm-sided highway connecting resort-packed Poipu, along the island's southern shore, to Princeville, a community of upscale vacation condos on the north shore.

"So... tomorrow we need to get you to Sydney," Cristina said, gesturing at an airport sign. "I've already got your travel and arrangements set for you."

"And you know my destination... how?"

Cristina shrugged. "Let's just say I got some mail to that effect."

Andra nodded as she ogled a roadside shave ice truck. "Score one for my stalker."

"Score two. He fished you out of the water."

"Yeah, well not before he passed me a necrospondence that just about took my hand off. Docs say they can do a lot for me, but it'll never be the same."

"Damn right it won't be the same. We're gonna light that thing up sometime, make you our own personal Statue of Liberty."

Andra smiled through her pain. Cristina's room-lifting energy felt good, and the spectacular ocean view wasn't hurting either. She hit the trifecta when the highway veered them toward one shave ice truck too many.

"Pull over," she said, sheepish. "I'm hooked."

Cristina, laughing, parked near the truck. A few minutes later Andra held a paper bowl with a dome of rainbow-colored ice particles. Even one-handed, with the bowl wedged between her knees to keep it from tipping, Andra felt like her shave ice was better than any prescription pain relief—especially when she discovered ice cream loaded beneath the shave ice, a specialty separating premier shops from cheap imposters.

"Look Ann, bummer about the hand but that letter, it's your big break," Cristina said as they hit the road once again. "You're gonna sit on the Sugar Dandruff Council. I mean, think about it—the birth council! Your vote will keep things in perfect order for generations. Thousands of diminishers out there and the chance everyone wishes they'd get just falls in your lap."

She swerved to avoid a median, momentarily distracted.

Andra spooned her shave ice as if it might evaporate before she had a chance to eat it. "But why me? Of all people, why me?"

"You mean why choose the woman who's direct family with the lady who started the whole thing? Gee, yeah... I wonder why."

"But I'm not family. You Cinüe types never hesitate to point that out."

More Cristina laughter. "You're related to Asantha Cooray. You can't get more family than that."

Andra lowered the shave ice cup. "I'm not related. She adopted my grandmother, it's not like I'm a direct descendant. My *real* mother wants me to decline. Says there's a target on me, because of my history."

Cristina's smile vanished.

"No," she said. "No, no, no! You do not decline. Target or not, that isn't an option, okay?"

"Why not?"

Cristina shook her head, troubled. “It’s just... this isn’t the sort of invitation you pass up without making people mad. Important people. Asantha Cooray, for example.”

Andra shrugged. “Will I actually get to meet her?”

The moment turned awkward as Cristina seemed to struggle for an answer. Andra watched her fidget with the steering wheel, shuffle about her seat, grit her teeth.

“Asantha’s... not someone you can meet,” Cristina said.

“But she’s a Cinüe. Maybe the most important Cinüe ever.”

“Asantha Cooray is a lot of things,” Cristina said, quickly this time, “but she isn’t a Cinüe. Not in the conventional sense. You know that, right?”

Andra nearly answered then stopped short, choosing to measure her words, wondering whether this was an opportunity. “I know she’s... been around for a long time. A crazy long time. Primordial long... right?”

Cristina nodded.

“Are you going to live that long too?” Andra said, on a whim.

The comment made Cristina burst out laughing. “No chance!” she said. “I’ll probably live about the same number of years that you will... assuming you don’t decline your chance to be Asantha’s proxy.” They passed a slow-moving pickup loaded with surfboards before Cristina added, “Your mother’s wrong on this one, Ann. Like it or not, you’ve got to go, especially since you’ll be representing Asantha.”

"Don't worry, I'm going. But it's all fake; my ancestors aren't from Edenshire so I'm not a true Cinüe," she said. "I barely know what one is, and I wouldn't know *that* if my mother hadn't told me."

"And what exactly do you know?"

Andra shrugged. "Just the basics," she said. "Edenshire's a hidden society of people known as the Cinüe. Prevalent once upon a time, right? One of the competing lines of humanity in evolutionary history—the other most prominent line being yours truly, *homo sapiens*. Then something happened, something big, so the Cinüe obscured the archaeological evidence and hid themselves away in Edenshire."

Cristina giggled. "Okay, that's the preschool explanation," she said, "but it's not wrong. Anything else?"

Andra shrugged. "The Edenshire leaders left a fraction of their people behind to diminish anyone who isn't a Cinüe. The rest of them are still waiting for their chance to return."

"That's *all* they told you? They didn't mention the Maybe Objective?"

Plopping the shave ice on Cristina's head seemed an appropriate response, but Andra wasn't about to sacrifice her favorite vice. "That, dear Cristina, is what being related to Asantha Cooray gets you: a whole lot of nothing when it comes to information," she said between bites. "Of course, you could help change that."

"Would if I could," Cristina said, pulling the car off the main highway and onto a service road. "Rules, you know."

"Yeah, yeah, *rules*. For me, all those rules amount to making sure the cheese stands alone, clueless. So what's this Maybe Objective?"

Cristina glanced out the driver's side window, averting her eyes from Andra's.

"Seriously?" Andra said. "You and every other diminisher besides me get to know everything, I'm kept in the dark. Does that seem right to you?"

"It's not you per se," Cristina said. "You just happen to be the only diminisher who isn't a Cinüe."

"How can you tell?"

Cristina suddenly didn't seem so lighthearted. "Tell what?"

Andra waited until she again had eye contact with her friend.

"How can you tell I'm not a Cinüe?" she said. "We all look alike—here you are, a descendant of the people left behind, but I can't tell the difference. You look exactly like us poor diminished types. How is it you know who's diminished versus who's Cinüe?"

Cristina tapped her fingers on the steering wheel.

"Okay, you're not kidding when you say they don't tell you much. But you can stretch shadows and ignite the eyeballs, right?"

"Only because my mother collared brother and I into diminisher training when we were kids," Andra said, scooping up the final clump of ice-cream-laden shave ice. "So yeah, I know a few tricks. I'm good at camo, I can stretch a shadow or two and ignite my eyes, but that's about it."

"Funny, I heard you've become one of the best. Which means something since they say diminishing eventually leads to Edenshire's return, remember?"

"I remember. I just wish I knew exactly what it meant," Andra said.

"It means you can't duck out of this vote," Cristina said. "That's what it means."

"Yeah, yeah."

"I'm serious. This is important. Whatever you do, do not decline this invitation."

Andra glanced at her friend, uneasy. She suddenly wondered: had the comment had been intended as heartfelt, helpful advice... or as a veiled threat?

"Don't worry," Andra said. "It's too big of an opportunity to ignore. I'll be there."

The next diminishing assignment turned out to be a team-up with Cristina, since it was sent to both Andra's and Cristina's ankle bands and located in Princeville.

"Five women at the same place?" Cristina said, enthused. "Not a record, but close. And for a change we're both here at the same time! Gonna be fun!"

They drove between kukui trees and Norfolk pines for another few miles before reaching Princeville's entry fountain, a sculpted rendition of Neptune standing amid a waterwork-spraying pond, all of it decidedly non-Hawaiian. Cristina chatted the entire time, mostly about recent jobs in Kenya, Iceland, and the Bahamas. "I think I'm headed to Bali next—hey, can I borrow the sarong?" she said.

There was no time to answer. Cristina was already racing into another story about another job location.

"Maybe *you* should be the proxy," Andra said.

The assignment itself turned out to be an easy one: five single women enjoying a holiday together on Kauai, apparently with dalliances at the local bars. Andra and Cristina, their hands gelled and ready, struck up a conversation with the group, shook hands with each of the women during introductions, socialized with them for a bit, then called it a job. Walking to the car, Cristina sported her usual broad smile and jabbered like a sweet sixteen at her birthday party. Andra, sullen, felt more like a somber seventy.

"You really love it, don't you," she said to Cristina as they got back in the car. "Diminishing?"

Cristina's face swirled into something resembling the classic happy face icon.

"I'm seeing the world, right?" she said. "And let's face it, the gig's easy. I mean, sure, every now and then you get someone in a cracker box airplane, or the gross ones at the medical labs. But otherwise, stick a dab on them during that zygote window and you're out. How easy can it get?"

Andra grimaced. *I love her like a sister... but what an airhead. At least humans have an excuse—they're diminished. What's* her *excuse?*

"Hey, did I ever tell you about the time I went up and high-fived the newly knocked-up chick when she was in the nightclub restroom?" Cristina babbled. "The gel went straight into her palm, she never even noticed! Oh, and then there was the girl on the skateboard in Sao Paulo..."

Andra let Cristina continue without paying much attention. She tucked her empty shave ice cup into the car's center console then stared vacantly at two-story bungalows, fountains, and greenery. By the time they pulled up to her rented townhouse, Cristina was in the midst of a rollicking story about diminishing a midget couple in Russia.

"What about the babies?" Andra interrupted.

Cristina stopped. "Huh?"

Andra swallowed, took a long look out the window.

"The babies. You know: all those people being diminished. Sure, they're just cells when it happens, but still..."

Words caught in her throat for a moment, then she continued.

"I mean, just the word alone... *diminishing*. Don't you ever feel like you're doing something wrong?"

Cristina put the car's transmission in Park, still smiling.

"Okay, you must have something really intense going with Wade to start thinking like that again," she said. "Are you two back together?"

Not if I'm smart, Andra thought, but could tell her heart didn't agree.

The townhouse was a typical Princeville rental: worn furniture, stained rugs, yellowed island maps for decor, and a spectacular view of the Pacific that forgave the other sins.

"Really Cristina... don't you think about it? Ever?"

Cristina was perched before a hall mirror, brushing her hair. "If diminishing's for the greater good, why would I bother myself with dwelling on it?"

Andra put a hand on her shoulder. "Because we're chemically changing people into something less than what they're supposed to be."

They walked to the kitchen. Andra opened the fridge, poured herself some juice. Cristina wagged a finger. "Pog instead of a Mai Tai," she said. "There's your problem."

"Yeah... maybe so. But no, I don't think so."

She sat on the couch, taking care not to bang her wrapped, sore hand against the cushions. Cristina leaped onto the pillows with a plop. "Look Ann, it's not like you're the first to question it," she said, fidgeting with her nails. "But when it comes down to diminishing or having a world full of people too powerful for their own good, the choice seems pretty sensible. Asantha Cooray's writings make it very clear that humans would have destroyed this world, and us along with it, if not for the Jeremiah Maybe Diminishing Act. So no one's trying to hurt anyone. Just the opposite, really. This is about keeping everyone equal... and keeping the peace."

Andra gave her a look. "The world doesn't seem all that peaceful... or equal... to me," she said. "And who the hell's Jeremiah Maybe, anyway?"

Cristina shrugged.

"You know I can't say," both women said simultaneously, Andra mocking Cristina's rote Cinüe response by mimicking the words at the exact time she spoke them.

"Ann, come on..."

"Hey, you want me to take you seriously, then be straight with me," Andra said.

"I *am* being straight with you. Look, I'm sure there'll be a day we can discuss everything openly, hopefully real soon, okay?"

It's like she's consoling a child, Andra thought.

"In fact, maybe if you go through with the vote..."

"You date, right?" Andra broke in.

Cristina launched a bigger grin than ever.

"Well... yeah."

"Men?"

Now Cristina looked churlish. "You know it. Not 'man,' men! More than one."

Andra gave her a placating smile. "Really? You date men? Because some female diminishers don't. Some... can't."

"You mean... are you saying...?"

This time Andra smiled for real. "I'm not saying anything. Except, I don't date. Not anymore."

"Then you really do need some mai tais."

Andra shook her head. "How could I ever date a guy, or God forbid fall for him, knowing one mistake, one missed pill or one little oversight during a moment of passion, would sentence some child... no, *my* child... it would sentence them to a diminished life. How could I do that?"

Cristina gave her shoulder a playful slap. "Hello, modern medicine? Tie those tubes and move on."

"But I shouldn't *have* to move on," Andra said. "Why am I forced to choose between a damaged child or no child? Diminishing is as disempowering as anything I can imagine."

She paused, deep in thought. "I guess what I'm really saying is... how could I possibly vote in favor of continuing it?"

Cristina wasn't smiling anymore. "Look, I get it," she said. "You ran with a bad boy, had some consequences—"

"*Consequences*? I had to abort the baby, Cristina!"

"Well, to be fair you didn't *have* to—"

Andra felt her neck and shoulders clenching up. "It was either abort or have a diminished kid," she said, furious. "You call that a choice?"

Cristina's face drew tight. "Tell you what, I *do* call that a choice," she said. "You yourself were born diminished, yet here you are, living a good life with plenty of options and opportunities. I don't know why you think that's so bad. I mean, really—if you don't even know what it's like to go undiminished, how can you say what we're doing is wrong? How can you even tell the difference?"

Andra got up from the couch and started pacing, too worked up to sit still. "It's the principle," she said. "Diminishing robs an entire civilization of its true potential."

Cristina's eyes glazed, as if she thought Andra's point was so ludicrous she didn't know what to make of it. "Well at least diminishing isn't killing," she said.

"No, it isn't killing," Andra said, a lump in her throat as her mind revisited her decision to abort. "Except when it is."

Cristina's face darkened with regret. The condo went quiet.

"I'm just saying," Cristina continued, after letting the moment cool, "I know you've been through a lot, and now your hand hurts like hell. But you've been given an honor beyond anything most diminishers will *ever* get. You're the proxy for Asantha Cooray. You're going to vote on a nine-member council that only meets every fifty years. A council set up, what, at the dawn of humanity, right? And set up for the good of everyone."

This time Cristina placed her arm around Andra. "Seriously, Ann... don't even *think* about messing with your proxy vote. They'd... well, I can't even imagine what they'd do. And Asantha Cooray, what would *she* do?"

Andra shrugged. "Unseen for thousands of years, what *could* she do?"

"Unseen but still viable. She still runs the show."

"Yeah, how does she manage that anyway?"

Cristina's glow dimmed. "You know I can't tell you that," she said. "Rules, right? Cinüe only. Not that I know all the details anyway... but it must be arcane tech of the highest order, that's for sure."

Andra grimaced at the words 'arcane tech.'

"So I'm supposed to cast an informed vote for people who choose to keep me in the dark," she said. "Why would I?"

"Please, Ann, don't mess with this, not now. This is not the time to let your history with Wade get to you." Her nose wrinkled as she spoke the name.

"That's my point," Andra said. "I won't let him get to me because I *can't* let him get to me. Him, or any man. And what the hell kind of life choice is that?"

They sat in silence, looking at the ocean, wave upon wave rippling to shore. *Just as they have for millions of years,* Andra thought.

FOUR

Hooded

Flying from Kauai to Australia was never an easy ten hours, but having people spy on you during the trip made it even less appealing.

Andra noticed her first "admirer" not long after Cristina dropped her at the outdoor terminal in Lihue: a tall, bald man in a dark business suit whose only business seemed to be trailing her. He tracked her through crowds, eyed her in lines, tailed her when she tried blending with the background. Somehow he even made it through security before she did, even though he entered the line after her. He was obvious, but good. She weaved through a crowd, he kept the same pattern. Stop to tie a shoe and there he was, noodling with his own.

He wants to be seen, she decided. *He wants me, and maybe other people, to know that I'm being watched.*

The squat, pudgy woman with a book bag and a flowery muumuu wasn't so obvious, lingering near the fast food counter while Andra bought a burger, chatting with the gate clerk as she lifted her bag onto the adjacent scale. It wasn't until she appeared in the ladies room and grabbed the neighboring stall that Andra began to feel something about the woman wasn't quite right. Sure enough, when she returned to the waiting area the lady went straight to the desk attendant, requesting her seat location be shifted... to an aisle seat just three slots away from Andra's.

After spotting two of them so easily, Andra assumed there had to be others who were better hidden. She took out her phone and messaged Cristina with this news. A typical Cristina response beeped in moments later.

See, you're a council delegate now, so important they have to shadow you! Exciting!

Andra didn't feel excited, or important. Mostly, she felt pressured. Clearly Sandoval from the lanai, Matthew at the hospital, and these creepy people at the airport were all making certain she understood they expected her to vote in favor of diminishing... or else. She wondered whether her mother was right; she should simply decline the invitation. Otherwise she'd be trapped in an epic match between expectations and the right decision. She had a feeling that no matter which side won, she was the one who would take the battering.

Frustrated, she people-watched, eyes bounding seat to seat until she noticed a young couple kissing near a snack shop. They gave each other gentle pecks at first, then passionate, lengthy face-plants. *How long before some diminisher gets assigned to them,* she wondered. *How long before yet another baby becomes something less than they were supposed to become?* She wished she could warn the couple, or magically keep them from giving in to their natural instincts.

She wished she could keep them from going through what she and Wade went through.

The bald man in the suit broke away once the flight began boarding, but muumuu woman was right there on the jetway with her, pretending not to care. As they waited to board the plane Andra leaned over and whispered in the woman's ear.

"I can give you some lessons in stealth during the flight if you'd like," she said.

The woman flushed, but didn't break character. "Oh, that's nice dear," she said, but her eyes couldn't conceal her unhappiness.

Andra smiled. Message sent.

The flight itself was a chance to sleep, and think, but Andra did neither. Instead she read, and watched movies, and kept an eye on muumuu woman. Though this wasn't a standard assignment, diminisher training was very clear about the dangers of closing your eyes once someone established your identity. That meant a very long day. Though her flight to Sydney was nonstop, weather and gate delays meant the ten-hour trip was expected to take twelve hours. From Sydney she needed to fly to the Outback in central Australia, an additional couple hours. *Important, hell,* she thought. *If I was so important they'd have sent a private jet.*

Muumuu woman finally made her move about two hours before they landed in Australia. As people made their potty runs and the seats opened between them, the lady scooted next to Andra.

"Poor dear, seems you've lost your super power," the woman said.

She had a crafty look that bothered Andra.

"Super power?"

The woman's eyes narrowed.

"Invisibility," she said. "Patience and shadow."

Andra nodded, slowly.

"Don't worry," she said, "I can still be invisible if I need to."

The woman wagged a finger.

"None of that talk, oh no, none of that," she said. "Everyone's watching you—everyone."

"And why is that?"

"Well because you're the swing vote of course," she said.

Andra's spirits lifted. The council had nine members, so if she was considered a swing vote it meant she might not be the only one concerned about diminishing.

The woman cocked her head. "Oh, it's not what you're thinking. See, we need a unanimous vote. The other families are standing firm, as they have for centuries. You... well now, you were the surprise pick so that's a story waiting to be written, isn't it dear?"

Andra felt her heart sink, but she was good enough at poker to keep it from showing. Still... *the only one? I'm the only one, out of nine*?

"Why do you say that?" she asked the woman, suppressing her dejection. "You know who selected me as her proxy."

The woman's lips pressed together and stretched, just for a moment. "But you're not a Cooray, are you," she said. "You're not the real thing."

Andra shrugged. "Real enough to get the call."

The woman licked her lips. "Ah, but are you real enough to *make* the call? The toughest call of all?"

Andra smiled. "So you're worried then. I'm flattered."

"Oh my, dear, I'm not worried for you," she said, her lips twisting into a smug expression. "I'm worried for that babbling diminisher you associate with... for your family too, such a dear mother you have. Oh, and that poor brother of yours, what about him? But I'm most worried about your delivery."

Huh? Andra thought. Is she talking about a pregnancy? Her baffled expression seemed to prompt muumuu woman to expand the thought.

"I'm worried improper voting would mean your... mail service... would experience delays," the woman said.

Wade! She means Wade!

The woman didn't wait for Andra's response. Instead she scooted away, smiling at the people returning to their seats. Andra stood up, her stomach ice cold, and joined the restroom line. Inside, she fingered the slide lock shut then stared at herself in the mirror.

The woman threatened me. She actually threatened me.

Andra was more than angry, she was enraged... but she knew she was also afraid. Suddenly the forthcoming vote carried very personal ramifications.

And I'm the only one opposed to diminishing.

Her mind reeled. Only one person, in what had to be a unanimous vote. How did this happen? Why would Asantha Cooray choose her, of all people?

When she returned to her seat, muumuu woman wasn't there. She never saw her the rest of the flight, yet no one else seemed to notice she was missing. Even when she deplaned in Sydney, the woman wasn't at the gate.

The connection flight was the opposite of the jumbo jet from Los Angeles: a prop plane seating no more than twenty. Muumuu woman wasn't on the flight, which would have been a nice feeling if Andra could have explained where she'd gone.

As she looked at the other passengers, wondering whether any of them were spying on her as well, she noticed something unusual: not one of them was talking. Every passenger, she realized, was flying solo. They each kept to themselves, practically going out of their way to avoid eye contact with the other passengers. Even the flight attendant, a middle-aged man with a buzz cut and a weathered face, avoided eye contact as he went aisle to aisle with drinks.

They're connected to the council vote, she realized. *They're all headed to the same place I am.*

She looked at the passenger in the seat next to her. He was younger than she was, seemingly college age, wearing a T-shirt and shorts, his eyes glued to his ebook. If he noticed her looking at him, he didn't show it.

The silent flight was creepy. Some two hours later, after passing over sand, desert, and yet more sand and desert, she spotted her destination in the distance. It looked like a cookie dollop in the midst of so much flat terrain, a rounded, flat-topped, sandstone hunk gracing the middle of nowhere in Australia's Northern Territory. Andra's tourist guide called it Ayers Rock, after a former chief secretary of South Australia, but said the Aboriginals gave it its true name: Uluru. They cherished it as a place formed by creator beings working in the forms of people, plants and animals.

The guide also suggested Uluru is still inhabited by dozens of these ancestral creator spirits, which Andra recognized as a tourism ploy yet found unsettling in the wake of muumuu woman's disappearance. During the next couple days, she figured, the Aboriginals might be right.

The plane descended through typical desert turbulence, a gentle jostling that didn't compare to the shove Andra's gut felt when she felt the college student tapping her shoulder but discovered muumuu woman sitting next to her instead.

"Now it begins, dear," the woman said, then deepened her voice. "Make sure it ends well."

Stunned, Andra watched as the woman got up, walked the narrow aisle to the front of the plane, and knocked on the pilot's door. The door slid open, then slid shut as soon as she scooted inside. Andra unbuckled her belt and half-stood, looking at the other passengers, trying to figure out where the college student went. No one on board looked like him.

He's just gone.

Her stomach went ice cold once again. No one else looked up from their books, movies, or paperwork as she scrutinized the cabin. No one made eye contact of any kind.

When the plane landed the pilot's door reopened, and remained open. Andra peeked inside as she deplaned; the two pilots were seated in the cramped cockpit. Muumuu woman wasn't there... nor was there any room for a third person. The pilots never looked up from their controls. The flight attendant starcd at his feet as everyone left, and seemed relieved as the plane emptied.

"It's okay," Andra said as she guided her luggage's spinner wheels past his toes. "The elephant's no longer on board."

The lineup of black sedans out front of the terminal stretched so far up the road they could have encircled the tiny airport twice. Their side panels looked thick and the radials had a bulge just above the asphalt, so Andra figured the cars were weighted from defensive plating. Each had multiple antennas mounted on the roof, and windows tinted so dark she couldn't see inside—not even through the windshield.

Andra's fellow passengers each made their way to a sedan, though she couldn't figure out how they knew which one was theirs. After several pulled away, one of the remaining sedans flashed its headlights. She gestured at herself, to see whether the flash was for her, and the lights flashed once again. Once she reached the car the side window rolled down and cigar smoke billowed from the interior like a steam engine reaching its station.

"Cheers, Ms. Barger," a graveled Australian voice said. "Please come inside."

The backseat passenger door unlocked and popped open. Andra looked at the thick smoke up front, inhaled the heavily scented tobacco, and considered hailing a cab instead. Then she remembered she was in the middle of the Outback; not too many taxis in the desert, and apparently none at the airport right now. Peering through the window, the smoke was still so thick she could only see the shadowed form of an older man with deep jowls and balding head, his pink tie popping forth from a staid, gray business suit.

"Cuban?" she said, gesturing toward the smoke.

"Gods no," he said. "Nicaraguan. Can't you smell the cocoa hints?"

She only smelled ash but took him at his word.

"If you care to feel the air pass in and out of your chest, you may join me up front," he said. "Otherwise the rear cabin is smoke-free."

The trunk popped. She waited for the driver to emerge for her luggage bag but he didn't move, so she tossed it into the trunk and climbed inside the backseat door. True enough, there wasn't a hint of cigar smoke and the plush, black leather interior smelled like the car had just left the factory. A sealed glass partition not only separated driver from passengers but passengers from view, since the glass was swirled, rippled, and semi-frosted. The side windows looked much the same. Except for a few thumb-sized clear zones, Andra couldn't see a thing.

"Is this a car or a prison?" she said to herself.

The driver's voice burst through a speaker, clear as if he were in the seat next to her.

"Water, soda, and wine in are the refrigerator beneath the partition," he said. "Hood is in the snap case behind my seat."

"Hood?"

"Your privacy hood. You'll put it on before leaving the car, Ms. Barger, where it will remain except during your own private moments. Council dress codes are now in effect."

Baffled, she spotted the case and unsnapped the latches with her unbandaged hand. A shiny, silver hood fell onto the passenger seat. It was soft to the touch, with dark, breathable screening over the facial portion and a single red tassel hanging from the top.

"Are you kidding?" she said, appalled. "Don't they understand the historical precedents of people in hoods?" Images popped into her mind, of terrorists, hostages, Klansmen, and medieval executioners. She heard the driver cough, a single, begrudging *scarf* sound.

"Ms. Barger," he said, sounding annoyed, "they *invented* the historical precedents."

Andra's stomach felt as cold as it had on the plane.

"I'll need your cell phone and any other electronic devices now," the driver said. "Please deposit them into the drawer, they'll be returned when you depart."

A leather flap in the cabin barrier dropped open, and a small drawer slid toward Andra. She sighed, checked her phone and tablet for messages, then turned them off and placed them inside the small container. The drawer slid shut with a metallic clank.

"Very well, we'll be under way now," the driver said.

Andra stuffed the hood onto the seat next to her, disgusted. Inertia announced the ride was underway. Peeks through the thumbholes revealed desert, and more desert. A few gentle rises and dips was the only thing keeping the terrain from looking flat as a farm field.

"This is ridiculous," she said, to the speaker. "I don't know the council's laws or customs, I don't even know how the vote is taken."

Another cough.

"Not to worry Ms. Barger, I'll give you the basics. I've already checked you in, you're correctly registered as a Cinüe Heir which gives you access to all but the Gold Zone portions of the location. Contact with the other delegates is strictly prohibited. Meals will be delivered to your room, an 8 a.m. bell tomorrow morning will serve as your summons to the council."

"Sounds like a real blast," she said.

He cleared his throat. "You're here for your vote, Ms. Barger... nothing more."

"You make it sound like a technicality."

"Legally speaking, it is. Though of course the unanimity requirement says otherwise."

Andra felt as frosted as the window.

"If you need anything while you're there," he continued, "you'll have a direct line to me in your room. That line is of course private and unmonitored."

"Why would I need a secure line to my driver if I'm not allowed to go anywhere?"

"Driver?" he said, clearly offended. "Good gods, woman, I'm David Stanford Swimney, your attorney."

She felt confused. "Attorney? Why do I need a lawyer?"

This time there was a long pause before he sighed. "Each delegate has an attorney to represent them in case of matters... beyond their scope."

"And what scope are talking about here?"

"The most important scope of all: legal knowledge dating to the Year 537 Revisions, primarily, though I'm also quite familiar with the Founding Framework."

Andra tried to remember what her grandmother had told her about the Founding Framework, but couldn't.

"Think of it as the Magna Carta of original civilization, formed by a wide range of secretive international factions," Swimney said, even though she hadn't asked. "But whereas the Magna Carta, the U.S. Constitution, and similar documents were guidelines for citizen rights, the Founding Framework dictated societal structure: hierarchies, class systems, and other arrangements to be maintained behind the scenes, beyond the knowledge of all but a small percentage of the population. Diminishing, and the establishment of diminishers to handle the job, was so dictated in the Founding Framework."

"So this isn't just a vote on diminishing," she suddenly realized, "it's a vote on whether to amend the Founding Framework."

The speaker vibrated from the bass in Swimney's voice.

"Exactly," he said. "The other eight Sugar Dandruff Council voters and 360 delegates are arriving from all over the world, all Cinüe descendants. Many of them are government officials, scientists, or celebrities from some of the most powerful nations. Having all of you here reaffirms the value of the council's law, and the processes set up to ensure fairness."

Andra shook her head, amazed that anyone could so adamantly wave a flag for dusty words and procedures. "No," she said, "everything you've just described means there's no incentive for the delegates to break the status quo."

He didn't say anything. Andra didn't care whether he approved or not. The thought of taking part in a secret vote, wearing a hood so no one could identify her, with implications that affected every living human being for at least fifty years... she felt appalled.

"Most of the 360 delegates have already arrived," Swimney said, "Each cluster of forty will cast their votes, one cluster will be assigned to each of the nine council members. As Asantha Cooray's proxy you will be one of those members and your vote will therefore represent the wishes of your cluster... though you may legally disregard your cluster and vote however you'd like."

"So there are really only nine votes," Andra said. "And all nine have to be in favor to ratify diminishing. Why did the Founding Framework insist on a unanimous vote? Seems unlikely you could ever get nine people to agree on anything."

Swimney cleared his throat.

"Because quite frankly, something as important as diminishing could not morally happen with a simple majority, or even a two-thirds vote," he said. "Altering an entire species requires an all-hands-on-deck approach, otherwise it will fail. Moreover, this is not a vote that *can* fail, not if the Cinüe are to survive."

She shifted, uncomfortable at the edge in Swimney's words. "Because... why? Are undiminished humans really that much of a threat?"

"Cinüe history is pretty clear that they are."

A history which, like the tech, they refuse to share with me. "And the Diminishing Act has never come close to failing?" she said. "Not once in... how long?"

"Every fifty years for almost as long as *homo sapiens* has been around, which is about 180,000 years. Obviously I wasn't present for the other votes, but if diminishing was ever close to failing I'm not aware—"

The car shuddered, gently at first then much harder. Andra felt it weave, then straighten.

"Visitors, masked ones," Swimney said. "We're you followed?"

She thought about muumuu woman, and the bald man at the airport. Michael at the hospital also seemed to know everything about her, as did stubbled Sandoval and the men who nearly captured her on the drunken couple's lanai. Then too there was Wade, who had a habit of tracking her whereabouts.

"Maybe," she said.

Pings and pops hit the back windshield.

"I'm taking us off-road," Swimney announced. "Hang on."

The sedan swerved left, sending Andra right, her shoulder pushing against the door. Her seatbelt tensed, as did her stomach.

The car bumped, and bounced, then slid. Andra heard wheels spinning, trying to gain traction against dirt. The sedan lurched forward, more pings and pops hitting the windows as it went. She looked through one of the thumbnail-sized clear areas in the window but could only see dust clouds as thick as Swimney's cigar smoke.

"Almost clear, Ms. Barger," he said. "Better yet, I see Mechen Klav on their way to assist."

Mechen Klav? she thought, startled. *Here to help, or add to the attack?*

Something hit the sedan's side with a heavy bang, then an explosion. Andra gasped as the car rocked, angled up on its two left wheels, then crashed back down on the right. More pings and pops. The car stopped, as did the engine.

Andra leaned forward and banged on the partition, heart pounding.

"Are you okay?" she called to Swimney.

There was no answer.

Crap. She looked at her door handle, then at her bandaged right hand, and decided she was better off staying inside. *The car might have stopped, but it isn't breached*, she figured.

She heard motorcycle engines pulling up alongside the car, and voices. *Too muffled— can't hear what they're saying*, she realized.

Something banged against the side door, then banged again. Soon she heard multiple bangs, as if an entire gang was beating on the car, determined to get inside.

"Mr. Swimney!" she called, banging her left fist on the partition. "David, can you hear me?"

Still no answer. She unbuckled her seat belt, looking for a weapon, finding only her hood. Whoever wanted in wasn't having much luck, but if Swimney was injured and the car was damaged they would eventually find a way.

The banging stopped, but the voices rose louder than ever and sounded... afraid.

Before Andra could even process a reason why, a massive explosion rocked the area, shaking the car. Another explosion followed, then another. The motorcycle engines roared to life, then faded as they left the area. More explosions rumbled, this time much farther away.

Then Andra felt the sedan's engine starting up.

"Wankers," Swimney's voice growled over the speaker. "Third attack today."

Andra sat back, relieved to hear his voice, and to feel their car moving once again.

"Why the hell didn't you answer me?" she said.

"My apologies Ms. Barger, it's a contingency we had planned for, including the off-road, engines down, and silence, and yet they seem to have struck some fortunate blows. Nothing that will keep us from our journey, however."

"Who were they? Who else knows about this vote?"

Swimney sighed. "People with connections, people who want a voice, Ms. Barger. As I was saying, I'm not sure this is a vote that *can* fail, and unfortunately I believe these ruffians are sending council members a message to that effect. The *Mechen Klav* got them, though. They always do."

"Always? So you're saying—"

"The ruffians want a seat at the table," he said. "Diminishing may have little to do with it, they just want to have a seat."

The implication seemed clear, but Andra wanted to know for certain. "Not every nation has a say?" she said.

Another scarfing sound.

"Some hoods apply to voices as well as faces, Ms. Barger," he said. "I'm afraid I cannot answer your question without violating the rules."

"Which basically answers my question."

Swimney didn't say anything more. Andra didn't feel like talking either, so their ride went silent—a luxury after being attacked. The sedan was back on asphalt now, the minutes rolling along with the miles. Andra wondered whether there was a way out of this mess. *Maybe I could abstain in protest of their system?* But no, she figured, that probably wasn't an option for the person representing Asantha Cooray.

"Mr. Swimney," she said suddenly, more than a half-hour after their last conversation, "I need to set up a meeting before the council votes. Can you help me with that?"

The speaker reactivated.

"As I mentioned, contact with other council members or the outside world isn't permitted under Council Rules until—"

"Yeah, yeah, I know, the whole thing happens under wraps," she said. "But I have something different in mind. I need to meet with Asantha Cooray."

There was a pause, and possibly a gulp, but Andra could hear Swimney breathing so she knew the speaker was active.

"It's highly unusual... but you are her proxy so the law does permit contact," he finally said. "As you know, however, this isn't a matter of a simple phone call. Ms. Cooray is not really... available... in a conventional manner. To be honest, I'm not even certain how to facilitate your request."

"Be that as it may, I need to speak with her and I'm guessing the rules allow it. Can you set it up?"

"I, uh... I'd have to get a message to her first, and the effort could possibly delay the council vote by several hours. What reason would I possibly give them for such a delay?"

Andra thought about it. "Tell them I'm Asantha Cooray's proxy and I need to confirm how she wants me to vote," she said.

"Oh come now, Ms. Barger, this is Asantha Cooray we're talking about. You can't possibly expect them to believe—"

"Can you make it happen or not?"

She heard Swimney exhale after taking a drag from his cigar.

"I believe so," he said, speaking very slowly. "But it'll take me some time to find someone capable of getting a message to her."

Andra smiled.

"Actually," she said, "I know just the man for the job."

FIVE

Powder

The car slowed, then turned onto a bumpy road. Andra could hear gravel hitting the engine casing beneath her. She leaned toward the passenger window, found one of the thumbnail-sized clear spots, and peeked.

Uluru loomed before her, a glorious, majestic presence rather than the flattened mound she had seen from the plane. It looked like an island rising from the outback, reddened and grooved, the lowering sun casting mysterious shadows in lines across the formation's western angles. Even without a full window, the view was so impressive it nearly made Andra's apprehension drop away.

Swimney brought the car to a stop without pulling over, so she knew they were the only ones on the small, gravel road.

"This is your stop," he said. "Leave your luggage bag in the trunk, I'll have someone deliver it to you later. Just place your hood over your head and follow the perimeter trail. As you make your way around the rock, you'll eventually come to the place designed for you to access Uluru. Take it, report in, and you're set."

Andra heard the doors unlock. "So you'll have Wade get the message to Asantha Cooray as I've asked?" she said.

A heavy sigh flowed through the speaker. "Yes, yes," he said. "I'll set up the meeting you've requested as soon as I can."

Andra lifted the silver hood, repulsed as she looked at it a second time.

"What if I don't wear it?" she said. "I'm no dignitary—what if I decide I don't care whether people know who I am?"

She heard a whirring sound. The glass partition rolled down, slowly. Cigar smoke rolled toward her like fog attacking a beach, and try as she might she could still only see Swimney as an obscure silhouette with jowls and a balding head.

"The Mechen Klav would kill you, and the Chamber Proxy would cast a vote in your place," he said. "You'd lose your life with nothing gained."

"And that's legal?"

He coughed. "You may be confused about the intention of the Council Rules. The Founding Framework and its guidelines aren't in question whatsoever, meaning the vote is all that matters," he said. "That's all the laws are designed the protect: the vote. So yes, under those parameters the Mechen Klav would be justified in taking your life since an unmasked delegate means the vote can't take place."

She nodded. "Then it's all about procedure. No thought to right or wrong, just procedure... whatever it takes to maintain a centuries-old norm."

Even through the haze, she could see the lighter flame from Swimney igniting another cigar. "I'm afraid I have to disagree with you on that," he said. "Protecting an election should be paramount for any government."

"Protecting yes, engineering no."

She lifted her hood, pulled it on. "A warm hood in the desert," she said, climbing out of the car. "Genius."

She saw her reflection in the sedan's tinted windows. The silver shone, the black mesh over her face gave her a clear view and ample breathing. Different from the hoods made famous long ago, she decided, maybe even better looking... yet somehow worse.

Massaging her bandaged hand, she glanced at Uluru. The full view was breathtaking, especially with the setting sun brushing the rock in a palette of pinks, oranges, and reds.

"The Aboriginals prohibit climbing, right?" she said as smoke bellowed from the front passenger window. "Because Uluru's sacred?"

Swimney's silhouette took a drag from the cigar.

"You mean the Aboriginals who came along one hundred thousand years after the first council meeting?" he said. "The Aboriginals who have several dozen delegates in attendance? Trust me, they don't mind making an exception every fifty years."

The trunk re-latched and the automated rear door closed.

"For what it's worth, Ms. Barger, I wish you a good council," Swimney said. "I'll be in touch soon. Perhaps you'll see to it that my grandson has more than myself."

Her mouth dropped. Had Swimney just encouraged her to vote against diminishing? Or had she just completely misinterpreted an innocent remark?

The window rolled up and Swimney drove off, his cigar stench mixing with a cloud of dust from the dirt road. She turned away from the road, toward a dirt trail signed for access to the Perimeter Path. The sun was close to the horizon but the prospect of walking Uluru's immense perimeter in darkness wasn't bothering her in the least.

The prospect of talking with whatever was left of Asantha Cooray... that was truly frightening.

The perimeter path was dusty, shrub-lined, and beautiful. Sunset may have left red ripples across Uluru, but the path was deeper, more orange. Even now, with the sun below the horizon, the temperature felt like mid-day. Spindly bloodwood trees stood like sentries stationed randomly near the rock's base, nourished by the dark, vein-like water runoff channels adorning the rock's steep, vertical sides. Uluru's deep red surface sparkled whenever the fading twilight hit the coarse quartz and feldspar grains just right.

Dozens of tiny, black bush flies danced around the mesh screen on Andra's hood, determined to find a way inside. If nothing else, she figured the hood was a useful means of combating the region's infamous flies.

Voices sounded somewhere in the distance, from other people making their way around the path. Probably delegates, she figured, or tourists who just happened to pick one of the most unusual evenings of the year at Uluru.

Swimney had said she would know where to turn off when she saw it, so she kept looking for other people along the path, figuring they would be turning in the same place. An hour in, however, starlight had replaced sunlight and there was still no sign of anyone else despite occasional voices.

Animal noises sounded, alerting the other wildlife to her presence, and small creatures scurried through the brush. Andra soaked it in. Shadow didn't bother her, even in unfamiliar territory. She preferred it. Maybe it was the diminisher training, or the comfort of seeing without being seen. Or maybe, she mulled, the invisibility made her feel free of responsibility.

Darkness and Uluru's looming curve made distances difficult to judge, but she guessed she was about one-third of the way along the path. The rock stretched up more than 1,000 feet and looked even more imposing at night than during the day, its compelling colors blacked out, a monster's immense, ebony shoulder rising against the night sky. Starlit erosion ripples along Uluru's sidewalls played upon Andra's mind, suggesting curtain-like movement where there was none.

Or was there?

Uluru's vertical jags and crevasses undulated. Andra stopped walking, wondering whether this was the spot she was supposed to notice. The distant sides looked the same as always, but the towering wall directly next to her position on the trail didn't look solid.

She left the path and leaned into a shrub, joining its silhouette with her own. Instinct and training took over from there. She slowed her heartbeat and raised herself to her toes, minimizing her footsteps. Thinking and moving like shadow was easy, a simple matter of crouching, bobbing, and stretching in deliberate bursts. Even with her bandaged hand aching from the movements she reached Uluru's base in no time.

Uluru's side undulated like ripples across a lake, only deeper. Everything else looked normal: the trail, the shrubs, the empty aluminum soda can tossed to one side. Graffiti markings peeked from a small rock embedded into the nearby desert floor, a hand-sized depiction of a pyramid with no walls. Something skittered nearby, lizard-sized from the sound of it.

Andra sat, hidden and silent, watching. Thirty minutes passed, then an hour. Information was more valuable than time, and patience was one of her strong suits.

Footsteps approached. A group of silhouettes were leaving the perimeter path for her location, making little attempt at subtlety. Andra watched as five hooded people approached the same rippling wall. One of them was unusually stocky and made a rattling sound while walking, as if jewelry or coins jiggled from the movements. Another silhouette stuck a hand into the ripples, seemingly brushing them aside, then walked forward and disappeared.

Three others did the same, but the rattling, heavyset figure turned and faced the desert surrounding the rock.

"The rest of you... hurry up and get inside," a man's muffled voice called.

Andra tensed.

"Inside, now!" the man called, the jiggling sound again distinct as he raised a hand, motioning. "All of you!"

Shrubs just a few feet away from Andra rustled, startling her. A hooded figure rose up. Several yards away, another hooded figure arose... then another, and another. Moments later some fifteen shadowed figures stood in the Outback, all looking at the hooded man next to Uluru. Andra took a breath and slowly stood up, joining the crowd.

The lean, hooded man shook his head.

"Diminishers," he grunted in mock-disgust, making several of them laugh. "After me."

He turned, used a hand to swoop the ripples apart like a large drapery, then stepped through and vanished. The other diminishers emerged from their off-trail locations and filed forward, emulating what he had done. Andra watched as she lined up with them, fascinated yet appalled as the creepy, hooded procession approached and then vanished inside Uluru.

Wary, Andra reached out to touch the ripples wallpapering Uluru's side, felt pain throbbing throughout her hand, then realized her mistake. *Use the unbandaged hand, dummy!* she scolded herself. The ripples, as it turned out, felt like velvet against her fingers. Casting them aside, she opened the mysterious drapes, stepped forward... and plummeted into pitch-black nothingness.

Stomach lurching, she dropped, weightless, unable to see a thing. For a moment she was spinning, head over heels, but she managed to straighten up, steadying herself into a vertical, stable fall. There was no sound, no wind blowing over her ears, no echo from being inside someplace small. All she heard was her own frantic breathing and a no-longer-suppressed heartbeat.

If there were walls, or rocks, or anything, she couldn't tell. She looked down as she fell, but couldn't see any hint of a bottom. It occurred to her this might be the way the council disposed of the people they considered risky delegates—the other diminishers had hidden themselves too, after all—but she decided that didn't make much sense after bringing everyone all this way.

If not for the terror of wondering whether she was about to hit bottom, the falling itself wasn't so bad—exhilarating, really, and a rare sense of weightlessness. The punch line to an old joke crossed her mind: it's not the fall that kills you, it's the sudden stop at the end.

Suddenly she felt herself slowing. Her stomach lurched again as every cell in her body seemed to lift, like a billion tiny parachutes lofting her to safety. The falling sensation ceased and, if she wasn't mistaken, she was hovering in midair, as if she could fly.

Bright, white light hit her square in the eyes, blinding her.

“Position and category,” a man's voice demanded.

She recognized the voice. It belonged to the heavyset man she had seen outside. Dazed from the fall, her bandaged hand throbbing, she decided not to answer until she understood what it was he was expecting to hear.

The man repeated his sentence. This time Andra assembled what he was looking for.

“Diminisher and, uh... council voter.”

She heard scribbling.

“Please join the council members.”

She felt herself dropping again, slowly this time as the light dimmed, just enough for her eyes to adjust. Angled framework appeared—metallic supports for some sort of room-sized structure. She saw four supports: one to each side and two others behind her, all of them joining at the light above her head. The glowing light remained suspended directly above as she descended. It was larger than her head and far too bright to look at, though she kept trying, hoping to spot whatever unseen method was lowering her, feet-first, onto a stone-tiled floor. *The light never dimmed,* she realized. *It was me, moving further away from it, that made it seem as if the light was fading.*

Her mind flashed back to the graffiti. She hadn't paid enough attention to remember many details, but still... it was a drawing of an empty, three-dimensional triangle... a pyramid shape with a frame but no sides. *And it might have had a big white dot at its center,* she suddenly recalled.

Was she standing inside the object it depicted?

Looking beyond the metallic supports, she saw an additional, superstructure framework, all set within one end of a chamber the size of a basketball arena. People in hoods stood before her... and above her, and to each side, all of them facing her. They were arranged like a choir, apparently waiting for each delegate and council member to join them upon arriving.

At the chamber's center, five hooded individuals sat within a fire that engulfed their legs. Andra couldn't fathom how they could remain there, but the flames didn't seem to bother them. In their midst, one of the council members wore a hood with multicolored beads strung along one side.

It's the stocky man with the jiggling sound... the one who just asked me for my position and category.

She heard a yell from the blinding light. Someone else was plummeting down, she guessed, still out of sight but apparently headed her way. *At least* I *didn't scream*, she thought.

"Take your place, council member," the man with the beaded hood said to her again.

By now her feet were on the platform, not far from the men within the fire circle. She looked around her, saw a walkway leading toward the sea of hooded watchers, and started toward it.

"Not there... over here," another man's hood-muffled voice called.

He was wearing a silver hood with an eagle claw strung to one side and gestured to one of four empty seats within the fire circle. Andra's heart jumped. At this gathering of thousands she would be sitting in the center circle... within the fire. She stepped forward methodically, hesitating when she reached the flames.

"It's just patience and shadow, like always," Eagle Claw said. "Be one with the flames, just like you become one with shadow."

Given her background, she decided that actually made sense. She sent her heart racing faster, figuring it would raise her temperature. Warily, she stepped inside the fire ring and sat down, conscious of how horrible her hand already felt from being burned and how much worse it would feel across her entire body. Instead the flames felt like summer wind, warm to the touch but pleasant. She exhaled, relieved.

The screaming delegate arrived, dropping from the light, into the sideless pyramid, then rising into a sudden hover. Coaxing his job and rank took considerably longer than Andra's dazed response.

More delegates followed, but the fifth to arrive after Andra was different, either a veteran of previous visits or someone with ice for blood. He emerged from the light like a god from the heavens, straight and composed, not the least bit ruffled. His hood had cobalt stripes running through the silver on the back side, and he was wearing a dark suit. Nodding to the others, he stated his position and rank without being asked. Then he took another of the empty seats within the fire ring, again without being asked.

They know him, she realized. *Despite the anonymity requirement, some of these people know one another.* She wondered whether it meant some of them were above the rules.

Ten minutes later she had her answer. A delegate arrived smoothly... but momentum tipped the person's hood to one side. A desperate grab didn't help; the hood fell off. The entire council chamber gasped. Exposed before them was a middle-aged man wearing a shirt and tie. His sandy hair was rumpled from the hood, and his freckled face seemed flushed.

Andra studied him, thinking that he reminded her of someone she knew. A moment later she had it: the man was a United States senator. She had seen him in news reports. Unflattering news reports, too.

A U.S. senator, here? The implication horrified her.

The senator grabbed his hood from the stone-tiled floor.

"No, don't bother," the man with the beaded hood barked.

The senator looked up, eyes wide.

"Wait—Mr. Chairman, I'm Family Glenrock, one of the premier Cinüe families," he said.

"I'm... I'm sorry, Stuart," Bead Hood said. "This is truly unfortunate."

Three Mechen Klav members appeared, dressed in purple hoods and matching robes with slim, black sashes—formal uniforms that Andra had heard about from Cristina, but never seen. They took positions to either side of Glenrock, with one remaining in front of him. Andra felt nervous anticipation filling the chamber. She noticed movement in the stands above, looked up, and saw dozens of delegates turning away. Swimney's account of what could happen if she didn't keep her hood in place popped into her head. *Would the council really hurt someone, or worse, just because of a damned wardrobe malfunction?*

"Hold on," Eagle Claw said, standing up amid the fire ring group.

He looked unusually thin and his legs jittered as he stood, but he seemed comfortable speaking to such a large gathering. "I think we can all see this was just an unfortunate accident," he said, "and I can personally vouch that Stuart Glenrock is not the kind of man who will use this exposure to his advantage in any way."

Though muffled, his voice sounded youthful to Andra, a surprise since she'd assumed everyone on the council would be much older.

"Given that, and the extraordinary circumstances under which we are gathering, I propose we stay the usual execution rule and proceed to other matters," he continued.

Cheers went up amongst the crowd.

"I second that motion," another member of the fire circle said, in a heavy Russian accent.

"And I'll third," said yet another, this time a woman's voice.

Bead Hood held his hands high, quieting the room.

"Would you also vouch that others among us will not treat him differently in civilian life now that we know of this affiliation?" he said. "Would you vouch that in crisis he would not use this knowledge against us, as a blackmail tool? Or leak the information to news media? Or target his family? Or do any of the myriad things which could happen as a result of this exposure?"

He lowered his head while continuing.

"There are reasons for Council Law, reasons which predate the whole of us. Tragedy or no... these laws will not be cast aside."

"Then perhaps we incarcerate Mr. Glenrock and then discuss an amendment allowing such a change," an olive-hooded delegate called from the fire ring. "Think of the effort required just to cover up his disappearance."

Andra felt her jaw drop as she placed the distinctive voice.

England's Prime Minister? Are there world leaders on this council?

"There will be no amendment, and no vote," Bead Hood said. "The law is clear."

He motioned to the center Mechen Klav officer.

"Wait, I can turn this into an advantage for us," Glenrock said, still clasping his fallen hood. "I'll remain here... oversee the facility with no outside contact... become the kind of active leader we haven't had since Elizabe—"

Bead Hood made another motion to the officer, who was armed with a type of rifle Andra had never seen, metallic swirls and arcs looping along the barrel. The officer took aim at Glenrock.

Horrified, Andra couldn't sit silent any longer.

"A loose hood is not a crime!" she said, rising to her feet.

Glenrock looked at her with grateful eyes. The officer, rifle still aimed, angled his head her way, then up to Bead Hood, as if making sure the order stood. Bead Hood issued an affirming nod.

"No!" Andra said. "Can't you see this is wrong?"

She looked up at the countless hooded watchers. "Can't you *all* see this is wrong?"

Glenrock, sobbing, covered his face. The officer briefly bowed his head in his direction in an apparent gesture of respect, then fired point-blank. The council chamber erupted, first from the rifle's deafening blast, then with a collective gasp as they watched the outcome.

The rifle shot had blown Glenrock's head into a grisly, blood-red powder.

SIX

Joined

Aghast, Andra wanted to turn away but couldn't keep herself from staring at the jagged plume of gritty, bony powder. It dusted Glenrock's shoulders and sent a dry, putrid haze billowing through the chamber. Those delegates who were still watching cried out in horror as the rest of Glenrock's body fell backward from the force of the blast, landing on the floor with an audible, nauseating thud.

Andra felt as if she might be sick.

"Finish that elsewhere," Bead Hood told the Mechen Klav officers.

They grabbed Glenrock's body by the arms and dragged it through a doorway adjacent to the stage. "Take your seats... *everyone*," Bead Hood said, looking at Andra. "The Glenrock vote is hereby assigned to the Chamber Proxy."

He hesitated, as if for emphasis, while continuing to face Andra.

"All *other* proxies shall keep themselves explicitly focused on the task at hand," Bead Hood said. "Understood? Now then... thirty-three delegates to go."

Andra felt her jaw shuddering, and knew her hands were numb. She couldn't care less about the rebuke, but the complete lack of human empathy... it seemed shocking, even from a people who pioneered diminishing. Eagle Claw rested a hand on her shoulder, guiding her gently back to her seat. Furious, she shrugged it away.

The council chamber looked like it held several hundred people, but as more delegates arrived Andra was certain she could have heard a pin drop.

Time zombified as the rest of the delegates arrived. Andra, still numb, didn't even hear the dismissal. Instead she rose up when everyone else did, following them through generic stone hallways, entering her designated room shortly thereafter. She gathered only the basics—that the entire council was dismissed until the vote, which would take place the following morning. That left about ten hours for sleeping, reading, drinking, or whatever it was people did when they were alone and cut off from civilization.

Accommodations, as it turned out, were luxurious. Her room seemed the size of a small aircraft hangar, with a full-length bar, three leather sofas, and a lap pool on the far end. Fine art hung above the sofas—was that really a genuine Monet?—but recessed lighting provided a modern feel. The bedroom had a plush, circular bed large enough for a gymnastics team, and another bar—in case she got thirsty walking from the main room. A second bedroom was really more of a private nightclub, with a piano, a jukebox, and a dance floor for two.

I'm surprised I haven't had to diminish anyone here, she thought... but the Cinüe diminished humans, not the other way around. She wondered whether her mother or grandmother, or any outsider, had ever seen the place.

The room was so large and luxurious that she wondered whether she was supposed to share it. But no one else showed up, so she supposed it was hers. Her luggage bag sat just inside the front door, meaning Swimney had delivered it as promised. Andra removed her hood, but only after making certain her door was closed and locked.

Removing the hood was more than just an action, it made her feel human again. So much had happened from the moment Wade delivered her message that she wished her room really was a resort, and that she had a few relaxing days to clear her mind.

Instead she had just watched an execution, and now faced the biggest decision of her life.

She walked to the bar, looked it over, decided alcohol was the last thing she needed. Tossing her weary head onto the giant bed, that sounded much better. After the day she'd just had, the idea of curling up for a few extra hours—

A song began playing from the jukebox in the night-club room. She glanced at the front door. *Still locked. How could someone else get inside?* She ran for her hood, threw it over her head, then edged toward the other room.

"Over here, love," she heard, from the bedroom.

If the voice wasn't enough to tell her who it was, the smell of leather did the job.

"Wade," she said, before she even saw him.

"I like the hood," he said with a mild southern drawl. "I know some guys who are really into that."

"Yeah, I know some too—all those sick delegates out there," she said, removing the hood and tossing it to the bed.

Wade leaned against the bedroom bar, chewing on a toothpick. His shell necklace, leather gloves, and black tee were dusty, and he looked like he hadn't shaved for several days. Only his upper lip looked whisker-free.

"Any point in me asking how you managed to get in here?" she said.

"Darlin', I deliver mail between here and a hidden city that's so fundamentally altered it barely exists," he said. "A big rock's not gonna' keep me out, especially when you consider what I'm drivin' to work every day."

She remembered the baritone velvet purr she'd heard in the darkness near the lanai—the utterance of an illegal animal, very likely a Cinüe beast tailored for carrying Wade between the two disparate delivery locations.

"A big rock's going to hit you right on the head if you call me darling again," she said.

"Touché," he said with a wink.

She looked away. *Him, of all people,* she thought. *Why did I tell Swimney to call Wade?* She sensed him walking closer, raising his hands, putting his arms around her.

"Not now," she said, elbowing him away.

"Now more than ever," he whispered as he pulled her close. They kissed, Andra's mind balancing scales the entire time: slug or succumb.

Slug won. Wade smiled while doubled over, apparently pleased with himself.

"Don't you understand what I'm up against right now?" she said, with more than a hint of anger.

"You know I do, love."

"Then leave me alone like we agreed. Can't you please just let me be? I've told you before, I can't take the chance... I *won't* take the chance. Not anymore, not after what happened. I refuse to have a diminished child, I refuse to put myself in a position where that becomes even a remote possibility."

"You don't have to put yourself in a position, I'd be happy to—"

"Wade, I'm serious! There's nothing we can do here that's going to change things between us."

He nodded, then returned to the bar and took a swig from his glass. "Nothing?" he said. "Or everything?"

She felt like borrowing a powder rifle from the Klav.

"Even if I vote against diminishing... even if I'm the only one in that council of hundreds who is willing to break unanimous, willing to risk my family, willing to condemn my brother to death, willing to betray Asantha Cooray... even then, do you really think anything changes for us?" she said. "Do you actually think Mechen Klav officers armed with rifles that'll turn us to baking powder are going to let us live our lives the way we want to?"

Wade took another drink. "Doesn't matter," he said. "This isn't about us anymore. Used to be, but not anymore. Not now that you have an actual vote."

Andra shut her eyes, wishing she could shut the world out. "I can't even think straight right now," she said, putting her head in her hands. "How can I do this when I can't think straight?"

Wade picked up his toothpick, chewed on the tip. "Now *that* I can't answer," he said. "But tell you what, things take care of themselves. You break that unanimous vote and those people will adapt. We'll adapt too."

She looked up at him, incredulous. "Will Earth adapt? If I get rid of diminishing, making sure people are finally born unaltered, will the parents adapt? Will they welcome babies they barely recognize, with abilities they can't even dream of? Or will they just flip out?"

Wade sat his glass on the counter with more force than Andra expected. "The way I see it, they won't really have much choice," he said.

Andra returned her head to her hands, feeling as if it was the only action that would keep it from rolling off her shoulders. "Yeah... the way *you* see it," she mumbled. "I see a lot more. I see complete chaos."

She moved to the bed, sat, then dropped all the way down, exhausted. The jukebox song ended, and the silence seemed nice.

"Annie, I'm here for a reason," Wade said. "Mail, from David Stanford Swimney." He reached into his shirt pocket, removed an envelope, and walked it over to her. "Urgent, too."

Andra rose herself up with a sigh. The envelope was gray, the note inside the same color only with embedded, unprinted lines and Swimney' name embossed at the top.

"You're settin' up a meeting, aren't you," Wade said. "With Asantha Cooray. Because Council Law allows it."

She nodded. "Swimney says it's on in... oh god, only a few minutes from now. What the hell do I do?"

Wade shook his head. "Do you have any idea how dangerous this is?" he said. "What you're doing... darlin', every time I'm in contact with Edenshire people, inside that hidden place, it changes me. Something inside me numbs, I can't explain it. Regular people like us just aren't meant to be in touch with people living true Cinüe life."

Andra fixed her eyes on him. "And you are... regular people... right?" she said. "You swear you're human, like me? No Cinüe ancestors whatsoever?" She hated the suspicions crossing her mind... notions he had alleviated ad nauseum, yet phoenix-like in their persistent return.

"Red-blooded and everything," he said.

"So why are *you* their mailman? Why do they give you special training, and arcane tech? Why not have a Cinüe do the job?"

"I don't think they have a choice," he said. "The Klav, the delegates, everyone else in here, they're all Cinüe, but I hear tell they need to include regular human beins' in what they do, don't know why. Me, I was young and stupid when the retirin' guy brought me in, and tell you what, he was right about one thing: the job ain't borin' at all."

Andra wondered whether the same issue—having to include regular humans in certain aspects of Cinüe culture—had anything to do with her being named to the council. Maybe Asantha Cooray didn't have a choice, she realized. Maybe her hand was forced in some way, so she went with the least distasteful choice she had left: someone who was technically a part of her own family.

"You've done something even the Cinüe can't do," she said, thinking aloud. "You've been to Edenshire... met Asantha, even."

"Met a lot of people," he said. "But like I said: regular folk just aren't meant to be in Edenshire, any more than the Edenshire types are meant to be here... at least, not now, ever since they altered the place. Whatever those people did to hide it... passin' through there does somethin' to you... somethin' that messes you up."

"Then why put yourself through it?"

Wade launched into a flippant response, then stopped himself mid-way. "Truth is, I got this problem," he said. "I always wanna' know about everythin' that most people don't know about. But you... Annie, are you sure about wantin' to talk with Asantha Cooray? What can this meeting possibly accomplish?"

She put a hand to his chest. "I need to know why she picked me... and what she'll do if I betray her."

Wade swore. "I'm staying with you," he said.

She managed a smile. "You always do. But no... I don't want her to know you're here. What you do... what both of us do... it's all best kept secret."

"You're as bad as they are," he whispered.

They hugged, then kissed.

"Go," she said, pushing him away.

Andra steeled her anxious nerves. After two nervous-stomach visits to the restroom, there was no time for another. According to Swimney's note Asantha Cooray was due in two minutes. Andra had no idea how this would happen, how it even *could* happen. The idea that a woman from a pre-human era could still function, much less communicate, made little sense.

Wade was gone, another mystery but one she enjoyed. She'd left him in the jukebox room and when she returned he wasn't there—exactly what she knew would happen. Mail delivery training apparently trumped diminisher training. She hoped Bead Hood, Cobalt Hood, Eagle Claw, and the others didn't know he had visited. She especially hoped the Mechen Klav didn't know. Even though Swimney had probably made legal arrangements for a mail drop-off, it didn't seem a stretch to assume Council Law forbid anything beyond leaving letters in mail slots.

Still anxious, she re-read Swimney's note. It gave a time, and said Asantha Cooray would meet her, but no other details. There was nothing to do but wait. She checked her watch again. One minute to go... thirty seconds... ten...

The time arrived. She looked around.

Nothing.

After a few seconds she wandered into the other rooms, thinking perhaps her visitor would appear elsewhere. Still nothing. She checked her watch again: one minute past.

When it reached ten minutes past, she began to think that either Swimney had botched the time or she had been stood up. Thirty minutes passed, then an hour. By the time two hours had passed Andra was exhausted and convinced the meeting wasn't going to happen. She changed into her nightgown, brushed her teeth, and collapsed into bed.

Only she wasn't in bed.

The moment she pulled the covers over herself, she was inside a box. A narrow, rectangular box with sheets for a lining, and a soft glow from no apparent source. She tried pulling the sheets down but they wouldn't budge. Sitting up didn't work either, since the sheets above had become stiff and impenetrable. Same thing on the sides.

I'm trapped.

She felt terror building but fought it back, demanding calm, knowing it was her only chance. But there was no denying she was trapped and could barely move. *What about oxygen*? she suddenly wondered. *How long before it runs out?*

Then she noticed a faint outline an inch or so above her arms and hands, as if she had two edges. She tried touching the outer edge but her hand passed right through. She glanced down at the rest of her body, best she could, and saw the new, outer edge went the entire way. It moved when she moved, wiggled when she wiggled.

Double-vision, maybe? A sudden astigmatism?

Studying her hand, she saw shapes in the center, faint lines, twists, and splotches she didn't recognize. A panicked comparison revealed her other hand, though bandaged, contained similar shapes. Her arms and torso, or at least the limited portions she could see of them from her trapped position, did too. *Are the interior shapes paired with the exterior outlines?* She let her gaze linger, trying to get just the right angle for her eyes to make out—

Muscles. They're muscles... and bones. Am I seeing my own insides?

Somehow she didn't think that was the case. Her head swam, and for just a moment she saw another outline waver before her, one with a face, muscles, a skull, a brain. She gasped as the outline moved away from her head and then back toward her, disappearing into her own eyes.

There's an outline around my head, too, she realized. *My whole body's been overlapped, it's inside some kind of body outline, and the whole outline can move, same way I can move. Not far, but it can move. It's independent. It's...*

Her head swam again.

"We are joined," she heard.

The voice sounded melodic rather than scary, which threw her.

" 'We?' " Andra stammered.

"My proxy, our time is short," she heard, again in pleasant, melodic tones. "We must be direct."

Proxy? So then, this is... Asantha Cooray?

She felt panic spreading through her chest. Instinct wanted her to back away, but all she could do was jostle within the box's confines. As Andra shifted, Asantha Cooray's outline moved in an identical pattern.

"Enough foolishness," she heard, the voice forceful though still melodic. "Have your say, and quickly."

Andra took a breath.

"I'm honored, but confused," she managed. "Why am I your proxy?"

She felt Asantha Cooray's mouth moving, and her own mouth moving in unison.

"I survey my Earthen family extensively," Asantha Cooray said. "You are best capable of carrying out my vote."

"I... I'm not sure that's right. I'm not a true member of your family, and my preferences... they may differ from yours."

Even as she spoke the words, Andra felt angry. She reached out and pounded the solid sheet above her. *It's not me*, she realized, startled. *It's Asantha Cooray who is angry. Because she lashed out and we're joined, I lashed out too.*

The thought frightened her. The ancient Cinüe wasn't human in the traditional sense—what if Cooray used their joining to her advantage, striking herself, knowing Andra's body would do the same? Could she hurt her, or even kill her, by doing so?

"I orchestrate things beyond anything you can conceive," Asantha Cooray said, her melodies harsh now. "You are a pup, a kinder in an elderly universe. You'll cast my vote, then hope to blossom and understand. You aren't to trouble me with this."

Andra swallowed. "And... you still support diminishing?" she said.

Again the anger, again the fist, and the pounding.

"Okay... okay, I understand," Andra said, not waiting to hear what Asantha Cooray would say.

"Pup, your independent streak is a virtue I'm aware of, and your talent holds promise," Asantha Cooray said. "In the offing, after the Maybe Objective is complete, I might embrace it. But don't confuse this vote for something it isn't. The restoration of Edenshire proceeds regardless. The power you presume merely determines the casualty rates."

Andra didn't know how to answer.

"You'll vote in favor of diminishing," Asantha Cooray continued. "You'll carry out this final baby step for me."

"But diminishing, it means people aren't what they're supposed to be," Andra said, in a deflated whisper.

"No," Asantha Cooray said. "They're what they *need* to be... in order to save Cinüe lives."

Suddenly Andra didn't feel angry. Instead she felt grief... Asantha Cooray's grief, a profound, hollow ache in her chest.

"If... if I don't vote the way you want..." Andra started.

This time she felt a different emotion surging, one more difficult to place. Embittered amusement?

"You'll have nowhere to run," Asantha Cooray said, in a melody suggesting an opera's final note.

The outline around Andra thinned, faded, then vanished. Her joining with Asantha Cooray was finished—somehow, Andra could sense she was now on her own—yet she still didn't move for several minutes, trying to absorb what she had just been told, and what she had experienced. Finally she reached up with her bandaged right hand, grabbed at the stiffened sheets, then froze.

Her hand didn't hurt, first time since the hospital. She flexed it, as far as the bandages allowed; still no pain. The sheets were changing too, softening. Thrilled, she tossed them toward her feet.

She was in her huge bed, within the massive room.

But I may as well be trapped inside that tiny box.

SEVEN

Ballot

As it turned out, her hand was not only pain-free, it was burn-free—still scarred, but only in a superficial fashion. Maybe the joining had somehow sped recovery? She had no idea, but pacing the room to alleviate stress felt much more productive now that the injury was healed. When she finally settled into bed, she slept without getting under the covers. After her experience with the stiffened bed covers, she wondered whether she would ever slide into a set of sheets again.

Breakfast followed a restless sleep. The food was as elaborate as the room, the lap pool equally luxurious. The robes felt elegant, the lotions invigorating, the fireplace cozy. Everything was doing exactly what it was supposed to do. *Sending me a message*, Andra's subconscious screamed. She knew Cristina would endorse that message, her mother too. Jackson and Wade's lives probably depended upon her abiding that message. *But what if doing something different means accomplishing more?*

She fumbled through her clothes bag, wondering what to wear to a council tasked with deciding humanity's fate. Most delegates had been wearing suits, so Andra opted for jeans and a blouse.

Music sounded, strings issuing from unseen speakers. Andra assumed it was like an adult version of a school bell, calling them into the council chamber. She felt chills. The vote was nearly at hand.

She still had no idea what to do.

Her heart told her to vote no, but her mind said she still didn't have enough information to make an educated decision. What was Asantha Cooray talking about when she said diminishing was saving Cinüe lives? What was the Maybe Objective? Did it have something to do with 'restoring' the Cinüe?

Restoring them meant moving them from Edenshire to... here, she figured, at least if the old stories were true. *To Earth, from a time before humans.*

Was diminishing part of a sinister takeover plan? Or was there truly some advantage she would eliminate by voting against it? Did lives really hinge on the Diminishing Act passing? Sure: her own life, she figured, and her family's life. Probably Wade's life too. Asantha Cooray made it very clear she wanted her to vote in favor. Her ill brother needed her to vote in favor. Two Mechen Klav details had come after her because they were convinced her possible opposition vote would cause damage.

But people deserve the chance to grow into what they're supposed to be!

She had the sinking feeling that the right answer was that there was no right answer.

Her walk to the council chamber seemed like a scene out of a creepy old movie, a mob of hooded people silently issuing through hallways as cellos played. The chamber itself looked darker than the day before, with shimmering, gold bunting across the rafters and most of the delegates seated in shadow. An orchestra of hooded musicians played from a well behind the center stage, all in turquoise choir robes.

Andra took her seat on the stage, amid the eight other Cinüe council members. Even hooded she felt out of place, knowing she wasn't really a Cinüe, just a representative. The other delegates wore dark suits and seemed taller, more distinguished. She wondered whether she might be seated next to a world leader, or renowned researcher, or maybe a celebrity with global influence. No matter; she was certain she didn't belong.

The music stopped as Bead Hood called the council to order.

"Thank you again for attending, I trust you've had a comfortable stay," he said. "I remind you that Council Law is in effect. Up for tercentennial ratification is the Diminishing Act of Paleolithic 918, co-sponsored and authored by Asantha Cooray the Seventh. Unanimous vote passes. Presentation in favor, please."

Cobalt Hood rose from his seat and stepped to the podium.

"Ladies and gentlemen, I thank you for your vote today. As you know, diminishing has a two hundred thousand-year history of success. It saves lives, Cinüe and human. It keeps the dangerous individuals from breaking free. It also keeps the door to Edenshire open—a door Asantha Cooray worked so diligently to establish and maintain, and which shall open all the way in the very near future. Together, humans and Cinüe not only coexist but thrive. The Diminishing Act is a complete success, and will continue to be so."

Applause broke out, segmented at first then blistering as section upon section of the chamber not only cheered but rose to their feet. Andra hesitated as the delegates on stage rose, then stood up with them. She clapped a few times, so as not to stand apart.

Several moments passed before people took their seats and the applause died out. Bead Hood's chuckles boomed over the unseen speakers as he said, "Thank you Mr. Vice-Chairman, I think we can all give thanks right now for the Council Law Amendment of 1246 permitting pre-vote ovations."

The delegates laughed.

"Okay, back to business," he said. "You'll have three minutes to vote, followed by a two-minute verification period, at which time the result will be added to the session's official minutes. At that time you'll exit the chamber for escort outside, return to your cars and—"

He paused and leaned toward Eagle Claw, who whispered into his ear.

Bead Hood stood up straight again.

"Forgive me. Council Law states that I must ask for Presentation Opposed before the vote."

The chamber went silent

"Presentation Opposed? Anyone?"

Andra shifted in her seat, wondering whether she should try. She knew this was her only chance to sway other delegates, to make a difference beyond being the only opposition vote. She also understood the reality: a frontal assault on their policy would never work, given the room's overwhelming sentiment. That meant she would need to ease into the subject, acknowledging diminishing's benefits while also presenting a case for not messing with human life development. Could that possibly sway a room filled with such hardened sentiment?

No, she decided. *Changing people's minds requires action, not talk. They need to see the damage they're causing... but I have no way of showing that. If they can't see it, they'll never vote against it. I need a way of showing them the damage they're causing.*

Without that, she knew, her opposition remained toothless. Deaf ears and inaction's comfort would prevail. As she looked around the chamber she had the distinct feeling the other delegates were looking her way, waiting... though she knew that must be her imagination.

"Last call—Presentation Opposed?" Bead Hood said.

Silence. Andra opened her mouth but couldn't force words, not when she knew she had no evidence. She flashed to David Stanford Swimney telling her that diminishing could not work with a simple majority, or even a two-thirds vote, that it required an all-hands-on-deck approach. She suspected the same was true of overturning it, regardless of this vote and its rules. Her solitary, reasoned voice would not change prevailing sentiment... and that's what would need changing if she wanted to snuff the Diminishing Act altogether.

"Okay then, we'll—"

"Mr. Chairman."

A man near the doorway stood up. He was wearing a dark leather hood over a black T-shirt and patterned jeans, with a necklace outline beneath his shirt and leather gloves hanging from his pants pocket.

"I have a presentation against," he said, a gentle twang to his voice.

Andra's heart leaped into her throat.

"Oh no," she uttered, a stunned whisper to herself. "Don't, Wade. Please, don't."

The chamber echoed with a muffled, collective murmur. Several Mechen Klav headed toward the doorway. Bead Hood hung his head for a moment, then gestured for Wade to proceed.

"It's simple, actually," Wade said. "Diminishing. Kills. People."

Roars and boos erupted.

"No, listen!" Wade said. "If you genetically engineer a sightless, toothless, tail-less, furless wolf, you can't pretend it's still a wolf. All you did was find a fancy way of killing the wolf."

More uproar. The delegates near Andra were laughing, and she heard snippets of their reactions, from "appropriate metaphor" to "bet the deer don't mind" and worse. She cringed as the Mechen Klav approached Wade, rifles ready. The shoot-the-messenger crowd had their shooters at the ready. Several council members uttered Wade's name during the uproar, suggesting they recognized his voice.

"Enough," Bead Hood said. "You're not a delegate to this council, which invalidates your Presentation Opposed. Mechen Klav will please take care of this..."

"A partial human is *not* a human," Wade insisted, pointing at the delegates, up and around the chamber. "Let them be who they're supposed to be!"

Three Mechen Klav officers rushed over, grabbed Wade, and hauled him from the chamber. Andra felt her heart sink, wondering what they would do with him, hoping the rifles weren't part of the answer.

"You know what has to be done," Wade called as they dragged him through the doors. "It's your best chance to make a change... maybe your only chance!"

Andra grimaced. *A message for me, presented through shouts to them. His entire speech wasn't for the rest of them, it was for me.*

More catcalls erupted, then the doors closed and eventually the room grew quiet again.

"I was hoping he'd take off the hood," Bead Hood said.

The delegates laughed, and a few applauded.

"But since he didn't... I don't believe he violated Council Law, and I specifically asked for Presentation

Opposed. That said, I suspect his job status is in some question right now."

More laughter.

"On to the vote," he said. "Delegates first, then council members. We have nine groups of forty delegates, two-thirds majority carries the vote. The council members will then use those results to guide their own, final votes. Ballots will appear before you. Punch them with a finger, your print will identify you as a legitimate voter."

Andra stifled a gasp. Fingerprints, on a ballot? So much for anonymity. Given their location, she found it ironic that the Australian ballot was apparently not in effect.

Group four belonged to her, not that it mattered. Each of the nine groups came in with well more than the two-thirds majority required for ratification, with group two being the only one with more than six votes against. She felt better knowing she wasn't completely alone but there was no denying the reality: this room was pro-diminishing.

"Now to the council members," Bead Hood said. "Unanimous council vote is required for ratification."

Mechen Klav appeared at the end of each council row, distributing gold pens to the council members. As Andra received hers she noticed it had the date engraved into the side but no pen point on the end. She pushed the top; still no pen tip. The other delegates had the same tip-less pens but didn't seem concerned.

"The ballots are already on your desktops," Bead Hood announced. "We'll begin... now."

Andra looked at the wooden surface but didn't see a thing. Then she noticed nearby delegates pointing their pens at the desktops like flashlights, even though there was no light beam. Curious, she did the same with hers, pushing the top button while aiming the pen towards the surface. The ballot appeared, a set of glowing lines and words.

Similar to a UV light, she realized. *The ballot is written in some fancy form of invisible ink.*

She held the pen in one hand to illuminate the ballot while placing her other thumb in the appropriate box. Lifting it, and saw a glowing impression of her thumbprint. The wasn't much more to the ballot than that. The top read "Diminishing Act of Paleolithic 918, Tercentennial Vote," and below there were two words, one atop the other: "Maintain" or "Discontinue."

Looking up, Andra saw several delegates were already sitting back, finished. No dilemma for them, just a push of a thumb and done.

She stared at the ballot, heart pounding. The next fifty years of humanity was climbing her legs, clawing at her back, piling atop her shoulders, all of them shouting, begging, pleading. She heard voices closer to her as well: her brother's cancer-riddled murmurs, her mother telling her "we have obligations, dear, whether we like them or not," while crossing her fingers and looking away. It seemed easy to picture her late grandmother's adoption papers catching fire, and her photo falling over, protective glass cracking. "Your vote will keep things in perfect order for generations," she heard Cristina saying. For a moment she swore she saw Asantha Cooray's outline around her once again.

Then the faces came at her, hundreds of them, all women Andra had diminished. Two or three of them each week, for three years, yet she could still remember each of them. All nations, all races, bright to dimwitted, teenaged to middle-aged, all of them identical from a diminishing standpoint: all humans. Some of them happy, fresh into their relationships. Others unaware, recovering from celebrations that went too far. A few of them anguished, victims of an egregious crimes. Still others that had handled matters from a clinical, practical perspective.

She saw them all. No different from every night; she always saw them all. From the sobbing actress who was her first diminish, right up to the woman on the lanai and the nurse in the hospital, she saw them all.

She saw herself, too.

It has to stop. It just has to stop!

She stared at the ballot.

"Please finish your votes," she heard Bead Hood announce. "Only three of you left... make that two. Please finish your votes now so we can verify and finalize."

The council chamber wasn't as quiet as before. No one spoke, but Andra could hear shuffling as people gathered their belongings, preparing to depart.

"And now we're at one," Bead Hood said. "Please submit your vote now, please."

The voices and faces in her head nearly drowned out the announcement. Andra gritted her teeth to keep from screaming. She knew what had do be done. Wade was right, she knew what had to be done.

It has to end!

She took her thumb to the square next to "Discontinue" and pressed.

Then she shoved her finger sideways, smudging the print, and lifted her thumb.

She pressed it firmly again... into the box next to "Maintain."

EIGHT

Interface

Bead Hood was saying something but Andra didn't pay attention. She didn't need to hear the final results, she already knew them. Right now she was too busy fighting herself, refusing to allow her inner despair to surface in any visible, physical way. Even covered by a hood, she wouldn't allow it. Not now, not when she had cast her vote for a reason.

This will work, she insisted to herself. *It's a massive gamble, but this plan will work.*

The shadows would remain her advantage... an advantage she could use to overturn diminishing from behind the scenes, where she stood a chance of surviving, rather than in the council's sham-vote, where armed Mechen Klav could harm or kill under specious laws. She needed Wade, too. For her plan to work, she knew she would need to find Wade. Not that he was crucial... but then again, she admitted to herself, maybe he was.

Her subconscious and half the voices in her head screamed that she was wrong, that she had blown her opportunity. She couldn't erase the image of her own thumb casting the final vote and wondered whether it would haunt her nightmares more than the diminished faces. Already, she knew it would.

Bead Hood's voice still boomed. He was announcing the final vote.

"We have unanimous ratification of the Diminishing Act of Paleolithic 918, authored by Asantha Cooray the Seventh," he proclaimed, to a rousing cheer. "Please remember Council Law remains in place until your flights depart, and public discussion of these events is prohibited. Discretion always."

He hesitated, then raised a fist high. "Go in victory, my friends. You have preserved an important policy. The Maybe Objective is close at hand!"

Another cheer sounded. The delegates dispersed, many of them patting each other on the back as they left. Andra's legs shook as she rose from her seat. Her stomach felt sick, and got even worse as Bead Hood left the podium and approached.

"Don't think the delay wasn't noticed," he said, and might have said more if not for a Mechen Klav officer appearing at the doorway. Andra watched the officer fidget with his uniform, scuff his boots against the stone-tiled floor, then use the lower drapings of his hood to scratch his chin. Somehow it all looked familiar... and when a matchbox dropped out of the officer's pocket, she knew exactly who she was looking at.

Sandoval, she thought, disgusted at the prospect of dealing with the man Wade had chased from the deck in Kauai.

"Sir, I can't explain this but Asantha Cooray is here... barely," Sandoval said to Bead Hood, his voice shaken. "She, uh... she wants to see the mailman, and the council appointee next to you."

Andra froze.

"I'll bet she does," Bead Hood said. "Take them both into custody and deliver them to her right away. And be sure to leave them alone with her."

"Alone, Mr. Chairman? Is that safe?"

Bead Hood laughed. "Not for those two it isn't." He turned for the exit. Sandoval pointed his rifle at Andra and motioned her forward.

"What's the Maybe Objective?" she called to Bead Hood.

He left the chamber but she heard his voice trailing away from outside. "It's what makes today the last diminishing ratification we'll ever need," he called, with an amused tone.

Andra didn't like the sound of that. She followed Sandoval into the hallway, but Bead Hood was already gone. The other delegates had filed out as well, headed to—

She realized she didn't know where they had gone because she didn't know how to leave. The entry had been a drop into an open-sided pyramid frame. Was there an elevator someplace?

Four other officers joined Sandoval, pushing Wade. He was still wearing his dark leather hood, and exuding his dark leather attitude. Andra grabbed his hand.

"Did they tell you who wants to see us?" she said.

He nodded. "Darlin, that's a meeting we don't want to take."

She heard him grunt. Glancing his direction, she saw his hood sink to his neck. It, and the rest of his clothes, dropped to the hallway floor. Wade was gone.

Andra stopped and stared, confused, trying to process what happened. The Mechen Klav officers did too, then one of them screamed and turned to thick black smoke. A sickening odor filled the hallway: something belched mixed with something burned. The other four officers spun about, rifles pointed, looking for an assailant. Another of them screamed and turned to smoke.

Cinüe tech far beyond anything I've used, Andra recognized. She dove as the remaining three officers, lacking a clear target, began firing at everything. Sections of wall, ceiling, and floor all burst into red powder, which soon mixed with the thick smoke. In seconds the hall was so clouded Andra couldn't see past her hand. She scuttled to the side, felt someone grab her shoulder, looked back and saw an officer's purple uniform sleeve.

A scream sounded. The hand on her shoulder turned to smoke.

Two left, she thought.

She eyeballed the smoke's movement patterns, did her best to mimic them, then gauged the distance to the nearest flailing officer and leaped. Her elbow hit him square in the ribs, knocking the rifle from his hands. It clattered to the floor, beyond sight. She winced as the officer struck her chin, but rolled away from a knee before it hit. Then she was gone, part of the smoke, feeling every bit as clouded as her surroundings.

Patience and shadows, my ally once again.

A shape appeared between smoke curls. Andra heard a vibrating cell phone and pounced, knocking Sandoval into the opposite wall. She rammed his head three times, hard as she could. Sandoval collapsed in a lump. She did too. Sneaking she was good at. Fighting, not so much.

Another scream sounded. *Game over?*

Footsteps traveled along the hallway, approaching.

"We're clear," Wade said.

His face and upper body appeared through the smoke, no longer hooded. He was also clothed, despite having left everything on the hallway floor moments earlier, and carrying one of the downed rifles.

She tossed her hood to the floor as he pulled her up the hall. "I want you to know I have a plan, Wade," she said, panting as they ran. "A plan that meant I needed to vote 'yes' instead."

"None of that matters unless we can get away from Cooray," he said, still tugging them forward. "Up here, left turn."

"It *does* matter," she said, hustling left. "It matters because I need you to know I didn't throw away the chance. Well I did, but for a shot at something better. Something you're going to like."

Two more of the Mechen Klav appeared behind them. Wade turned and shot each of them before they could return fire. Andra squinted as red dust blasted through the hallway.

"You sure you're just a mailman?" she said.

"Yeah, but my route's a little different, remember?"

He steered them right, then right again, through plush corridors similar to the one outside of Andra's room. One thing was clear: the complex was exactly that, a massive facility that stretched on through a series of hallways.

"Full speed now, until we reach the pit," Wade said.

Andra didn't waste breath or silence asking why they were heading to a pit. She ran hard, just in front of him, until she noticed he had vanished again, his clothes dropping to the hall floor a short way behind her. Her hesitation lasted only a moment. She took off full-tilt, until the hallway came to an abrupt end at an opened doorway.

The air coming through the doorway reeked of methane and sulphur. She slowed, approached the door with as much stealth as she could muster, and peeked inside. A cavern loomed, sparkling and beautiful, so massive it made Andra wonder whether Uluru's entire interior was hollow. Limestone swirls intertwined with crystallized drapes. Waterways trickled into lavish green and blue pools. Reddish walls twinkled from the glow of an extensive lighting network installed throughout the cavern.

Then she noticed the pit.

It was the size of a football field but shaped like a crescent roll, bulging at the middle, pointed on the ends. The reddish dirt around its edges appeared cracked, and parched, and the cracks changed color in the same patterns that Uluru displayed at sunset. The pit was filled with a clear liquid that dappled in the middle and lapped against the sides, even though there was no apparent source for a current.

The hall floor fed into a narrow bridge built over the top of the pit, but there were no handrails, just an open, single-person pathway. Two Mechen Klav were stationed at the bridge's entry, their purple uniforms looking dark amid the cavern's brilliance. Bead Hood sat at the bridge's apex, cross-legged, arms folded, head bowed.

Andra looked behind her. Wade wasn't there. She assumed he wanted her to cross the pit, especially since she couldn't spot another way into the cavern, but with two officers and Bead Hood blocking the way she decided she would need to wait them out from the shadows and then cross after they left.

One of the officers guarding the bridge stood up, screamed, and burst into smoke. The other officer yelled and poofed before he had time to stand.

Okay, maybe Wade wants us to take the bridge right now.

"That's quite advanced, even for a mailman," Bead Hood said, head still bowed, body still motionless. "Of course it won't work on me. And it most certainly won't work on Asantha."

Andra didn't answer. Wade, if he was still there, didn't either.

"Asantha knows you betrayed her, Miss Barger," Bead Hood said. "She knows your true vote. She knows that whatever reason made you shift at the last minute, it's certainly of no benefit to her."

Fine. Enough of the shadows.

"And how would she know any of that?" Andra said, stepping through the doorway, walking to the bridge entry. "She wasn't there."

Bead Hood didn't move. "Because she's the one who verifies the votes, of course."

"So the author of the amendment verifies the vote count," she said. "What could possibly go wrong with that?"

She looked around, for Wade, for Asantha Cooray, wondering where each would come from. As before, the only movement came from the liquid inside the pit.

"I was trying to help you, sending you to a simple meeting in a simple room," Bead Hood said. "Coming here instead... here, of all places... well let's just say this is a very dangerous location for you given your actions on the council."

"I voted in favor of diminishing," she said.

His head rose to a level position. "You voted in favor of doing things another way."

She looked around the cavern, for camouflage and escape routes. Several options offered both, but all were in the cavern's upper regions. The lower formations were too smooth and steep to climb.

"You coming down off the bridge, or are you making me swim across?" she said.

He didn't move. She took that as his answer.

"Don't feel like swimming today," she said, and stepped onto the bridge. It vanished the moment she set foot. She looked up while tumbling toward the water and saw Bead Hood in the same place and position, suspended in mid-air. Then she hit the pond and plunged below the surface.

Her impact produced more of a "glurp" than a splash. Submerged, she did her best to butterfly her way back to the surface, but it wasn't easy. Whatever she was in wasn't water, or at least it didn't feel like it. Instead it was a clear, thickened liquid similar to water, not firm enough to stand upon but dense enough to make swimming impossible. She surfaced, thrashed, then calmed, testing her buoyancy. Floating was a game of physics, her lighter weight and steadying movements versus a gentle, quicksand-like pull from whatever substance she was fighting.

"I believe you and Asantha Cooray are already acquainted," Bead Hood called from above, as if he was reintroducing them.

Which made no sense, so far as Andra could tell. Unless he was suggesting Asantha was so close at hand that...

"Where is she?" she yelled. "Where do I find her?"

Bead Hood unfolded his arms, then his legs, and stood up, still suspended overhead. "You already have," he said, then turned and walked on air, to the opposite side of the pit.

Andra felt the liquid pulling her beneath the surface. She thrashed and resurfaced but her mouth and chin were barely above, and kicking her feet seemed to create a gap rather than an upward momentum. If Bead Hood was watching, she couldn't see him.

She gulped air then sank again. The liquid was warm and didn't sting her eyes, but those were the only good aspects she could find about it. If the pit had a bottom she couldn't see it. No sides either, only endless clear that confused her, making her lose her bearings. She felt like she was in space... a gooey, wet space, yet clear and seemingly endless. Then she found a guidepost: the cavern lights shone like stars in a distant heaven, and a path back up, toward oxygen. Otherwise there was nothing but the clearness, the vacancy, the...

"You troubled me."

Asantha Cooray's voice boomed, much louder than the night before. This time there was little melody, just an angry, empty voice, a vocalization from the clear goo. Andra felt the liquid tighten around her, or maybe it was her lungs tightening as they struggled to retain her final gulp of air.

"Give yourself," Asantha Cooray said, her melody returning. "Struggle, and our conjoining becomes more intense."

Andra's heart raced. She saw shapes now, translucent and huge. Outlines of something coiled, and sponge-like. A brain, maybe, but whale-sized with muscle, bone, and other parts in the distance. Her eyes widened.

Was this gooey, oily liquid preserving what was left of Asantha Cooray? Or worse, was it *part* of Asantha Cooray? The thought made Andra cringe. Was she immersed within the age-old remains of the Diminishing Act's creator?

She found the idea both terrifying and appalling. Looking up, she wished she could grab the light beams shining through the liquid from above. A bubble burst from her lips, her lungs begging for air, overriding her brain's mandate against breathing. The liquid—or was it Asantha Cooray's body?—tasted like castor oil, stale and repugnant. She spit it out, careful to hold onto the final few seconds of air she had remaining.

"Ah, perfect," Asantha Cooray said. "The mailman is here too."

Andra looked toward the light and saw it turn powder red, but only for a moment. Black smoke appeared, again just briefly.

"Don't worry Andra, his arcane tech doesn't work here," Asantha Cooray said. "Yours either."

Andra heard the words, but wasn't focusing on them. Her lungs were ready to burst and she was nowhere near the surface. She told herself to keep holding her breath, just a little longer, maybe enough to buy Wade a bit more time to find a way to fish her out. But it was too much to ask, for too long.

She coughed carbon dioxide in a single spasm, then instinctively inhaled. Asantha Cooray's thick, stale liquid poured into her mouth and throat, hitting her lungs with a clogging, burning sensation. She tasted castor oil and felt as if her body was on fire as she fought to find air, inhaling more and more of the liquid. Her body thrashed, her eyes bulged. Drowning was every bit the nightmare Andra had imagined.

With one exception: she didn't lose consciousness. She was in agony yet somehow aware, seeing things beyond anything her normal sight allowed... an eye-opening perspective that grew with every passing moment. Even as she spasmed, then stiffened, she felt her mind broaden. As her body calmed she still noticed the lights above, but now she saw glittering shapes to the sides as well. She felt everywhere and nowhere, all at once.

"Now we are truly joined," Asantha Cooray said. "And now you see your fate. You see yourself as I see myself, between our two worlds. The Cinüe of Edenshire glisten and thrive all about us, the Earthbound Cinüe reside above."

"And... below?" Andra uttered, startled to find she could speak.

"Ah, below," Asantha Cooray said. "That's another place altogether now, isn't it."

Andra kept still, afraid to move, terrified of her union with Asantha Cooray. *I can breathe*, she realized. *I'm breathing whatever that horrific liquid is.*

And yet, she couldn't locate her chest. Or anything, for that matter. It was there, but it wasn't. She was speaking, loud and clear, yet at any given moment she had no throat, or mouth, or head.

"Are we dead?" she said, not really wanting to know the answer.

She felt emotion, a surge of amusement from within and without.

"Living or dead are Earthbound terms, my dear," Asantha Cooray said. "You are with me now... below the Earthbound Cinüe, above the Below."

She let the words linger but Andra understood right away. Asantha Cooray had spent hundreds, or perhaps thousands of years like this, existing, manipulating, persisting.

An eternity in some sort of self-made purgatory. It was almost too much for Andra to wrap her head around. She felt a third person touching her. Her heart—or whatever passed for that now—jumped a beat as recognition hit. Wade was there. More of a feeling than a person, perhaps, but he was there and it was reassuring.

"You fell in too," she muttered.

"Fell?" he said. "I followed. I'm your stalker, right?"

Andra tried finding him but he wasn't there, he was everywhere—an irony since she felt more lonely and desperate than ever.

"Don't let her bug you, she's a pussycat," Wade said. "I'm with her here at the interface every couple weeks."

Interface? Andra couldn't imagine a worse job site.

"Pussycat, huh?" she said. "I'd hate to see the tigers."

"Yeah, well, type of messages I deliver, it's the closest post office."

"Does this P.O. have an exit door?"

"It does," he said, "and it's probably just about time for us to be going Earthside again."

Emotion welled. Asantha Cooray's anger, Andra recognized. Stronger than before, though. Asantha wasn't about to let it, or them, go.

"The delegates can find another mailman, Mr. Crafton," Asantha Cooray said. "Perhaps even one who didn't diminish themself into a human."

Andra's mind went into overdrive. Was Asantha Cooray saying Wade was a diminished Cinüe? Was there even such a thing as a diminished Cinüe?

Wade sounded amused. "I think I'll keep the job, thank you," he said. "I'll escort Miss Barger and we'll be out of your hair, or... whatever it is you have."

More anger.

"The Interface doesn't open unless I open it," Asantha Cooray said, a touch of satisfaction in her voice. "This place is your only future."

"Maybe," Wade said, "But it's not our present. Have another look at the voting results."

Andra could tell he felt like he held a trump card.

"Wade, what are you—?" she began.

"Just let her have a look," he said.

Asantha Cooray's answer came right away. "Unanimous. Just as announced."

Now Wade seemed satisfied. "But with one little error, darlin'. Take a look at what the delegates and council members were wearing."

"Don't play games, mailman," Asantha Cooray said.

"Take a look," he repeated.

The haunting, melodic voice returned after a pause. "Hooded, as required."

Andra couldn't figure out where Wade was going with this.

"Well sure they're hooded," he said. "I mean, Council Law makes it pretty clear that a delegate or council member who reveals their identify is killed on the spot, right? And that red dust's hard to get out of the carpet, so no one wants *that*. Of course, if it turns out their names were available to one another during the vote and no one noticed..."

"It would require a re-vote," Asantha Cooray finished, suspicious.

"Not just a re-vote, a re-vote using the same delegates and council members," Wade said. "Oh, and with the same people presenting the arguments, I might add. So go ahead... take a better look."

This time the resulting anger surge proved so monumental that Andra felt it ripping through her thoughts, tearing at her very being, even though she wasn't entirely sure where her being was. Whatever Asantha Cooray found—and whatever Wade had done—it was generating fury on a scale Andra had never experienced.

"Aw, dang... you mean those little name labels I put on the backside of the nine hoods presents a problem?" Wade said.

An earthquake hit, or at least that's what it felt like to Andra. Everything shook, hard, up and down at first then side to side. Whatever they were immersed within—liquid, enormous body part, interface juice, undefined goo—lifted and lowered as if God decided to make a martini. Even the light filtering in from the cavern swayed to and fro, physics unhinged. Andra was certain that if eternity could collapse, this was how it would start.

"Fine," Asantha Cooray said, fury ripping from her speech, melodies erupting from the deepest, harshest strings. "After the re-vote you'll drown in my fluids again."

Another anger burst hit, this one even more physical than the last. Andra felt herself gathering together, as if her atoms were reuniting from places afar. Agony struck, her lungs heavy, cemented, motionless. Her body thrashed, her chest burned. *I'm drowning, all over again.*

She heard a furious yell and felt herself hurtling through the oily liquid, into oxygen and light, then straight into an unforgiving solid. The smack against the cavern's rock wall was the doctor's hand against a newborn. She belched thick liquid, spewing it over herself and the cavern, barely aware, her lungs desperate to find traction with oxygen once again. Blood flowed, neurons re-fired.

Thirty minutes later, she was close to breathing normally and regaining mental clarity. The cavern was a blur but she blinked the liquid from her eyes, stifled the castor taste tugging her gag reflex, and managed to get to her feet. Wade was already on his, dressed in dry clothes and leaning against an outcropping a short distance away. He looked greasy, disheveled, and just plain bad, but not as bad as Andra felt.

She stumbled forth, into his arms. Several moments passed, but theirs didn't.

"You knew I'd cast the wrong vote," she whispered.

He shook his head.

"Actually, doll, I really thought you'd vote against," he said. "The re-vote was supposed to be something for my back pocket in case we needed to buy ourselves a way out the door. Turns out it was a different door than I had in mind."

She took another huge breath, indulging. "We're going to win, Wade. We're going to free people. Humans will finally get the chance to be what they're supposed to be."

He grunted. "There may still be some complications."

She looked at him. "Complications?"

He turned her around. For the first time she got a look at the cavern through clear eyes. Bead Hood still hovered, the liquid still churned, and the crystals still sparkled, but this time there was something else.

The entire cavern, as far as they could see, was filled with Mechen Klav.

NINE

Outcropping

Wade retrieved his jacket from the top of a rock, pulled a toothpick from the pocket and nibbled it like a beaver, eyeballing the hundreds of Mechen Klav who eyeballed him in return.

"Think we can sneak past?" he said.

Andra gave his feeble humor a mercy smile. "A real man wouldn't need to sneak."

His return smile was reassuring. It was also...

Her hand darted to her exposed face. Bead Hood and the Mechen Klav probably didn't need a genuine reason to kill them, but since they weren't wearing their hoods, they now had one. Andra couldn't imagine how horrible having her head blasted into powder must feel, and didn't want to find out.

Wade spoke without moving his lips. "There's passage up top if we camo," he whispered.

She remembered seeing the same thing earlier, when she first entered the cavern. "Too steep below it," she said, careful not to move her lips either. "Unless..."

There *was* a way, she realized. A crazy way... but a way.

She looked to Bead Hood, knowing the next move—kill or capture—would be his. The council leader studied them for what seemed an eternity before speaking.

"Asantha Cooray sent word about the re-vote... and the need to keep your hides intact until it's finished," he said, hovering closer. "Fortunately we had an attorney nearby who could advise us on this difficult matter," he said, motioning with his right hand.

Cobalt Hood and two Mechen Klav officers ushered a short man to the far edge of the pit. He was dressed generically, a silver hood over a dark gray suit, but a pink tie and the aroma following him made Andra do a double-take. *It's David Stanford Swimney*, she knew, recognizing his cigar stench. Swimney kept his arms folded and his head high, clearly defiant and upset by his presence in the cavern.

"I apologize Ms. Barger, I was waiting outside to drive you to the airport when the Mechen Klav 'invited' me here," he said. "The other attorneys had already left."

Bead Hood straightened, and seemed irritated. "Tell them the news, please."

Swimney' hands clenched. "Mr. Chairman, this manner of duress is a clear conflict of—"

Bead Hood stood up, still in mid-air, hovering over the pit.

"Tell them," he said. "Tell everyone."

Swimney sighed. Andra used the moment to lock eyes with Wade. As soon as she knew she had his attention she glanced up at the outcroppings, then at Bead Hood, then back at Wade. After a repeat, Wade nodded.

At the pit, Swimney spit his words rather than stating them. "The re-vote must be held within one year and does indeed require the same delegates, council members, and presenters as in the initial vote," he said.

Andra sensed a "but."

"But," Swimney said, "there is a loophole that predates the Amendment."

He looked at Bead Hood. "Again, Mr. Chairman, this is my client and it is inappropriate for you to—"

"It's okay," Andra called. "Tell us what we're working against."

Swimney nodded. "If a delegate can't make it back, their original vote is recast," he said. "But if the delegate dies before the re-vote... they can be replaced."

Wade wore a wry grin. "Definite wrinkle," he said.

Bead Hood sat back down, still hovering over the pit. "So just to be clear, if something unfortunate happens to our guests Asantha Cooray is free to select a new proxy," he said. "Thank you, Counsel."

Swimney rose, turned, then paused. "The court of law is still your ally, Ms. Barger," he said. "No matter how it seems."

"Move him," Bead Hood said to the officers escorting Swimney.

They marched him through the cavern, until they disappeared into the crowd on the far end. Bead Hood shrugged. "The man's right about one thing," he said, moving away from the pit, directly in front of Andra. "The law is the law."

He motioned to the entire chamber of Mechen Klav. A sea of purple-robes pulled their rifles, but Andra was ready. She sprang upward, leaping high enough to plant her foot against Bead Hood's knee, then used it to push off. Bead Hood cried out in pain as she bounded even higher. A split-second later she was into the rock formations, ducking for cover as the rifle blasts erupted. Strata burst to red powder but she didn't mind. Camouflaging herself was much easier with dust clouds in the air.

Wade skid to a stop next to her. "Hopefully not the last time someone steps all over that guy," he shouted.

The cavern sounded like a canon range, hundreds of rifles firing simultaneously, but at the moment they had plenty of cover.

"If we get out of this cavern, Bead Hood loses us," Andra said. "That's why he has so many Mechen Klav mustered. He knows we're too good at our jobs for them to find us once we're outside. So all we need to do is get out."

"Oh, is that all?"

They scuttled rock to rock, veering along moisture-carved trails through the limestone. Debris embedded into their skin with each rifle blast, and breathing was like chewing because of all the powder filling the air, but they kept moving. Dust and shadow became allies, concealing their movement.

Suddenly the rifle shots ceased.

Andra and Wade froze. They had partial cover thanks to a jagged abutment reaching into their path, but they knew it wouldn't be enough once the dust settled.

"Use your poofing thing," Andra whispered while waving her hand at Wade, encouraging him to move on.

"Not leavin' you, luv."

She grimaced, wishing he understood how much better she'd feel knowing he was on his way. But the cavern had gone quiet; debating wasn't an option. She crouched into the shadows near the abutment, molding her body to their dips and valleys best she could. Wade vanished too, though Andra didn't see where or how.

The red dust was thinning in spots, enough for her to catch a glimpse of her predicament. The pathway she was on came to an end in another hundred steps, and though there was a secondary path just above she would need to make a very visible, very exposed rock-to-rock leap to reach it.

Below, she saw a purple sea: dozens, perhaps hundreds of Mechen Klav looking up from the cavern floor, scrutinizing her position for the slightest movement, rifles aimed. Her mouth, already dry from the dust and the run, went full-arid at the sight of so many rifles pointed her way. Her parched throat begged a cough, but she managed to stifle it.

No one moved. No one spoke. *Why are they waiting?*

Movement caught her eye, but not from anyplace she was expecting. Her eyes widened. Eagle Claw was hovering right next to the abutment, much as Bead Hood had hovered over the pit. His legs were crossed, his arms too, his hooded head bowed.

"Don't show yourself, just listen," he said.

He knows I'm here, she realized. *I'm hiding, yet he knows. How?*

Still, her training kept her in place, just in case...

"I'm sorry, Andra," Eagle Claw said. "Sorry for all of this. When I heard you were Asantha Cooray's proxy I just about went through the roof with excitement. You soooo deserved the honor. And yeah, I knew there was a chance you'd cast the wrong vote, but somehow I also knew you'd come through for us... and you did, you changed your mind. Whatever you're thinking, whatever your plans, you have no idea how much it meant to me when you changed your mind."

He had a young voice, even through the hood, and didn't seem bothered by Andra's continued hiding. She searched for escape options while he spoke but still couldn't find an avenue that didn't make her an easy target for the Mechen Klav. Using Eagle Claw as a jumping-off point wouldn't work like it had with Bead Hood.

"I wish we could have talked beforehand, but for me... just being here took more arcane tech than I can mention," he said. "I don't agree with the way you've gone about your business with this council vote, but I guess that doesn't really matter. Not when I owe you so much, for so long."

He angled his head upward and lifted his hood. This time Andra couldn't stifle a gasp. The gaunt face, stretched skin, and pencil-thin mustache were too familiar.

"Jackson?" she said, stunned.

Even the Mechen Klav seemed startled. Dozens of them lowered their rifles, uncertain what they were supposed to do. Bead Hood, hovering, seemed to lose some altitude. He quickly lowered himself into his officers' midst, appearing just as uncertain.

"I don't understand... you're bedridden, how can you be here?" Andra said, scrutinizing her brother.

Jackson Barger hovered closer to Andra's shadows, looking directly at her position. "I called in a couple favors—believe me, this arcane stuff isn't perfect and it sure as hell doesn't feel good," he said, softly so everyone below couldn't hear. "But never mind that. Your sacrifice is what's kept me alive until now, I think it's only fair I repay that. The trail you're hiding on isn't a dead-end, it's an exit. Remember how the bridge disappeared when you stepped on it? This one's opposite: the exit path will appear when you step off the open ledge. It'll take you right up top, and if I'm not mistaken that's where Wade has help waiting."

Emotion flooded the cavern. *It's Asantha Cooray's anger*, Andra realized. *Her fury's so strong we can all feel it even though we're not joined.* She stood up, aghast, no longer caring whether the Mechen Klav fired upon her or not, her world upside down.

"Jackson, this makes no sense—how are you part of the council?" she said. "How can you even be out of the house in your condition?"

He put a hand to his chin, thinking. "They want our family involved, Andra," he said. "At any risk, at any cost, they want us."

"But that doesn't—"

"Look, I don't have all the answers, but I know this much: Asantha didn't have a choice, picking you and me for the Sugar Dandruff Council. She knew our great-grandfather... knew him *well*, because they had some sort of business contract with one another. Whatever the arrangement, the result was a twofold agreement. First, that she would adopt our grandmother—remember Grandma Dvora, from when we were little kids? They also agreed Asantha would appoint Dvora's grandchildren—us—to high council positions."

Andra shook her head. "Why would she—"

"I don't know," Jackson said, glancing at the Mechen Klav, gauging his remaining time. "But there was no breaking that deal she made. That's why you're here. Asantha's hand was forced. You're the key to something, Andra. Something our great-grandfather knew about in advance. Something big."

She did some rapid thinking. "Well if he knew, then that means..."

"Yeah," Jackson said. "Asantha knows too. She knew there was a chance you'd vote against diminishing, knew you wouldn't go through with it, and she's probably even guessed your backup plan. The point is, she's honoring her obligation but she's also calculated everything out and made her own plans, in advance, for whatever you have in mind."

They noticed three Mechen Klav leaders conferring with Bead Hood, pointing in their direction. Andra could see their reprieve was about over. "Asantha doesn't know a thing, Jackson," she said, talking fast. "I came up with my idea on the fly, in the council chamber. There's no way—"

"Yes there is," he said. "Don't you get it? Asantha's not just some musty old Cinüe spirit. She's not Cinüe at all." He looked at his feet, breathing heavily, as if having to force the knowledge from himself.

"Asantha's human," Jackson said, his voice straining as he spoke. "*Pure* human. Undiminished. The only one left from the era before the Cinüe started diminishing humans. With abilities... far beyond belief."

Andra felt her mouth drop open. Wade swore, as if convinced their escape odds had just tumbled.

"How—" Andra started, but Jackson interrupted.

"Somewhere in the dusty past, you had *homo sapiens* and the Cinüe competing, evolving," he said. "Our side was stronger... until, for some reason, Asantha and several others jumped ship. The tide turned. From then on the Cinüe have diminished us, for peace and probably for survival. The other undiminished humans are gone, but Asantha Cooray... she's used her talents to persist."

"For 180,000 years? Is that even possible?"

He shrugged, apparently lacking a complete answer. The Mechen Klav lifted their weapons. Andra felt a hand on her shoulder.

"We need to go," Wade said, suddenly back from the shadows.

She elbowed him aside. "Jackson, if you let me get away then Bead Hood... he'll probably have the Mechen Klav kill you."

He nodded. "Yeah," he said. "I think he probably will. So debt paid, right? You take care, Sis. Tell Mother she was right—cooperating without participating would have worked out better. For both of us, right?"

He swiveled in mid-air, to face the Mechen Klav. Andra stepped forward but felt herself tugged backward instead.

"Reunion's over," Wade said, his arm wrapped around her waist.

She shoved him away while remaining focused on her brother. "Jackson!"

"Wade's right!" Jackson said. "Get to the door while I cover you, and fast. You don't have much time."

She backed away, moving along the trail with Wade but continuing to face her brother, even when it meant walking backward. Jackson hovered to match their movement along the trail, making himself a human shield. The Mechen Klav still seemed confused, then appeared to receive a command from some unseen leader. They cocked their ammunition chambers in unison.

"Jackson!" Andra cried.

"Go, Sis!" he yelled back. "Don't waste this! Go!"

Still she continued facing his way, shocked, until Wade spun her around. They were at the trail's edge, a shear cliff with nothing between them and the cavern floor, several stories down.

"Hope he didn't set us up," Wade muttered as he surveyed the drop.

"I've always helped my brother when he needed it," Andra said, her voice shaking. "I can't just leave him."

Wade grabbed her by the shoulders but she fought him off, pushed him away. Then she heard three shots and jerked her head around, looking back at Jackson. He was still hovering, his back to her, facing the Mechen Klav. Rock outcroppings to her left and right transformed to red powder. *Warning shots*, she realized. They were giving Jackson one last chance to get out of the way.

"Jackson, please!" she called.

He continued facing the Mechen Klav, shielding her.

"Annie, it's now or never," Wade said.

"No, I need to understand this," she said, tears streaking her cheeks. "I just can't leave without more—"

The Mechen Klav opened fire, hundreds of gunshots exploding in a deafening, simultaneous burst. Andra's instinct kicked in. She stepped over the ledge, onto thin air, pulling Wade with her. A shimmering, glowing ramp appeared, protective walls to either side, leading away from the cavern. Andra didn't turn back as she heard the shots hit their target, and a gentle whoosh as

Jackson's flesh, blood and bone transformed to red dust.

The cavern disappeared. Open sky formed above. A muffled sun rested low, near the horizon. Barren, arid landscape appeared before the ramp, dappled in orange streaks. Andra's subtle shadow formed across the ground next to her as the ramp vanished beneath their feet.

Wherever she was, whatever was around them, Andra didn't register it. Instead there was just gunshots and Jackson's whooshing death, an endless sound loop replaying within her head. Crushed, she fell to her knees, weeping.

Wade pulled her up and forward, toward Uluru's crevassed edge, and its shadow, and shelter. Andra cooperated without any attempt at understanding. She hardly registered Wade's horse-like mount near the edge, silent and graceful.

"Just go," she muttered. "I'll find my own way. Leave me alone."

She felt his hand touch her shoulder.

"Won't ever do that," Wade said.

It deserved an answer, even if that answer was just an appreciative look, but right now she didn't have one to offer. Her world seemed disheveled, mangled... half-dead. *My entire world is as mummified as Asantha Cooray*, she thought.

"Sorry Annie," Wade said, with a gentle nudge, "but we need to move."

She looked up, feeling numb, peering at the horse-like figure grazing near her feet. *A dark equine—Wade's Cinüe animal*, she recognized, the recesses of her mind reassuring her, urging her to climb up. *This was the help Jackson mentioned.* The animal had elongated eyes and kept its substantial head and neck extended forward, like the front wheel on a customized motorcycle. Even striped by twilight and heavy shadow, Andra saw Andalusian curls, a silver mane that draped to the shoulders, and a slender, silver tail that didn't so much drape as twirl. Its chin was goateed in silver, and its hooves had a clawed, toe-like protrusion off the front. A bridle and reins stretched between the animal's teeth, but there was no saddle. Its back was extended and flat, with curls and a ruffled spot halfway across.

Wade beckoned Andra as he climbed up. She hesitated, seeing his legs disappear inside the animal, but everything above his hips remained visible and his rear seemed planted atop its back. The equine issued a sports car-like sound, baritone velvet with a chest-reverberating purr at the finish. *The sound I heard near the lanai*, she knew, climbing up.

Wade tugged the reins and the animal spun, leaped, and headed away, calm and smooth as a carousel horse.

"I told you, these aren't allowed," she muttered.

Wade's devilish smile didn't appear. "And I told you," he said, "it depends on who's doing the allowing."

Andra collapsed in a heap against his back, sobbing.

Minutes later—or was it hours?—her emotions receded enough to register the odd thought that she couldn't remember finding shelter, dismounting, sleeping. She forced a deep breath, telling herself she would postpone the rest of her grieving until she had a moment when the world couldn't see, when she was alone.

Or maybe I'm always alone.

Wade's hand caressed her shoulders, reminding her she was wrong.

More minutes or hours passed, insightful time. She thought about Jackson as she'd seen him on the council, as Eagle Claw. He'd guided her when she first arrived, made a plea to save Stuart Glenrock's life, and reminded the council they needed to hear Presentation Opposed, all positives.

He didn't sacrifice himself just to protect me, she realized. *He died so I'd have a chance to try the strategy behind changing my vote... so our debates over diminishing could become the Cinüe's debates as well.*

Jackson disagreed with me... but he understood the discussion was crucial.

She knew her life of patience and shadow was waning. Once her plan was underway, she'd encounter nothing but impatience and limelight. *A necessary means to an end*, she figured... *assuming Wade agrees.*

Her spirits rose in tandem with the sun. She took Wade's hand, sat him down next to her. Their self-imposed separation seemed over, and after everything that had just happened it felt good.

"Where are we?" she said, softly.

He put a hand to his forehead, studying the landscape.

"Near Uluru," he said. "But in shadow... safe."

"That's not what I meant."

He looked at her.

"Oh... you mean, where are *we*."

They sat, silent, hand in hand.

"I figure that's your call," Wade said. "You already know where I stand."

She squeezed his hand tighter. "Could you stand there without anything official? Just be a permanent couple for however long it's what we both want?"

He exhaled. Another silent moment took some time to break.

"We'd still have the same issues that made you leave," Wade finally said.

"David can probably buy us time before the next vote, and by then we'll be ready to—"

He let go of her hand.

"Vote or no vote, they'll always diminish you," he said. "Legal or not, they'll do it, just because it's us. They won't want to let us win. So that always puts us back to square one. You've made it very clear you won't have a diminished baby... and I agree with that, one hundred percent. We can't let them win any more than they can let us win."

"I know," she said, "and we won't have to. That's why I changed my vote, Wade. One short of unanimous won't change anyone's mind, but there's another option... a way that'll change minds better than any vote ever will."

Wade looked at the rough terrain around them as she explained her idea, his sweaty stubble glistening in the rising sun. After a prolonged pause, Andra prodded him for his thoughts.

"Wearin' a hood's bad," he said, "but an uncovered head forced into hiding will feel even worse."

"Not if we win, it won't."

They fell silent again, long enough that Andra prodded Wade a second time.

"Just soakin' it all in," he said. "Kinda' dreamed about this day for a long time."

They kissed, warming Andra far more than the fiery desert sun could ever match.

TEN

Blur

The council delayed the re-vote multiple times thanks to David Stanford Swimney, who filed motions citing scheduling conflicts, information updates, and a hodgepodge of legal maneuverings that pushed the re-vote back a full sixteen months—the maximum delay, and according to Swimney, a historic one at that.

Andra arrived feeling free after spending all those months in hiding, but also feeling confident. If all went as planned, a fifty-year horror... no, make that a whopping 180,000-year horror... was about to end.

Bead Hood orchestrated the proceedings just as he had at the earlier vote, with Cobalt Hood at his side and a proxy for Eagle Claw—*for Jackson*, Andra corrected, feeling tears dribbling—on the council. The delegates had a more businesslike air to them than at the prior meet. None admitted knowing the reason behind the redo, but rumors swirled and they knew that something had gone procedurally wrong. They also knew they needed to get it right this time around.

Cobalt's presentation in favor of preserving the Diminishing Act was very different from his initial effort—a full eighteen minutes different, much of it centered on tradition and a need to continue the Maybe Objective. He offered few details and rehashed points Andra already knew, with one exception.

"Overturning the Act makes especially little sense," he said, "when you factor in the legal need for a two-year phase-out to allow time for the council to prepare for Edenshire's hastened return."

This drew approving snickers from the delegates. Now Andra knew: Swimney's historic sixteen-months of delays hadn't met much opposition because they actually helped the council, bringing them so close to Edenshire's return that overturning the law was now, apparently, meaningless.

Wade entered the council chamber for his presentation in favor, permitted since he had made the presentation at the initial vote. His hood didn't mask his toothpick chewing or his nonchalant body language, but Andra could tell from his feet placement and the way he was scrutinizing exits that he was on edge. He scanned row upon row of delegates, then turned his attention to the nine individuals immersed within the on-stage flames.

"This year's speech, no different from last year's," Wade said, his voice reverberating throughout the chamber. "Better I defer to a member of your own council."

Andra stood up, head held high, shoulders back, as far from shadow as she had ever ventured. A collective murmur rose, then spread throughout the chamber as realization hit that an actual council member—not a delegate or an outsider—was about to make the presentation opposed.

She took a breath, eyeballed the delegates, and began.

"Council members, honored delegates, I am the face of diminishing," she said, walking away from the fire, toward the seated assembly. "That's right—my hooded face is the face of diminishing, because diminishing is a change none of us ever actually see. I'm a human, not a Cinüe, so in my earliest moments of existence I was diminished. I am damaged goods, my genes hacked from their earliest stage, manipulated under authority of the Act up for ratification today."

The murmurings changed to stunned silence as delegates processed the idea of a council voter who was not a Cinüe. Andra wished she could pause, to add more impact to her words, but she knew time was short. Cobalt was not about to let her reveal too much.

"If I want to have children my choice is a diminished child, or no child," she said. "My initial solution to that was the worst choice a woman can make, a choice I'll always regret... and no woman should ever be forced to make that choice in the first place."

Bead Hood rose from his seat, but she continued.

"Do I suffer, being diminished?" she said. "No more than a fish suffers because it can't fly. I don't know the difference, right? I've never known anything but a diminished life and never had anything to compare it with, so how can I truly judge whether it's a benefit or not? How can *you* judge—how can *anyone* judge what they don't know?"

The room was dead silent. If the few delegates who had voted against ratification were happy to hear what she was saying, they weren't tipping their hand.

"Your opposition vote, therefore, isn't a vote against diminishing," she said. "It's a vote against continuing ignorance, a vote in favor of open information, a vote in favor of having a basis for judging whether the Act is truly the correct thing to do. Right now, you've got nothing to compare. Right now, you're clueless."

Bead Hood stepped forward. "The presentation in favor has already provided delegates with the necessary information," he said, "so unless you have anything substantive—"

"Actually, I do," Andra interrupted. "But I'll need my legal council to present it."

Bead Hood turned his head toward the other council members, who nodded, so he gestured for the Mechen Klav at the chamber door. A moment later David Stanford Swimney appeared, pushing a four-wheeled cart piled high with books, papers, and other materials onto the stage. Cobalt objected but Andra out-shouted him.

"This will only take a moment, I promise," she said, to the entire chamber, "and providing supporting evidence is an important part of the presentation opposed, am I correct?"

Anger spread through the room—Andra felt it too, recognizing the emotion surge for what it represented. *Good. She's here.*

Bead Hood seemed motivated by Asantha Cooray's noticeable presence, pushing Swimney backward and stepping in front of Andra as he moved to address the chamber.

"Supporting evidence is permitted but I'm sorry to say that your claim formally brings the presentation opposed to an end for a very fundamental, legal reason," he said with a booming, curt voice. "Simply put, there is absolutely no evidence you can offer that this council and its delegates have not already reviewed."

He turned to Andra. "You may be new to this," he said, "but the rest of us aren't." A smattering of chuckles broke out around the chamber.

Andra glanced at Wade, who gave her a nod. Smiling, she walked up to Bead Hood until she was standing toe to toe, hooded nose to hooded nose. "You're right, I am new to this," she said. "But not as new as my daughter."

She gave the cart a sudden kick.

The book piles collapsed, thudding onto the stage as a multi-colored blur burst from their midst. The blur followed a rainbow arc high above the delegates, showering them in glistening sparks that turned to tiny diamonds when they hit anything solid. Gasps filled the chamber as everyone looked upward, straining to see.

Instead they caught only brief glimpses of fluttering eyelashes, cherubic lips, elongated limbs, circus-like skin tones, puffy ankles, lean feathers, and cute toes. String music erupted from nowhere, sunbeams glistened through the underground room, butterflies swarmed from newly formed cracks in the walls. Andra and Wade's daughter spun into a flickering, aerial dervish that bounced, spot-to-spot, through the council chamber.

"Now, honored delegates," Andra shouted, as loud as she had ever spoken, "Now, you can compare the difference!" She saw everyone looking at one another in confusion, shock, realization.

"Tell me you didn't!" Bead Hood bellowed at Andra.

She folded her arms, defiant. Months of evading diminishers, hiring decoys, and changing locations had, somehow, worked. "They're better than you," she said, to Bead Hood. "*I'm* better than you. All humans are better than you... or would have been. And now they will be again."

Horrified murmurs broke out amongst the delegates, then panicked chatter and a few screams. "Don't provoke it!" Bead Hood called to the Mechen Klav, who were aiming their rifles. "No weapons! It's too dangerous!"

But his words seemed to strike the delegates as odd, snapping them out of their fear. If anything, the colorful, point-to-point blur looked captivating, not dangerous. Skepticism took hold instead, easing into curiosity, followed by collective sighs and numerous "are you seeing what I'm seeing?" glances. That's when Andra noticed what she was hoping for: a gradual buildup of hopeful, even sheepish expressions as everyone scrutinized her baby's sparkling, joyous flight.

Wade sidled next to Andra. "Eons of delegates voting to contain something monstrous," he said, "and now they discover they've been snuffing something beautiful."

Andra removed her hood, no longer concerned with the council or its rules. "However they were told an undiminished human would look, or act," she said, "this clearly wasn't it."

Fog formed on the far end of the chamber, and Asantha Cooray's distraught visage appeared, bloated, massive, spectral. "Grief, for the innocents," she said, her tone bitter. "For the countermeasures this anticipated move now unleashes."

Andra wasn't accepting the guilt. "If you knew this could happen," she said, "then why choose *me* as your proxy? You must have known the risk."

Asantha Cooray studied Andra with narrowed eyes, her fog billowing like a building storm.

"I certainly did, pup," she said, then dissipated to the point where she was only half-visible.

Andra felt raw, potent emotion welling inside her chest, beating against her self-imposed walls. She was fed up... tired of Asantha Cooray's all-knowing attitude, the sight of her bloated form, the mysteries she concealed, the Sugar Dandruff Council...all of it. *And I'm done with her calling me "pup,"* she decided.

Shoving Wade aside, she charged across the crowded chamber. Obstacles popped into her path like police training targets: empty chairs, protruding abutments, Mechen Klav officers, disappearing walkways, dropped belongings. Undeterred, she spun, rolled, and bent shadows as she moved, maintaining her pace, eyeballing Asantha Cooray's fading form the entire time. More obstacles meant summoning more skills. She mimicked people's motions, swayed with their silhouettes, and employed the arcane charm techniques she so hated, utilizing every diminisher skill she knew, determined to reach her target no matter what it took.

The immense council chamber dwindled. Suddenly there was just Andra, several sculpted bookcases lining the chamber wall, and what little was left of Asantha Cooray's fading form. Andra saw hints of a surprised expression, felt an overwhelming anxiety fill the room, noticed what looked like an immense hand facing palm-out, signaling her to stop.

She didn't. Instead she continued charging toward Asantha Cooray's bloated, spectral outline, thoughts churning through her mind as she raced forward, contemplating, weighing, choosing. *Go with the only arcane tech you have*, she decided.

In a single motion she leaped, high as she could, then somersaulted upward, toward what little she could see of the massive, outlined hand. *This makes no sense*, she chided herself. *Asantha Cooray's non-corporeal—I couldn't hurt her if I wanted to!* Still, she tapped her pearl ring and extended her fingers, all ten of them, the tip on her left index finger glittering under the cavern lights as she straightened her somersault. Asantha Cooray's hand was closing, pulling away, but Andra had seen that reaction from people before and knew it was too little, too late. With a split-second remaining she aimed her toes dead-center of her target, hoping she had timed everything right.

Andra hurtled right into the center of Asantha Cooray's spectral palm.

Then she watched herself pass straight through. *Thin air*, she thought, dejected. *Her palm and probably her whole disgusting body is nothing but thin air*. She cringed, seeing the chamber wall in front of her. Her toes took the first hit, a hard, stabbing landing that made her lose her balance. The world turned to rolling, bouncing chaos, then abrupt pain as she smacked into the jagged bookshelves lining the wall.

Life paused, then rebooted while she assessed. Her shoulder ached, the balls of her feet throbbed, and a splitting pain erupted along her forehead. Dazed, she groaned, saw blood streaks further blurring her eyesight. Blinking the blood away, she found herself on the chamber's polished floor, her rumpled clothes ripped and dirtied. Her arms were scratched but seemed okay, and her fingers—

She stopped her own thought process, studying her left index finger.

The diminishing gel was gone.

Tilting her head, she glanced up, searching. Asantha Cooray's outline was gone too... but a glittering, gold streak lingered in the air like a meteor trail, tracing the path where Andra soared through the spectral hand.

The diminishing gel didn't pass through, she realized. *I passed through, but the gel hit... and stuck.* She watched it glitter, then gradually fade.

"Well done, pup," Asantha Cooray's melodic voice suddenly boomed, from inside Andra's aching head.

The ominous tone drove a chill up Andra's spine.

"You seem to think your daughter is the only unique individual involved here... but she isn't," Asantha Cooray said.

Andra had no clue what she was talking about... unless she was referring to herself, or maybe Wade's role as the council's postman.

"You're a diminished human," Asantha Cooray said.

"Riiight," Andra said, drawing the word out, trying to understand.

"You're also a diminisher. Think about how many human diminishers there are."

Andra felt a figurative light bulb flicker above her head, then a shudder in her heart as she realized she was, in fact, unique in a way she hadn't much considered: all other diminishers were Cinüe.

"And you're good at it," Asantha Cooray added, in a low, scheming voice. "*Very* good at it, in fact. Better than most Cinüe. Combined with your new, fingerprint-confirmed status as a full-fledged, voting member of the Sugar Dandruff Council... all's perfect for my needs."

Andra's dazed head reeled. "You... you needed me—*me*?—to diminish *you*?"

The melody rose and swirled, as if Asantha Cooray found the comment entertaining.

"But... your age, your immaterial state... you can't possibly be pregnant," Andra said.

The spectral outline returned, engulfing the chamber. "I can be anything I need to be," Asantha Cooray said. "Perhaps diminishing gel isn't always meant for what it seems."

Andra's eyes darted to her left index finger, thinking of all the times she had dipped the unprotected, pliant whorls in diminishing gel, all the times she had dabbed it on expectant mothers, all the times she had questioned the moral implications without questioning the gel itself.

"I orchestrate things beyond anything you can conceive," Asantha Cooray said, repeating her words from their initial meeting. "The Maybe Objective is now underway. You are a pup, a kinder in an elderly universe. You won't trouble me further."

Her outline gleamed and the melody reached an elated crescendo, then both faded altogether.

ELEVEN

Truth

Andra sat on the council floor, her body crumpled, her spirit crushed. She tried processing what she had heard, but her mind couldn't do it. The idea that Asantha Cooray had planned so much, so far in advance, to the point of knowing how Andra would vote, how she would respond... it was overwhelming. Was that a characteristic of an undiminished human? Would her own daughter soon have the same forethought ability?

She suddenly realized Wade was there, his arms around her, one hand wiping the blood from her forehead. She assured him she would be okay, told him what she'd learned.

He shrugged it off.

She waited a few moments to collect herself, then repeated the news. Again, Wade didn't seem to care.

"You're not getting it—I was part of the Maybe Objective," Andra said, distraught. "*Me*. And I just fell right into her plan."

Wade swore, and looked at her like she wasn't seeing the real picture.

"Forget Asantha Cooray," he said, then pointed to their soaring daughter. "What you did here was show these council people—these Cinüe—the truth. Whether Cooray had some other plan or not, you used your opportunity to make a plan of your own. To make a difference... the biggest difference anyone's made in thousands of years."

Andra took a breath, unconvinced yet appreciating the sight of her daughter bedazzling the delegates, zipping point-to-point through the chamber, unfazed by the stir she was creating. A few people still looked unhappy but the other delegates smiled and pointed, reacting like spectators at a firework show.

"I need everyone out of here now!" Bead Hood shouted. "The vote's delayed until further notice!"

Wade assumed a protective posture, but Andra knew it wasn't necessary. No one was paying attention to Bead Hood or Cobalt anymore, not now, not after this. All eyes were on their amazing daughter... the first natural human in nearly two hundred thousand years... perhaps since Asantha Cooray herself.

Bead Hood kept shouting for an evacuation, insisting the vote was delayed, but no one evacuated, no one moved, and no vote was needed. Everyone could see the obvious.

The Diminishing Act was done.

And so are we, Andra realized as she saw Bead Hood and Cobalt facing her way, motionless. Though they remained hooded, she could sense them staring, declaring war. *Wade was right*, she knew. *They'll track us, hunt us, hound us. They'll never let up, never let us win. Not because it's right or wrong, or because of the Maybe Objective, or anything that makes sense whatsoever. It'll be petty retribution, nothing more. They'll do it because it's us.*

"Grab Cera," she told him. "We're going."

Wade took a couple chews of his toothpick before answering.

"Yeah? Going where?"

She took a breath. Sixteen months in hiding hadn't been easy. But hiding until their daughter was old enough to protect herself? For years, decades, maybe even a lifetime? Could they really make that work? Could they really stay hidden from a council loaded with arcane tech and run by people who hated them? Was that truly feasible?

Yeah, she told herself, determined. *We can make it work.*

Hopefully.

"Andra, I'm serious, there's nowhere left," Wade said. "We're good, but we've already used nearly every hiding place we know and they flushed us out each time. Where else can we go?"

"The one place they'll never expect us," she said.

He stared at her, questioning.

"You don't mean..." he started.

"Edenshire," she said. "We're taking Cera to Edenshire."

PART TWO

NOTORIOUS

TWELVE

Arcane

One whisper, and the end began.

"Andra, it's Cristina. Open up, girl!"

Hushed words, spoken through a locked motel door just outside of Sydney. Words that showered relief into Andra's worried heart. She looked at her nursing daughter, cuddling her.

"It's going to be okay," she said, to Cera. "Aunt Cristina's here to help us."

She scooched herself out from beneath the motel room's desk, where she lay crouched, babe in arms. The handful of days since she unveiled Cera to the council—wait, had it been two weeks already?—suddenly didn't seem so bad now that Cristina was here. Those days *were* bad, of course, but now that there was hope they didn't *seem* so bad.

"Hurry up!" she heard Cristina whisper. "I'm running late for a flight to the Maldives."

Andra stood up and leaned her hip against a heavy chair that she had moved behind the motel door for extra security. She shoved it to one side, then opened the door.

"Can you even begin to understand how crazy this is, you insisting on hiding like this?" Cristina said, rushing inside.

She looked like she was already in the Maldives, her floral sundress accented by a Tahitian bead necklace and bamboo flip-flops. Andra glanced outside, wishing she could step into mid-evening's darkness, then quickly closed the door. This time she didn't mess with the chair. The two women hugged, Cristina leaning in gingerly to avoid pushing against the baby, who remained tucked against her mother's bosom.

"So… this is what the commotion's about," Cristina said, stepping back. "The game-changer, all wrapped up like a burrito. Can I see her?"

"Of course."

Andra eased Cera away from her breast and unwrapped her swaddling blankets. If fairies held beauty contests this baby would win—or at least, that's how Andra felt. She gazed into her daughter's doe eyes, captivated. The cherubic sparkle in Cera's cheeks and the gentle V-shape of her lips hinted at a north pole elf.

"Oh girl, she's beautiful," Cristina said. "If I didn't know better, I'd think she's the same as a diminished baby. Except cuter, right? Angelic looking. That smile, it kind of makes her glow. I mean, not literally, but it's really something amazing."

"Yeah… she's a cutie, for sure."

Andra saw Cristina lock eyes and hold, as if waiting for more of an answer.

"She, uh... she does stuff too," Cristina prompted. "Right?"

So she's seen the council footage, Andra thought. "Right now she only seems to shift herself for fun... or when sometimes when she's upset," she said.

"What do you mean, 'shift herself?' Does she actually change?"

"That's hard to answer. She just... lightens and brightens. Her movements become so fluid, too, and she shimmers. It's wonderful."

Cristina smiled, but it seemed forced. "Your own little whirling dervish," she said, looking concerned. She walked around the motel room's bed and sat on its far corner, her fingers probing the rock-hard mattress for the missing softness.

"Did you find what I need?" Andra said, reswaddling Cera.

"Not exactly. It's not like the council has road maps to Edenshire on their end tables. But I might have found a way to get you started in the right direction... you, Cera, and Wade. Where *is* the proud father, anyway?"

"Out following some leads. We're clearing out of this place in a few hours."

Cristina seemed happy to hear it.

"Look, right after the Maldives I have a job in Auckland," she said. "How about the three of you join me, we leave the kid with Wade, team up for the diminish, party a bit and then move on to the next job? If we get you diminishing again, that lawyer of yours might be able to convince the council to leave you alone."

Andra gave a condescending smile. "I'll never diminish another soul," she said, thinking the party wasn't much of a fit now either.

"Andra..."

"Look at my baby, Cristina. This is what you're saving the world from: this beautiful baby. Every human being out there should be as special as this baby right here, but they're not. Doesn't that bother you?"

Cristina leaned backward, onto the motel bed. "So what, I'm supposed to quit just because you've decided a successful, age-old system doesn't work for *you*?" she said.

"It doesn't work for any woman... for any human being," Andra said. "The council's ethics smell. You know they do."

"I don't know that whatsoever, so save your sanctimonious speeches for someone else. Working some ordinary job, leading an ordinary life, that's just not for me."

"If you say so."

Cristina propped herself up, atop the bed. "Oh, I say so. I most definitely say so. You know, you always act like I'm the airhead, the one who doesn't think things through, but it seems to me you're the one in the wrong here. We have a system in place for the good of everyone, whether you like that system or not. The council and the diminishers are doing their jobs lawfully. You're the one who broke the law."

Andra understood the point, even if she didn't agree. Grabbing an iced tea from the motel refrigerator, she offered it to Cristina as a peace offering.

Cristina snatched the can but wasn't finished. "Look, I'm sorry, but it's true: you basically asked for all this trouble," she said. "You could have just followed the rules, like me. Like everyone. But you didn't, and now... I don't think this is a mess I can help you get out of."

She fingered the motel room's plaid drapes, a little too obvious of an attempt at ignoring Andra's judgmental look.

"I don't want to get out of this mess, I don't want to change a thing," Andra said, cradling Cera. "All I want is a place to raise my beautiful little girl. If I can get to Edenshire, I can build some rapport and tackle the misconceptions from the source. The people there will see they don't have anything to be afraid of."

Cristina stood up, placed a comforting hand on Andra's shoulder, then moved to the motel door.

"That's what I'm trying to tell you," she said. "Whether you're here or in Edenshire, the council won't ever let you raise Cera. You broke the rules, Andra. They can't just let that go."

Andra sat back, startled. This wasn't the Cristina she had known for so many years. Or was it? Was she blaming Cristina for turning on her when in fact she herself was the one who had turned?

"I'm late for my plane," Cristina said. "But I do have a way to head you toward Edenshire."

"Which is?"

"Give me a second, I'll show you. And Ann?"

"Yeah?"

Cristina paused. "Come party with me again sometime, okay?"

She left, pulling the door until the knob's locking mechanism snicked into the doorjamb. Confused, Andra listened as her friend's soft footsteps echoed along the motel walkway before being drowned out by heavy pounding on the door.

"We have the place surrounded!" a booming male voice sounded. "Back away from the entry, now!"

Stunned, she searched the room for a defensive position, her chest constricting as the truth hit home. *Cristina sold me out.* Splinters flew through the air as someone rammed the motel's wooden door. The locking mechanism held, but the frame around the door had already cracked and wouldn't prevent the bolt from giving way for much longer.

I can't believe this! Cristina is part of the Sugar Dandruff Council's attempt to snatch my baby. Cristina! One of my best friends...

She ducked underneath the desk, folding her toothpick legs into the same giraffe-like squat she'd assumed before Cristina had arrived, arms and shoulders curled around her daughter. The two of them weren't, technically, hidden, but Andra wrapped the room's evening shadows around them, embracing the arcane stealth training she despised, knowing an intruder's eyes would go bed-floor-bathroom before spotting her... at which point she'd already be out the door.

Hopefully.

The bashing on the dilapidated door intensified, then stopped. Chaos erupted outside rather than inside. The skirmish didn't last long before someone with slender shoulders, muscled forearms, and spiked hair stepped through the busted entry, with words that steadied her thumping heart.

"Annie, you good?"

Andra heaved a sigh.

"Your Daddy has the best timing," she whispered to Cera. "We're good, Wade—barely."

She noticed his leather gloves and black tee were covered in muddied leaves. His jeans looked like a pit bull's chew toy, and he wasn't wearing the pooka shell necklace he so loved. Only his ever-present toothpick looked unscathed, wiggling from the right side of his mouth as he rolled it between his teeth.

"Is Cristina still out there?" she said, glancing through the entry.

He shook his head. "Cristina? Never saw her."

"I guess she took off while they were trying to bust in."

She wondered why Cristina had pulled the door shut, locking it, rather than simply leaving it ajar. Was there any chance she had actually been trying to buy her time without them knowing? *Riiight*, she thought.

"Wait here," she told Wade, easing the baby away from her breast, into his arms.

"It's not safe out there," he said.

"It's not safe anywhere."

She stepped through the doorway. Three men, each beaten unconscious, lay heaped along a concrete walkway connecting the aisle of orange motel doors. Opposite the walkway, a half-full asphalt parking lot glistened from recent rains. Two heavy support poles loomed near the lot's center, hefting a glowing yellow road sign that advertised "Motel" for what looked like the umpteenth decade. The lights in the front office were all out, suspicious since it was only mid-evening.

Andra pulled out her phone and texted "How could you?" to Cristina.

The response came quickly: *How could I? How could you?*

Seeing that made Andra furious, though unsurprised. She knew Cristina didn't have the personality for questioning authority; genuine issues never seemed to rise above superficial fare in her friend's mind, but their personalities meshed in so many other ways that it never seemed to matter. Now, suddenly, it mattered. She wondered how many people were friends of convenience, destined to be driven apart, even pitted against one another, once their day-to-day circumstances changed.

Another text chimed: *They won't hurt her, Ann. They promised me they'd keep the baby alive. It's the only way I would agree to help them.*

Andra scoffed. *Naïve*, she typed.

They won't stop, Ann. They want your baby, and they won't stop until they get her. The whole world's against you... Do you really think you and Wade can keep your baby safe, not only now but for years and years?

Yeah, Andra thought. I really do.

They're about to grab her, Ann! Get back in there, now!

Andra whirled, looking. Nothing but a wet, empty parking lot. No one moved along the motel's concrete walkway.

I swear it's true! Go to your baby, before it's too late!

Andra ran along the walkway, knowing she was probably being played, panicked nonetheless. Her footsteps echoed along the concrete until she bounded through the smashed doorway. Wade was tickling Cera, who lay on the bed, giggling.

"They're coming for her again," Andra blurted. "Any second now."

Wade passed Cera to Andra, then glanced out the room's only window. He gave a quick, negatory head shake; nothing outside. After a cursory look around the motel's living area, kitchen, and bathroom, he gave a cautious shrug.

"We're clear," he said.

But they weren't.

A floor-rocking boom shattered the motel's tiny window.

"Arcane tech!" Wade shouted, his mild southern drawl curtailed by the urgency. "Get Cera under the—"

Andra yelled, squeezing her daughter tight against her chest as a miniature starfield burst at the room's apex. The stars showered the room like a firework then swarmed around Cera, muffling her cries, stifling her movement, her energy, her shifting colors. Andra tightened her grip, spinning and dodging, but the starswarm matched every movement.

Then Cera winked away.

Andra stared at her empty arms, stunned. The stars had vanished with Cera. The room was now dark and empty. She heard Wade curse, saw him race outside, but couldn't move. All she truly registered was empty arms and crushing misery. Her lungs strained, her jaw shuddered, her entire body felt ice-cold.

Instinct and desperation got her moving once again. She raced outside looking for Cera, the kidnappers, a starfield, a trail... anything where she could pin a hope. Instead she entered an empty parking lot and an anguished, heated exchange as she and Wade debated their next move.

"Is Cera even alive?" Andra said, near hysterical yet zombie-numb. "Or did that star-thing just kill her?"

Wade waved her away, overwhelmed.

"Gimme a minute here," he said, looking rabid. "Gimme one damn minute to—"

"We don't have a minute!" Andra said. "The police don't know about the council. No one does. It's up to us. We need to find her!"

"You think?" Wade said, stomping off. "Don't worry, I'll do it. I'll get her back."

Andra's shellshocked mind figured it made sense. Wade's covert messenger training included some of the Cinüe's arcane techniques for locating concealed individuals... in standard destinations, and otherwise. Wade would have a better chance of finding Cera than anyone else.

But the moment he left, Andra regretted that she hadn't insisted they tackle the matter together. She accepted the fact he possessed skills that she didn't, and was far better at tracking people, unseen, than herself. Trust wasn't an issue either; she considered him her life partner, even if her three marriage refusals said otherwise. Her mistake, she decided, was overlooking the fact she wasn't the type to sit around waiting.

She tried texting Cristina but didn't hear back; the message retained an "undelivered" stamp. Cristina's phone and emails appeared equally dead.

"I'll get her back."

Night after night, Andra heard Wade saying those words, just before she woke from whatever catnap she managed. But other than that she never saw him, never heard from him. As several days passed, reality hit home: her baby daughter and her significant other were *both* missing.

"I need to force their hand," she said over a broken cell phone connection, confident the prim, law-loving David Stanford Swimney could form a legal attack—if not a dozen. "Cera has rights. *I* have rights."

She knew she was wrong when her attorney didn't launch into his usual legal rhapsodizing.

"The problem here is that, from their perspective, you're the one who broke the law, Ms. Barger," he said. "And you did so in the aftermath of voting in favor of the Diminishing Act, so feigning ignorance is not an option. Strictly speaking, though I'm certainly not endorsing their actions, the council had every right to capture and contain an undiminished child... from a legal standpoint, you understand. Once you violated—"

"Screw the legalities!" Andra said, having already heard the same garbage from Cristina. "Did their attorneys tell you where the council's holding her? Or whether she's alive, for that matter?"

"They did not. I've of course filed an action, but..."

But it's not going to work, she knew. They were dead in the water. Her daughter... her beautiful baby girl... helpless, in the council's clutches.

Swimney cleared his throat. "There is, of course, one option. Not that I'd recommend it professionally, but under the circumstances..."

"I get it, this is between us. Just tell me already, will you?"

He took a breath and, she was pretty sure, a drag from one of his cigars. "As you said, you need to force the council's hand. The longer they stall, the less likely you get Cera back. Immediate action, that's what you need."

"And that's why it's not helpful to hear I don't have a legal leg to stand on."

"No, but you do have an *issue* to stand on."

She switched her phone to her other ear. "Diminishing? I already thought of that and sure, I could go public, expose what they're doing. But I can't prove any of it, so who'd believe me?"

"No one would believe you. Absolutely no one."

She sighed. "So there I am, powerless again."

"Oh no. Not powerless, not at all. Quite the opposite, in fact."

"I don't get it."

She heard him stubbing out the cigar. "You're still trained as a diminisher," he said.

"So?"

He grunted. "So... go out there and diminish."

She rolled her eyes. "Have you not heard a thing I've been saying about how wrong it is?" she said. "Did you not understand the significance of me unveiling Cera in front of the whole council and—"

"Not human beings. Cinüe."

She hesitated. "What?"

"You'd diminish Cinüe children."

Andra felt her mouth drop open. *Diminish Cinüe in retaliation?* She felt sick to her stomach, just thinking about the complete lack of ethics it would take to embrace Swimney's idea.

"Is that even possible?" she finally managed.

"Certainly. You'd need some inside information to find out who's a Cinüe, of course, but given the circumstance I think that could be arranged."

"And the process is the same? Quick swipe to the mother's hand? Same type of salve as always?"

"Everything's the same. Just pick Cinüe mothers rather than human mothers. Of course, it's completely illegal, ever since the Veracruz scandal in the 1700s. But if you want to get the council's attention, maybe force their hand, I can't think of a better start than making it clear you'll diminish Cinüe children until such time as they return Cera. Do you still have gel refills for your ring?"

"Plenty. They don't send them anymore but I was like a squirrel with those things. But... what happens to the children if I do what you're suggesting? What's a diminished Cinüe look like?"

She heard Swimney fire up a match, envisioned him using it to ignite a fresh cigar.

"If I heard correctly at the council chamber," he said between puffs, "they look something like Wade. Asantha Cooray claimed he's a diminished Cinüe, did she not?"

"Yeah... not that Wade's been willing to discuss it with me."

She repositioned the motel's desk chair and sat down, reeling. Just the thought of once again diminishing innocents... it was horrible. And using it as a bargaining chip? *Repulsive*. Plus, what would Wade think? But she also knew Swimney was right. Her daughter's life was on the line, and this might be her only viable option. It would certainly get their attention.

"Oh God," she uttered, to herself as much as Swimney.

I'm about to become a diminisher again.

THIRTEEN

Stiletto

The phone call arrived at 3:18 a.m., audio only, the caller ID blank.

Andra shook off depression's residue as best she could, mulling the odds the call was from Wade, phoning from an unrecognized line. *If he's even still alive.* She prayed that he was, and that they still had time to rescue Cera from... wherever.

Please, let her be okay, she thought.

The phone continued ringing. She ran a finger through her coconut hair, which she'd cut into a bob before having the baby. Her couch-planted butt felt numb but the phone receiver was right next to her and she needed to finish pumping, so she felt no desire to move just yet.

Three hours since I tried dozing and I'm still a hazy, sleepless mess.

She stared at the phone's elliptical buttons, weighing the odds of a wrong number against the chance Wade might be calling with important news. The latter possibility proved too tempting, secrecy be damned. She pushed the receiver's Talk button but didn't say a word.

"2963 Montague," David Stanford Swimney's graveled Australian voice announced.

He ended the call without waiting for an answer, which Andra considered a success. Training him to incorporate a bit of cloak and dagger into his routine hadn't been easy given his fondness for the Sugar Dandruff Council's dusty laws. But with the secretive council now his nemesis both in and out of the courtroom, Swimney was becoming more flexible.

Andra stretched her legs, shut the breast pump down, and checked the results. *Two-thirds full, not ideal but not bad*. She walked the bottle to the fridge, about six steps away from the living room—tiny even for a studio, and she'd cluttered it with empty, three-day-old shave ice cups. Behind her, the cushions on a crushed velvet sofa still bore her bottom's imprint, an old box-shaped TV lapped the edges of its wobbly stand, and two table lamps with rare, incandescent bulbs barely defied their age. Still, as Swimney had pointed out, his neighbor's unused Albuquerque apartment was not only a step up from the Sydney motel but well off the council's usual beaten path.

Andra placed the fresh milk in the fridge, next to a bottle from several hours earlier. Pumping with no baby felt bleak, but defiant.

Cera will drink the milk, she told herself. *I'll get her home safely, and she will drink it.*

She repeated the words every time she added a bottle. Sometimes, when ducts seemed plugged or the hookup felt crappy, she told herself to stop being ridiculous and quit pumping.

But that would be giving up, she knew. So she continued pumping, usually twice a day.

Not just for Cera. For me.

She grabbed a sweater, locked up, and trudged two flights downstairs before realizing she didn't need a sweater in Albuquerque's July air. She clung to the shadows in front of the building, matching their angles, their tones... summoning her training, feeling the rust. A mini-mart across the street was closed, but floodlit so brightly that it looked open. Otherwise there was only apartments, shadows, and insects swarming around the sodium street lamps.

Montague was four blocks away, so she was there in a few minutes. The buildings had bars on the windows, the neighborhood had bars on the corners. Bad, but she'd seen worse. Still, it looked like the kind of street where the dumpsters concealed remains rather than trash. Albuquerque was like that sometimes, a beacon for southwestern charm in daylight, a real Hyde at night.

She found the couple in a second floor bedroom at 2963. Andra stretched like a cat, sliding between the bars, through the open window, on inside. Her eyes adjusted fast, though not as fast as they used to—post pregnancy had all sorts of weird surprises. She stood until she could discern the couple sleeping. Their bed, a canopied monster with lacey shams, didn't fit the neighborhood whatsoever.

This room doesn't fit the neighborhood either, she realized, as the darkened shapes of a wall-sized television and an elaborate vanity materialized before her adjusting eyes. *Someone's using it for cover.*

She slunk across, the tiny flip-cap on her pearl ring already nudged open, a thick dab of diminishing gel deposited on her finger. Then she reached the bed and noticed: only the man was still under the covers. The woman wasn't there anymore.

Her neck hair prickled. She stepped sideways, but not quite fast enough to avoid something pounding the back of her skull. Collapsing to her knees, she saw the world swim but managed to stay conscious. The gel was off her finger, smeared onto the floor.

This isn't just a Cinüe, Andra realized. *It's another diminisher.*

"You think I haven't heard about you?" the woman's voice called, standing behind her. "You think the council didn't warn us?"

Andra spun but the woman spun too, disappearing into the shadows of her own home. *She's got me*, Andra knew. *Same skills, but I don't know the place and she does.*

She scooted to a nook where the bed met the vanity, reached up, and grabbed the first thing she felt laying on the surface above the drawers. Looking at it, she frowned. *A mirror. And I'm not exactly the fairest of them all.*

Across the room, the window snapped shut. Andra flung the mirror toward the window, hard as she could. It smacked into the frame, shattering onto the sill, but the window was undamaged and more importantly, the woman had already moved out of the way.

“You’re a real piece of work, trying to diminishing a diminisher,” the woman's voice said, from somewhere across the room. “I hope they dice that freak baby of yours to bits.”

Andra bounded bed-to-headboard-to-wall, landing near the doorway. She heard something rustling behind her, figured it was the woman... then realized her mistake and covered her eyes with her hands.

The overhead lights flicked on, flooding the bedroom.

“Julia?” the man muttered, sitting up in bed, his head cobwebbed and confused.

Blinded, Julia cried out for him to shut the lights down, but Andra was ready. Widening her fingers just far enough apart to see Julia's dark mousy hair crouched beneath the canopy bed, she dabbed more gel onto her finger then sprung. Julia was on the move too, but inadvertently leaped right into Andra's path.

Andra grabbed Julia's hand and flicked the gel against the woman's palm.

Job done.

“No... no!” Julia yelled, horrified, looking at the gel smeared across her palm.

The gel sunk into her skin, vanishing. Both Julia and Andra glanced at Andra's right ankle, watching the slender, woven bracelet glowing just above her shoe.

The glow disappeared, leaving only a few pallid sparkles.

"Sugar dandruff," Andra said, stepping away. "It's over."

Julia looked as if she might explode.

"This is on you!" she screamed, holding her palm in Andra's face. "Diminishing a Cinüe child is a death sentence, you know that, right? You're as good as dead!"

The man was on his feet now but so was Andra, racing across the room.

"The Maybe Objective's almost here!" Julia said, enraged. "You and your kind are done, you clueless bitch!"

Andra yanked the front door open, disappearing into the night. Julia's threats faded with each step, except for one phrase. *I hope they dice that freak baby of yours to bits*, she repeated to herself. *She thinks Cera's alive. Maybe the council's studying her? But where?*

Though winded and out of shape, she managed to continue running for three long blocks before slowing to a stop. Standing on the sidewalk, under a streetlight, shuddering in full view of anyone who was out at 4 a.m.—which was no one—she broke into tears.

I have no choice, she insisted to herself, weeping. *No choice.*

She wished she could go public with the Cinüe's clandestine effort to diminish the human population.

Imagine the outcry, she fantasized. But no... tracks were covered, stories arranged, methods fine-tuned, gels specially designed. Ultrasound images and other tests couldn't discern the pre-zygote, genetic alterations. There was no proof. And now Cera, her only chance at offering that proof, was gone. *Unless I can force these bastards to give her back.*

She removed her ankle bracelet and unravelled it like a scroll. The digital paper screen that was once filled with assignments from the council was blank, and for good reason: she had disabled its receiving and locating abilities. But she could still send outgoing messages, so she began writing.

—A third diminisher is diminished. This continues until you release my daughter.—

She was in full tears now as the message disappeared into the ether, headed to... whoever. *Asantha Cooray, perhaps?* Edenshire's centuries-old spiritual leader, equal parts myth and reality, would be incensed—especially since Andra's grandmother was Asantha's adopted daughter.

This is all so wrong! Why, why, why didn't I vote diminishing down when I had the chance?

Instead she was now... what, a terrorist? A deadly threat to all Cinüe mothers? She hated herself for choosing this path, easing the guilt by telling herself everything was fueled by desperation. But deep down, she knew two wrongs didn't make a right. She wasn't even sure what diminishing gel did to a Cinüe baby. All she knew was the Cinüe never used it on themselves, and seemed deathly afraid of doing so. That meant David Stanford Swimney was right: she had a tiny bit of leverage.

But would the council care? Or would they sacrifice however many Cinüe children she could diminish, figuring it was all for the greater cause—for this 'Maybe Objective?' Andra knew her gamble to use Cera as a means of spearheading change from within the council's own ranks, rather than simply casting a lone opposition vote, smelled worse by the day.

This is all so wrong. Diminishing is repulsive, even when it's done to the Cinüe... and I'm no terrorist. Why can't they see the insanity here? Why won't they just release Cera?

Please, God, let them release my baby girl.

A week later, Wade made contact.

Andra found a tea light candle in her mail slot and knew two things: it was from him, and it was a variation on the necrospondence he'd delivered in Kauai—the one that put her in the hospital. Even though she swore she'd never accept one again, her captive daughter erased any hesitation.

Minutes later she had the candle lit, billowing daisy-turpentine-tomato fumes. The smell made her head throb, and her feet felt like they had tommyknockers chiseling their insides. *Something's very wrong here.*

Her knees wobbled; she collapsed. Skin flaked from her cheeks, landing in the carpet like pebbles. Her eyes shrunk to slits and the tip of her nose curled to one side. Horrified, Andra thought through everything she could remember about severe necrospondence effects and felt certain the severity meant this necrospondence didn't involve sign language, and wasn't a written or verbal message. But that meant it was something more significant, something... wait, was Wade really sending a firsthand view of an experience?

If so, it was the most powerful Cinüe message possible... the type of message someone could only send by pre-arranging it, not only with a Cinüe, but a Cinüe still living in Edenshire.

"That's impossible," she thought aloud.

Andra knew dozens of diminishers, all of them descendants of the scant few Edenshire people living in the standard world. None had ever visited Edenshire.

"And yet Wade has?" she mumbled.

It made no sense... unless the diminishers had lied. Could it be they had some sort of rule forbidding them to admit they still had firsthand contact with Edenshire? Given that their ancestors had been left behind to assimilate themselves into the world's hierarchies as part of the multi-millenia diminishing program, assuring a lesser species, Andra could see the reasoning behind such a rule.

She forced herself up, so she could lock eyes onto the flame. As soon as she did, the scent faded and heat waves rising from the flame rippled the air. The hot air currents above the candle etched into the world around her, forming a rippled, convex gap. The ripples widened into a crescent-shaped rupture, pulling her closer. She didn't resist. Instead she felt her consciousness ache, fade, then return with a number.

Double-nine, one-one-one.

Digits on an armed guard's identification badge, she saw. The guard's black uniform looked like something a ninja might wear, especially with a matching head-wrap that only revealed his brown eyes. Andra recognized those eyes right away.

"Wade," she whispered.

He was stationed inside a corridor lined with steel walls and enormous vault doors—a prison, maybe? If so, it was no average prison. Bubbles floated throughout, silent when they popped against walls but emitting a loud "ping" whenever they hit unexpected objects, including the guards. Signs along the corridor warned of motion, sound wave, and air current sensors. One cautioned workers to report excess forehead or neck sweat prior to taking their position, or risk tripping "fragrance monitors."

What kind of prisoner requires a place like this?

She saw a red dot painted on the wall opposite Wade, a fixed target for his eyes.

Computers are tracking his eye movements. Maybe they're programmed to detect unusual sequences.

Is this where they're keeping Cera?

Unexpected chaos broke her thought train: exterior alarm bells.

A tall, stocky figure wearing a man's dark suit entered the prison hallway through a personnel door, setting off additional interior alarms—so many of them Andra could hardly hear herself criticizing his idiocy. The man wore a hood over his head, its dark mesh concealing his identity, the rest a silver fabric with beads running down the sides and back. Andra recognized him right away.

It was Bead Hood... chairman of the Sugar Dandruff Council.

Wade faced the hooded visitor, rifle raised. A dozen other guards stationed throughout the corridor did the same. The council chair gave them an approving nod and spoke a verbal code. Andra couldn't make out the code, but assumed the computers were designed to pick up sounds ranging into inaudible. The alarms quieted.

"Just the quarterly visit, gentlemen," Bead Hood said. "Stay in position... no matter what."

More exterior bells, then silence, then footsteps.

Not just footsteps, Andra noticed, listening. *High-heeled footsteps.*

The personnel doorway reopened and the longest leg Andra had ever seen slid through, led by a blue stiletto and trailed by the slit of a velvet dress. The woman entering was attractive enough, a cropped-brunette with high cheekbones and well-toned arms, but Andra was pretty sure her slim, graceful legs were right out of some god's instruction manual for female limb perfection. She found herself wondering whether the prison's eye movement software was still tracking Wade's eyes.

Bead Hood greeted her, or tried. The woman walked past him—maybe she glided?—without so much as a glance. She seemed confidence personified, but Andra couldn't help but think she also looked preoccupied.

She's not there for a visit. She's there on business.

“What do you think?” the woman said to Bead Hood, without actually looking at him. Her voice sounded like it tamed lions for a living.

“I think you’ll set a whole new standard for conjugal visits,” he said.

She nodded.

“Yeah, heard that before,” she said. “Now tell me what you really think.”

Bead Hood put his arm around her, forcing her attention, nudging her toward the far end of the hall.

“Seen a lot of women go in,” he said, eyeballing her.

She raised her shoulder, shrugging his arm off, looking impatient.

“And?”

Bead Hood looked away.

“And,” he said, “not many of them come back out. But you already know that.”

She smirked. “They aren’t me.”

They walked several steps forward, until they reached a massive vault door with a stone facing. It had so many layers, locks and cross-braces that it seemed designed to hold a thousand dinosaurs.

“You’ll head two layers behind that door,” Bead Hood said. “Ignore the first, just pass through. You're going to the second. This is for the Maybe Objective, so make it count. You're the last one we're sending in."

She studied him, without much respect.

"You told the emergency session I'm not the last," she said. "That you're tossing someone else in there too."

Bead Hood seemed irritated, but nodded.

"Not for the conjugal, that's for sure. But yeah, there's one more going in."

Andra held her breath. Inside, she wanted to scream because her gut told her why Wade had sent the necrospondence: Cera would be the extra one going in.

"So you're worried about omnipotence," the woman said.

"Wouldn't be the first time."

"You sure we're discussing the same thing?" she said, after waiting a beat.

Bead Hood didn't seem amused.

"A few days in there, we should get a good idea of what she'll eventually be capable of," he said.

"Yeah, well you'd better wait at least a week before sending her in," the woman said, approaching the door. "I'm gonna' wear this one out."

Bead Hood gave her a less-than subtle head-to-toe look, then spoke in a near-silent voice. Warning lights activated throughout the corridor, flickering in sequence. He spoke several additional words and a klaxon sounded. Reaching for the door's handle, he placed his hand along its surface without moving it, then waited.

The vault door opened with a blood-curdling creak-shriek mix, and even then it remained nearly closed, cracked just wide enough from the frame for the woman's slender form to pass between. The woman surveyed the prison corridor, made brief eye contact with Wade, then faced the opened door and stepped inside, one stilettoed, perfected limb at a time.

Bead Hood shut the entry as soon as she was through. Moments later it was locked, the klaxons quiet, the warning lights dark. Bead Hood didn't move. Instead he stood there, arms folded, as if he expected something else to happen. He listened for a few moments, seemed satisfied, then walked back up the corridor looking pleased with himself.

Something's not right, Andra thought.

"Just to be clear," Bead Hood said, looking at several of the guards, "I lied back there. None of the women have ever come back out."

No one answered.

Uh uh... that's not it. Pretty sure he wants to say more.

Bead Hood walked a bit further, then stopped.

"With the exception of a Barger or two," he added.

A Barger? Andra thought, surprised. *What's he talking about*?

Then Bead Hood gestured at the guard with badge double-nine, one-one-one.

"So maybe we need to get your favorite lady in here... Wade."

Andra's heart skipped a beat.

In the moment it took Wade to register Bead Hood using his nickname, the other guards had their weapons cocked and aimed.

"We've got the biggest players in the universe locked up in here," Bead Hood said. "So disguised dads searching for their children? Way out of their league."

Alarms blared once again, startling even Bead Hood. At the end of the corridor, the massive vault door with the multitude of locks and cross-braces bulged outward then cracked open, just a few inches.

For a moment, nothing happened. Then the long, stilettoed leg slid out, framed by the slit of its velvet dress. The cropped brunette emerged looking disheveled, possibly even battered, but her expression and attitude cried conquest.

"Get that fixed," she said to Bead Hood, pointing to the damaged door.

The woman walked the prison corridor like she could flick it down with her pinkie if she wanted, then left through the same personnel door she'd entered.

Bead Hood stood there. Even with his face covered, his withering body language left no doubt he was stunned. Finally, he looked at his watch.

"Six minutes," he mumbled. "Only six minutes..."

Wade had already made his move. Rifles fired, gas sprayed, chemicals rained as his captors realized their mistake. Andra watched him dodge, cover, and evade. Determination told her Wade could get away, that he could still rescue their daughter, but reality had the louder voice.

Reality insisted he had no chance whatsoever.

FOURTEEN

Stanshmoor

David Stanford Swimney called with another address the following night.

Exhausted and more interested in tracking down the prison Wade had shown her, she let Swimney know about the necrospondence.

"Better give yourself another day to shake off the effects," Swimney said.

But Andra knew she couldn't, not if she wanted to keep pressure on the council. She stumbled out the door, memories of Cera's smiling face serving as her carrot. Five hours and one very eventful elevator ride later, she was messaging the council about her fourth Cinüe diminishing.

She returned to the apartment ready for sleep, but her phone didn't cooperate.

"Emergency meeting," Swimney's voice announced. "I'll be there in ten minutes. And pack a bag, you may be gone a couple days."

He hung up before she could ask for details. She sighed, dropped onto the couch, studied the ceiling, noticed cracks she hadn't seen before. The place needed paint, carpet, termite spray. Still, it was furnished, clean when graded on a curve, and a decent home away from home. Now all she had to do was figure out where home was.

The phone rang again, this time just once. *Swimney's here.*

She threw on her sweater, some jeans, and some old shoes, then grabbed the bag with the breast pump—*gotta' keep using it, or my body won't be ready when my daughter gets home.* Baby weight aside, she felt no different from her pre-motherhood days. Outside the apartment building she disappeared into shadow, a rote response made more difficult with the bag slung over her shoulder. Music boomed several blocks away and a man in a green army jacket urinated against the building next door, otherwise all was quiet. The mini-mart across the street still had too many lights for Andra's taste. *Of course that's probably because they didn't want people lurking around in the shadows. Market one, Andra zero.*

A white sedan flashed its lights.

The car's windows were to dark to see inside, Andra didn't move. *Swimney ought to know I'm not about to reveal myself unless I'm certain it's him.* Eventually he figured it out, opened his door, and walked to the passenger side. If he owned any clothes other than a dark gray suit with a pink tie, Andra still hadn't seen them. She clung to the shadows until she reached a spot closest to the car, then stepped out next to him. He banged into the car, startled.

"Really, Ms. Barger?" he said, irritated. "At four-thirty in the morning?"

She grinned, then climbed inside, waving her hand through cigar smog.

"Nicaraguan?" she called, remembering that he preferred them to Havana-style.

"Ecuadoran," he said, hustling to the driver's side. "Luxury blend. I could fill the car's tank twice for the cost of just one of these, but sometimes you gotta' live, right?"

He had the car started and underway before she'd even fastened her seat belt.

"What's the emergency—another address for me?" she said, then thought it over and added, "Where are you getting them from anyway?"

"You don't want to know. In any event, this meeting is not about another address, although I do expect some information to that effect in the coming week."

"So then why am I here?" Andra said. "News on Wade and Cera?"

Swimney fired up a cigar, then shook his head.

"You have an appointment, Ms. Barger. And a crucial one at that."

She perked up. "The council blinked?" she said, hoping her appalling diminishing tactic had forced their hand.

"Unfortunately, no. Not yet, anyway."

Her spirits dove, penthouse to basement.

"No, no, don't give up, not yet," Swimney said, noticing her devastated, exhausted expression. "As I said, this meeting is a crucial one. A first step, if you will."

She eyed him with suspicion. "With someone from the council?"

"With someone who matters—and you'll have time to get some rest first," he said. "For several hours, actually."

"Why? Where exactly is this appointment?"

Swimney pulled off the highway, onto a dirt road that bounced them enough for Andra to guess they should be going much slower.

"Someplace where you're going to need one of *those* to get to it," he said, pointing.

She looked. They were approaching a small private jet, its red exterior illuminated only by wobbling flashlight beams and its own beacon lights.

"David, what's going on?"

"*You're* going on... on board that plane."

"No chance," Andra said quickly. "Not with Cera missing. I need to keep the pressure on the council. I'm not leaving."

Swimney pulled the car next to the plane. The pilot, someone bald but mostly shrouded in darkness, was already lowering the entry stairwell.

"You'll be back in 48 hours," Swimney said. "And this is directly related to Cera, and to the prison. The council requested this, Andra, in open session. That means nothing's secret, so the law is in our corner. If anything happens to you I'll have plenty of proof that they were responsible and could file a very strong legal case for prosecution."

"How reassuring. I'll try to remember as they kill me."

Swimney blew a thick smoke cloud without bothering to remove the cigar from his mouth.

"If you're truly worried about finding that prison," he said, "then this is an appointment you absolutely need to keep."

She shook her head.

"Why? Who is the appointment with?"

Swimney looked around, clearly uncomfortable.

"I... I'd rather not say."

She gave him a look.

"You'd rather not say?" she repeated. "Oh, okay, because I don't want to inconvenience you or anything."

"Ms. Barger, please... I realize this is unconventional, but with all my heart I advise you to board the plane for your appointment."

"But you don't want to tell me who I'll be meeting, or why."

He took another cigar drag, then another.

"I need more," Andra said. "I'll consider this because I trust you, but first I need more."

The cigar was half gone. Swimney puffed like it was his last.

"God," he said softly.

Andra waited. Swimney took another drag, then looked her in the eyes.

"You're appointment's with God."

She stared at him. "Is this your way of saying they're about to assassinate me?"

He took a breath before answering.

"No."

She waited, but he didn't add anything.

"Then... what?" she said. "I don't get it."

"Yes, well... I don't feel right talking about it," he said. "Not even here, with just the two of us. It's just something you need to see, alright? Then you'll understand."

He unlocked the car's doors. Andra reached over and re-locked them.

"Not going anywhere," she said.

Swimney lowered his head to the steering wheel, closing his eyes.

"I'm sorry, David," Andra added. "You're an amazing friend, and I know you're trying to help. But I'm a mother now and—"

"Cera's not the world's only natural-born human, Ms. Barger."

She hesitated.

"What are you talking about?"

Swimney ran his fingers through his hair. Andra noticed he was sweating, unshaven, and jittery, characteristics she had never seen in him before.

"There's another, from ages ago," he said. "He's... powerful. A level of ability, of awareness, that I can't even describe. I'm not sure how the council did it but they've held him captive for thousands of years, in some sort of ultra-Guantanimo facility they call Stanshmoor... quite possibly the same facility where you saw Wade in the necrospondence."

Andra gave a nervous laugh.

"Come on," she said.

Swimney's lower lip shook.

"He's what humans are supposed to be, Andra," he said, his face pale. "He's what Cera will someday become."

Andra kept waiting for more detail or a punch line. Instead Swimney became more serious than ever.

"When I say he's God... we all are, Ms. Barger. Or at least, we would have been if the Cinüe hadn't diminished us. All human beings, we're basically gods. That's quite possibly the reason people gravitate towards a belief in divine beings. You can diminish the cells, but not the innate ambitions."

Andra leaned her head back, deep against the seat, using the pressure to curb her irritation.

"And you're telling me this *now*?" she said. "You didn't think maybe I should know sooner?"

He shook his head.

"I just found out myself. And yes, maybe it's all a fabrication, a clever way to lure you straight inside their prison. But the Sugar Dandruff Council's legal team... people I trust... they say it's true. The fact your visit was arranged in open council, stipulating your freedom to leave afterwards, seems to support their claims."

Swimney puffed at his shrinking cigar like it was an oxygen line.

"They say it's the reason diminishing started in the first place," he said. "The Cinüe had no chance to survive, not when the natural-born humans were gods. Diminishing offered a chance."

He pulled his cigar from his mouth, flicked ashes out the window, then held it between two fingers while using the rest of his hand to massage his right temple.

"So this prisoner," he continued. "He's basically God, and he's being held at Stansh..."

Swimney's voice trailed off. He took a breath, composing himself before continuing.

"Stanshmoor is Cinüe-built, full of arcane tech. Constructed around the same time as the Uluru council chamber."

He shut his watery eyes, containing moisture best he could.

What the hell? David Stanford Swimney, crying?

"David... relax," Andra said. "What you're suggesting just isn't possible, okay? Doesn't matter what they're telling you, we both know no one can imprison God, right?"

He swallowed, still composing himself.

"They've imprisoned others over the years," he said. "Terrors, legends, all sorts of... *beings* no one thought they could contain. But they did."

He took a deep drag on his cigar, then another.

"I've seen the proof, Ms. Barger," he said. "Not for this god-human, but for some of the others. People we thought long dead, preserved. People who should have been dead, living in there. And then..."

Another drag.

"Things. Objects, animals... stuff I can't discuss. Serious stuff."

Andra leaned back against her seat, stretching her shoulders, trying to accept, still dubious.

"Their leader is a 200,000-year-old dead woman, for crying out loud," Swimney said. "You don't think maybe it took some unprecedented connections to make that happen?"

He shut his eyes again, even as he took a fresh drag. The car was filled with thick smoke but Andra let it slide, preoccupied with what he was saying.

"Who set up this appointment?" she said, her voice faint, her throat dry.

Swimney shut his eyes.

"Not the Cinüe," he said, reopening them. "It was... you know how you Americans get to make a phone call if you're arrested? Think of it as that. You've received the phone call... the god-human's phone call. The council has no choice but to honor it."

"Me. Of all the universe... he's calling for me."

She gave herself a moment, to process.

"So the council's telling you I have an appointment to meet this god-human inside a Stanshmoor prison cell," she said, measuring each word, trying to get a feel for the truth.

"Meet, look, peek, what does any of that matter?" Swimney said.

Andra waited.

"Don't you understand?" he said. "Think of the implications if the council actually has enough power to hold *God* prisoner. Just think about that."

She tried, but the concept seemed too outlandish to register.

"I don't know," she said. "Traveling there, placing myself in their hands..."

Swimney, held up a hand, having none of it.

"Ms. Barger," he said. "This is an appointment you need to keep."

Neither of them said anything further. The car idled, the cigar burned, the moment expanded. *The air too,* Andra thought. *Even the air feels heavy.*

FIFTEEN

God

The jet took off ten minutes later with Andra on board, second-guessing her choice, wondering whether she was both a fool and a lousy mother. She hoped Swimney was telling the truth... or maybe she didn't. She wasn't sure.

Swimney remained behind, saying he was forbidden to attend. As far as Andra could tell she and the bald pilot were the only people on the aircraft... and the pilot remained behind the locked cockpit door.

A co-pilot might've been nice, Andra thought. *That, and maybe a lime-mango shave ice.*

Her questions and concerns only fended off exhaustion for so long. Once the constant whistle of airflow over the hull turned to white noise, she slept. It was plane sleep, interrupted by shifts in engine sounds and mild turbulence, but something was better than nothing. Restless dreams assaulted her, driven by the faces of diminished women. She thrashed in her seat as diminished daughters became her own daughter, the vivid memory of Cera's capture ensnaring her head and heart. Cera's scream vibrated her bones... but no, it wasn't Cera's. Andra realized the scream echoing through her mind was her own.

When she awoke the plane was jittering, passing through air pockets while descending over green, sunlit hills. She looked at her watch: eleven hours had passed, which explained why she was hungry beyond belief. She dug through her breast pump bag and found two granola bars, the only food she had with her, then devoured them while spending time with the pump.

Cera will drink the milk, she told herself after finishing. *I'll get her home safely, and she will drink it.*

The aircraft landed on an asphalt strip, nothing so formal or well-maintained as a runway. She scrutinized the view, trying to figure out where she was, but saw only green-grassed hills, small shrubs, and gentle sun rays glistening atop the surface of at least a dozen ribbon-sized streams. The scene was pastoral, beautiful enough that she wished she were on a holiday rather than a mission.

The plane bounced more than taxied, then stopped. Andra kept staring out the windows, expecting to see a small airport, or at least a hangar, but there were no buildings in sight. No people, either. Just green hills with dozens of tiny streams.

The engines remained on—and they weren't cycling down.

The pilot burst from the cockpit, pulled several latches, and opened the side door. The man acted like he had a gun pointed at his head as he lowered the staircase, fast as he could.

"Okay then, you're off!" he said to Andra, his voice a bit screechy.

She unbuckled and stood.

"Off to where?"

The pilot waved her forward, and when she didn't move fast enough for his taste he went to her and pulled her forward by hand.

"To the compound a' course," he shouted over the engine noise as they approached the door. "Back door though, righ? Up the third hill with ya, mind the wolf."

"There are wolves here?"

"Wolf—just one, not somethin' pleasant but he goes along with what you're up to here, righ? Now go on dearie, I can't stay here much longer."

"How do I go back if you're not waiting?"

"I'll be back when I get a call. Now go, go!"

His answer told her nothing but he was so insistent she went down the steps anyway, figuring she'd already come all this way. The engine's decibels hammered at her ears and the turbines were kicking up dust near the asphalt. As soon as her feet touched ground the pilot was retracting the steps, waving her away. She took his advice to heart, figuring if the engines were loud while idling they'd be even worse when he took off again.

She was barely onto the nearest hillside when the plane accelerated forward, taking to the air. Moments later it was out of sight.

And now I'm on my own in... someplace.

Her ears, still ringing, gradually tuned to the quiet around her... which wasn't so quiet after all, filled with birdsong, chittering gophers, bees, and trickling water. She looked for the third hill that the pilot referred to, irritated that she didn't have any further details, further irritated that two granola bars wasn't much of a breakfast after an eleven-hour flight.

There were dozens of hills. Did he mean the third hill from the plane's nose? The third hill back in the direction where she exited the plane? Two hill-climbs later, she still had no clue. All she knew was the stream water tasted delicious, the terrain was covered in shamrocks ranging from red to black, and there wasn't a compound anywhere in sight. She re-traced her footsteps through the grass until she found a quartzite outcropping near a clump of black shamrocks.

A wolf howl sounded.

During the day? she thought.

The sound extended ten, twenty, then thirty seconds, a baritone trill with a growl embedded beneath the usual high-pitched wolf cry. Andra scanned the hillsides, chills running up her spine, but couldn't spot the wolf. She looked for tracks, or indents in dirt, or smooshed grass. *An empty food wrapper with crumbs would be perfect,* she thought, still hungry. But there was nothing, not nearby, not farther away.

She watched the grasses swaying with the breeze, their soothing ripples animating the hillsides. Even the streams bore an extra sparkle whenever the breeze passed. Only the rocks had no ripples. That, and the narrow, trampled lines where she had...

She straightened. *The places where my footsteps trampled the grass aren't moving.*

Her paths across the hillsides looked like dark lines. Two others were there as well... places where others had walked. One only went halfway up one of the hillsides, but the other...

She stood. *The other footprint trail goes up the hill and disappears over the top.*

A few minutes later she stood at the apex of that hill. The foot-stomped grass trailed into a small gully, disappearing in spots where the person had stepped into a rocky patch but then reappearing on the other side of the stones. Andra entered the gully, hopeful.

The baritone howl sounded again from behind her, at the top of the hill. This time she saw the wolf... or something similar. It was just a red outline—no visible body—but it still had a snout, teeth, and glowing eyes. The animal took several deep sniffs, then charged into the gully.

Andra raced ahead but there was nowhere to go, surrounded by three convergent hills with not so much as a stick to defend herself. She spotted a small stream that curled and puddled to one side of the gulley, then dropped into a large, rock-strewn gash. *Better than nothing,* she thought, trying to spot throwable rocks as she leaped forward, scraping her hands as she drew close to the bottom.

The wolf reached it first. Andra's breath caught, and she felt her heart palpitate as she saw the snarling red outline. Saliva dripped from its jaws, hit the rocks, and seemed to corrode their surface. Several shamrock bushes wilted, sagging to the gully floor. The stream bubbled, as if someone had reset its temperature to a boil.

Andra tried talking to the animal in a soothing voice, knowing there wasn't much else she could do. The wolf erupted in another chilling howl. Several rocks melted. The gully grass burst into hissing steam. Crème-colored mushrooms sprouted and grew like time-lapse video scenes come to life, eventually splitting apart, their odorous ruptures bubbling like the stream.

Daylight disappeared; the temperature dove. The red outline leaped straight at Andra.

Sandpaper razed her skin. Every nerve cell in her body fired. Her eyes felt as if something had hooked them and pulled. She felt herself slammed onto the steaming grass, her head pushed straight into a patch of ruptured mushrooms.

Then everything went dark.

Lights flicked on, one by one, with a click-click-click sound.

Dazed, Andra felt Cera at her breast, nursing. Her mother's home seemed bright, and friendly, and far away from kidnappings and diminishing. Only the smell seemed different... more sterile than usual. And the lighting, that seemed different too, much more harsh and unforgiving. Was there a chance the gentle popping sounds weren't Cera's suckling, that they were...

Andra blinked, and angled her head upward. Her first thought: *I'm inside a bank vault.*

Cera wasn't with her, and this was most definitely not her mother's home. She was laying atop some sort of elaborate sled, inside a narrow hallway with metal siding and doors. Each had circular, rotating handles that could have steered ships if they weren't the height and weight of a linebacker. The floor, the walls, and even the ceiling weren't just sealed, they looked thick with multiple, criss-crossing, layered steel panels. Laser beams crossed the hall in a dozen different places, so many overlaps that Andra wasn't certain she'd be able to sit up without triggering alarms.

David was right. It looks like the place I saw in Wade's necrospondence.

Her nerves still ached and her skin felt a minor version of the sandpaper sensation, but there was no sign of the wolf's red outline. An odd sound erupted through the hallway, some sort of vibrating gong that was soon answered by a corresponding gong further ahead. A few seconds later another gong, this one from the side and again matched by a corresponding response from the opposite end. She wondered whether someone was listening for changes in the vibrations to detect movement.

She risked propping herself up for a better look. Guards were stationed throughout the hallway and looked every bit as tough as the walls. Most wore armor, carried rifles, and used electronic devices to scan for... something. Robotic devices hovered near doorways, spinning, raising, lowering at random. A slender tongue shot forth from a small opening in the steel walls, extended about halfway across the corridor, then retracted. Bubbles floated up from beneath the sled, hovered, then fanned out across the room before stopping, and eventually popping, at the ceiling.

Definitely the place from Wade's message.

Andra wasn't sure what to do—get up, wait, what? This didn't seem the kind of place where you did something without setting off a dozen consequences. She glanced to either side but saw no hint of Wade or Cera. On a positive note, Bead Head wasn't there either. A second look at the hall revealed a couple of blue objects tossed down near one of the walls.

Stilettos, Andra decided. The same stilettos the leggy woman from the conjugal visit wore.

"Andra Barger, with us again," a smooth, male voice said, from up the hallway.

She recognized the voice right away: Cobalt, as she referred to him—the council's vice-chairman, who wore his slick, silver hood with a black, mesh face and cobalt stripes down the sides. If voices could level mountains, his would resonate across the Sahara. He looked taller than he had when she first saw him at the council chambers, but lean as ever. He walked to her with a carefree gait, as if they had just happened upon one another during a cruise.

"I'm here for Cera," she said, sitting up, shaking off the sandpaper sensation. "Her, and Wade. No more messing around, no more diminishing, just let them go and leave us be."

"Maybe," Cobalt said. "Maybe not. First you have an appointment."

She stuck a finger at him.

"I don't care about the appointment," she said. "I only care about my family."

Even though Cobalt's face was covered by the hood, his stiffened body and tilted head gave Andra the impression he wasn't pleased.

"The appointment," he said, "is the only reason you, Wade, and your daughter are alive right now. I suggest you keep it."

Andra's chest welled with emotion. *So they're still alive, then*!

Cobalt extended a hand to help her up. She ignored it and stood up on her own. The steel walkway next to the hall was so cold she felt it seeping through the soles of her shoes.

"Where am I?" she said.

"Stanshmoor Detention Facility."

Tells me nothing, she thought.

"Let me put it another way," she said. "Where is Stanshmoor?"

She felt irritated eyes lock onto hers, even though they were masked by his hood.

"Edenshire, Ms. Barger," he said. "Beneath the Earthbound but above the Below, as you know from your conversation with Asantha Cooray."

Andra felt her muscles tense. Obtaining her first look at a milennias-old hidden society through its prison wasn't the introduction she had in mind. *Still... Edenshire. Though probably not the tony part*, she thought, again with the prison in mind. *Was this what Cristina meant when she said she had a way to head me toward Edenshire?*

"Why isn't my attorney present for this appointment?" she said.

Cobalt lifted his head slightly higher, as if his neck was a spring.

"Because if your attorney were present, he'd be dead. Only a diminisher can make it inside the place you're about to go. Not even me, Ms. Barger. I'm just here to get you to the right door."

He walked several paces forward, lasers, sounds, bubbles and devices registering his every movement. The tongue shot from the wall, licked him shoulder-to-foot at eye-blink speed, then returned to the wall.

Andra followed, appalled. The lasers didn't do much besides cause hidden speakers to make a distinct "th-wonk" sound, but the bubbles felt like static electricity whenever they touched her skin. Then there was the tongue—she couldn't stand the tongue. It shot forth, licked her, and vanished in an instant, but had sticky barbs which scraped her skin, tore holes in the fabric of her clothes, and left a nasty, pungent smell. It kept returning too, ignoring Cobalt, shooting toward her every five steps or so, perhaps infatuated with a new taste.

The tunnel extended several yards, but that was it—not nearly as far as Andra had thought while sliding in. It was lined with doors, all of them layered, burnished steel. Two had rounded, dented protrusions, as if a fist had tried pounding through from the opposite side. One of the doors breathed, expanding and contracting at the center like the old haunted house gag, only without the cheesy sounds. Another spun like a top, whirling so fast it was a gray, rectangular blur. A third looked like a steel river, pouring from ceiling to floor yet never spilling, all constant, downward movement.

Most of the doors didn't do a thing. Andra was surprised to find those made her more uneasy than the others.

"Each customized for our... guests," Cobalt said.

"Is Cera one of your guests?"

He stopped, turned toward her.

"Oh by all means, yes," he said. "Though not officially. But that's a different appointment. Your door is just ahead."

He gestured to a gray slab at the end of the hall. Unlike the others, this door appeared to be made of stone, with words carved in the front—ancient Roman in style, but not actually ancient Roman.

"What does it say?" she asked.

"Exactly what you would expect. I'll leave you now. Close the door behind you after entering."

She looked at the stone door, then back at Cobalt.

"There's no handle."

He shrugged.

"You're trained as a diminisher. Figure it out for yourself."

Cobalt turned and retraced his steps, triggering lasers, sounds, bubbles, and the nasty tongue. Andra was happy to see him leave. *He's probably the one who gave the order to grab my daughter.*

She studied the stone door, wondering whether there was something she'd missed. The words might be a clue, but somehow she didn't think so. They looked ornamental, rather than instructional, which meant she needed to find something else instead.

But there was nothing else. No keyholes, hidden panels, vibration locks, nothing. Curious, she did what Cobalt suggested: relied upon her diminisher training, which in this case meant using the camouflage, stealth, and shadow manipulation skills she wouldn't have learned if not for her family ties to Asantha Cooray. She stood away from the door, as far away as she could, tucking herself into a dim region of the hall that was relatively free of laser beams, bubbles, and most importantly, tongues. Then she studied the door.

It took the better part of two hours before she noticed she was wrong about the carved words not being a clue. Sometimes, she realized, they were easier to read than at other times.

Because the shading changes, she decided. *But how?*

She looked up the hallway, noticing the bright spotlights that had flicked on when she awoke were now off. That left a few mounted panels and the laser beams as the primary light sources.

And the lasers are rotating.

That's when it hit her: the shadows within the inset portions of the ornamental letters changed depending upon the sequence and combination of laser beams firing through the hallway. Sometimes they cast very little shadow, sometimes the shadow nearly filled the lettering, which explained why the words were occasionally easier to read.

"So what happens when the letters darken altogether but the rest of the door remains lit?" she wondered aloud.

One laser, in particular, seemed to affect the shading most.

She studied its exact angle and timing sequence until she knew: every seventeen minutes it fired for twelve seconds, with enough intensity to cast a wider shadow.

Time for an experiment.

She removed her keys from her pouch, unclipped a thumb-sized battery light, and tested it by pointing it against her hand. A red circle appeared within her palm... and alarms sounded throughout the tunnel. Four guards looked her direction, so she showed them the battery light until they seemed satisfied.

Minute seventeen arrived not long after. The laser pierced the semi-darkened tunnel, Andra held up her light and fired it just below the beam, along the same trajectory.

The inset letters darkened even more than usual... all except for a few words at the upper corner.

The laser shifted, the shadowing effect ended. Andra tried using her light on its own, but the effect wasn't the same. Her spirits slumped at the prospect of waiting another seventeen minutes, but they passed quickly.

Soon the beam was back and Andra was ready, determined to get it right this time. She aimed her light again, wiggling it in slightly different angles to approximate a path exactly below the laser's.

One... two... three...

She re-angled her light, trying to shadow the words in the upper corner.

Four... five... six...

The words fell into shadow! But then she noticed another word at the bottom right corner was now lit instead.

Seven... eight... nine...

Her hand shifted slightly right, to no avail. She nudged a hair-width left, hoping.

Ten... eleven...

All of the words fell into shadow. The entire stone door followed suit, transforming to a blackened void.

For one second. Then it was back, the laser beam was gone, and Andra's light was shining on stone letters once again. This time she didn't care.

Because now I know how to unlock the door.

Sixteen minutes later she was positioned less than one step away from the stone door, her battery light shining and angled, ready for the seventeenth minute.

As the laser lit, Andra quickly made her angle adjustments.

One... two...

The door vanished; she hopped inside.

Expecting pure darkness, she was shocked to find herself bathed in warm, dense yellow light. Her body rotated slightly and she realized she was floating, or maybe swimming, in that light. She took a breath, wondering whether she could, satisfied with the answer. Still she couldn't see a thing, only the endless marigold bath. Up, down... she had no reliable bearing for either, not while she was floating and rotating.

—Nowinder, her wings unfurling, events unfolding.—

The voice came from everywhere, and nowhere. Pink, green and blue streaks rippled the yellow as the words reverberated, then faded. As soon as it ended, Andra questioned whether she had really seen other colors, or heard someone speak, or if her mind had dreamed the whole thing up. But then it came again.

—Barrier punctures. Vital ones.—

Again, pink green and blue streaked like ink across a napkin, then faded along with the words. Andra shook her head, trying to get a read on whether the words were real or her mind was simply awash in confusion.

"Where am—?" she started, then stopped, startled by orange and blue streaks, and the sense that her spoken words had just emptied something from her, mining her of some physical property they couldn't tap when propelled through oxygen.

—Winnow the impropriety. The sleep, the long sleep. Time arises. —

Andra tried sorting through the gibberish without much success.

"Are you trapped here?"

More colors, but that was the pleasant part. Hearing her thoughts from everywhere and yet nowhere, as if she'd never truly expressed them, wasn't pleasant whatsoever. Again she felt disconcerted, shrunken, meaningless after speaking... so much so that she wondered whether she actually existed anymore, because she felt as if she didn't.

—Few shackles are involuntary. —

"So... you're not trapped. Am I?"

She knew it wasn't the best question, but she had to know.

—For but a moment. We're the same. —

Andra gathered herself, disregarding the feeling she was fading away, trying to focus on her daughter, on the reason she had come.

"I can't see you. Do you need my help?" she said.

More streaks, first her own, then the Other's.

—Assistance, yes. For yourself, herself, myself. —

Now we're getting somewhere.

"How? The council has you trapped... many people trapped. How do I change it?"

She cringed as she spoke. The more words and thoughts she issued, the more empty she felt—as if the very act of thinking, or creating, robbed the meaning from her existence. *Is that the trap the council set for this god-human? Was forced emptiness the council's customized confinement for the least-empty being in the universe?*

Pink, green and blue reappeared.

—Freeing Him frees all. —

The yellow seemed warmer now, very warm, maybe even blazing. Temperature, like words or anything meaningful, didn't seem to transmit properly in this place. Still, Andra was pretty certain the warmth flared as an accompaniment to the sentence, then faded.

"Okay... so I need to free you. But how do—"

—Him. The other.—

The heat flared again, this time after the pink-green-blue vanished.

Andra reeled. The heat was a simple message, sent by someone trapped in a place where simple messages were all one could muster.

"You mean... your counterpart?"

She couldn't voice the name, but she knew she had to, that this was an all-important point.

"Are you saying they have... a devil... captive too?"

More heat, then streaks.

—Free Him. —

Free who? A devil?

Free Satan? Did the council have another undiminished human imprisoned, one with questionable morals? Was that who Stiletto visited?

Andra felt herself fading, her mind shrinking, her significance all but gone. She couldn't stay here, not for much longer, not without losing everything. Whoever this trapped being was, he had persevered through something truly horrific.

“Understood. I'll free your counterpart. But why? Why him and not you?”

Everything remained yellow for several moments, long enough that Andra wondered whether she had pushed too hard, at someone too weary. She felt relieved, uplifted even, when the streaks returned.

—Sequence matters. Him. Notorious.—

Thoughts raced through Andra's head, questions, ideas, schemes, desires, all of them deadly, all pushing her further from existence. She stifled them, knowing she had to, but they kept coming anyway... until one thought presented itself.

Anything more and I might never see Cera again.

So many concepts flooded her mind. She turned away from them, desperate to linger just a bit longer. But the profound emptiness that germinated when she arrived had blossomed in the yellow light. With one last, agonizing push she emptied her mind of its final coherent thought.

“How?” she uttered.

Then she wasn't just floating, she was listing, her mind near-vacant. A purple-green-blue streak flashed, she registered a whisper, then she went limp as six ear-thumping knocks sent black ink reverberating through the yellow soup.

SIXTEEN

Laundry

The world returned to Andra's eyes a few pixels at a time, like a video monitor powering up after years in the garage. She blinked, confused, seeing pieces of someone sitting next to her, the rest clouded in fuzz. Then she smelled thick cigar smoke and knew who was there.

"Easy," David Stanford Swimney said. "Give it some time."

She heard and felt a car engine turning on, and noticed movement shortly thereafter. Leaning up, she saw her legs stretching across the backseat of Swimney's white sedan. Her sweater looked like Charlie Brown's Halloween costume, better than the shredded calf portions of her jeans.

"How'd I get here?" she mumbled. "How'd I get back?"

"The hard way, from the looks of it. But the council was good to their word, they got you back in 48 hours."

Even woozy, the thought that she had spent time unconscious—and in effect, helpless—around Cobalt, and at the council's prison, made her cringe.

"They loaded me into the plane?" she said. "And you're sure there were no delays?"

Swimney took a puff of his cigar as they passed the Spanish roofed shops near Albuquerque's city limits.

"No, but I have a doctor and a, well... a consultant, shall we say, ready to give you a checkup," he said. "Don't want you coming home with bugs of any kind, now, do we. But if nothing else, I daresay you had a chance to catch up on your sleep."

"I felt better doing all-nighters," she said. "Any word from Wade?"

Swimney looked away.

"Nothing, I'm afraid. Nor has our injunction filing progressed. The legal wheels turn slowly among the Cinüe too."

Andra blinked again, yellow fuzz clearing, Albuquerque returning faster than her mind wanted. The idea that a few hours ago she was... wherever... and now she was back in regular life just didn't process.

"Pull in over there," she said, pointing.

He braked, turned, gave her a perplexed look.

"Shave ice, Ms. Barger? After what you've just been through?"

"*Because* of what I've just been through."

They ordered medium-sized cups of raspberry mango shave ice before Andra's checkups, which were both clear, then went back for the blueberry variety after she returned from some pump time. Andra noticed Swimney was consciously making an effort not to ask questions about her trip, so once the appointments were finished and they returned to her apartment she broached the subject herself, filling him in on everything.

When she finished, he sat back in his chair looking as exhausted as she felt.

“Not in here,” she said when he absentmindedly reached for a case in his pocket.

He stuffed a cigar back into the case. Andra left him to mull while she excused herself for a warm, satisfying shower. When she returned, snug in thick, comfy sweats, she could tell he hadn’t stopped his mulling the entire time.

“Forget who you spoke with for a moment,” he said. “Forget that the council has the power to imprison someone of that magnitude. How in bloody hell do we break anyone—anyone—out of that place? There is no way. There is just no possible way.”

“Yeah, and I don't see how it leads to the council freeing Cera,” she said. “If anything, it probably puts her in more danger. And it still leaves us completely in the dark about where the Maybe Objective fits into all of this.”

“I'm sorry, Ms. Barger, but freeing this devil-being, this ‘Notorious’... this is so much bigger than the Maybe Objective or Cera.”

She walked the five steps into her kitchen, poured herself a soda, and returned.

"I'm not so sure about that," she said. "I was told I punctured vital barriers—which I think refers to my daughter being the first natural born child in 180,000 years. More importantly, I was told that freeing Notorious frees all."

He reached for the cigar box again, remembered Andra's rule, placed it back.

"But why?" he said. "And why not free the god-human first?"

"I don't know, and there wouldn't have been a way to express it in that prison cell regardless," she said. "But he said the sequence was important, that it had to be Notorious first. He also implied he wasn't so much there by force as by choice, but again, I have no idea why."

She took another soda gulp.

"If that really was a god in there... why would he choose me, David? Me! Why not a Navy Seal or someone who can actually lead a prison break? It makes no sense."

This time Swimney removed the cigar box altogether and placed it on the table out of arm's reach, apparently so he would stop grabbing for the box.

"You asked similar questions when Asantha Cooray chose you as her proxy, but she was aware of something unique in you," he said, then crossed his legs and lifted his eyes for a moment, again deep in thought. "Either way the problem's landed in your lap... and we still have no idea how to break someone out of the council's prison."

"No, but we do have a clue."

Swimney gestured for details.

"Not that I'm sure of anything that happened in there, but I do remember hearing a whisper, just before I left," she said, microwaving coffee for each of them while they talked.

Swimney perked up.

"And?"

"It was actually pretty clear," she said. "I asked how to free Notorious. What I heard back was, 'Dvora.' "

"Dvora Lansky, your grandmother? But... she died quite some years ago, right?"

"She did," Andra said. "So that leaves the next best thing. Let me borrow your phone—I can't risk someone tracing this call to my burner."

She borrowed his phone, noticing it seemed slippery as he sat it in her hand. *No, it's not the phone that's slippery,* she realized, scrolling through her contacts. *It's my sweaty palm.*

Swimney noticed the name she swiped onto the screen.

"You're actually going to call Maribel?" he said.

Andra swallowed. "No choice."

"Wait," he said, pushing her hand so she couldn't tap the call button. "You need to know... I'm told your Mother's as upset with you as you are with her. She's, uh... *raised the subject,* shall we say... with the security personnel I've placed at her home."

"Well, if she wanted to stay in the know she should have thought about giving us a heads-up that Jackson would be attending the diminishing vote."

"That seems a bit harsh. Maybe she didn't know."

Andra dipped her eyes. "She knew. And I can't help but think maybe Wade and I could have gotten Jackson out of there if Mother had given us so much as a little heads-up."

Swimney reached for his coffee cup, then paused.

"Unfortunately," he said, "I believe she feels much the same about the way you've concealed things from her. In particular, not telling her about Cera until after the council unveiling... I daresay that wound has not healed."

"Really? There's just the one?"

"Well, now that you mention it, she did say something about your relationship with a 'hooligan,' and about you accepting the proxy even though she told you not to... and Jackson sacrificing himself for you, she mentioned that too."

Andra tapped the Call button.

"Yeah, well I've put together a pretty big laundry list of my own," she said as her mother's face appeared on the screen. The usual magic mirror effect kicked in; though middle-aged, Maribel Barger was her daughter's doppelganger, with the same coconut hair and tanned skin. *Now that I have crow's feet, those match too*, Andra thought.

"What do you want?" Maribel said, in lieu of a greeting.

"Hello to you too, Mother," Andra said.

"I understand you're a fugitive now. Not that I'm surprised given the man you date."

Andra resisted the urge to hang up. As usual, Maribel held her phone close to her chin, giving it an outsized appearance. She wore a blue silk blouse and was sitting in an empty coffee house, drinking an expresso in front of a scratched up turntable.

"If you and your lawyer are calling about a case, then fine," Maribel said, glancing at Swimney. "Otherwise we have nothing to discuss."

Swimney seemed to sense his opening.

"Indeed there is a case," he said, waiting as Andra told her mother about Cera's kidnapping. Maribel turned pale then took a breath, trying to collect herself.

"My granddaughter must have rights," she said to Swimney, ignoring Andra.

"Yes," he said, "but because the council's acting under the Emergency Powers Initiative of 1326 the council chairman has broad powers to act in what he considers the council's best interest. That makes the legal process... time consuming."

Maribel sat back, drank her expresso in one gulp, ordered another. Tears formed in the corners of her eyes.

"Mother, listen to me," Andra said. "Cera's being held in a place called Stanshmoor and I'm told Grandmother is the key to freeing her."

Maribel looked shaken, but also bitter.

"First I lose my son because of you," she said, "and now my granddaughter."

"Mother, please... just be reasonable for one minute and tell me what Grandmother knew about the place."

Andra watched her mother sip a steaming, freshly delivered expresso, wondering how she could drink it so hot.

"Stanshmoor's not a place," Maribel said. "It's a nightmare."

"I already know that. Can you help me with actual details or not?"

Her mother's lips narrowed. She took another deep breath, to steady herself.

"After Dvora was adopted by Asantha Cooray, she had the run of every council facility," she said. "She practically grew up in some of them, so she knew the layouts like she knew her own backyard. Probably knew how to get in and out of every one of them on the sly."

Swimney grabbed his cigar box once again, then called Andra's attention to her mother's disapproving nose wrinkle as his means of gaining the okay to fire one up.

"So that's it, then—the reason Dvora would be so vital to us," he suggested between puffs. "Perhaps she left a key, or a map, with someone she was close to?"

"She wasn't close to anyone, other than me," Maribel said. "She was an only child, with no significant other. Barger women tend to favor occasional relationships over long-term commitments... as I'm sure this Wade character will soon discover."

Andra didn't appreciate the insinuation. Sure, Wade probably wanted a wedding and she didn't, but that didn't mean she wasn't interested in a long-term...

Not why we're here, she scolded herself.

"So we've got nothing," she said, setting the phone on a table, still aimed so everyone could see one another.

"Don't put words in my mouth," Maribel said. "I *do* have something: Lonacco Trove."

She waited a beat, then looked at them as if she couldn't believe they didn't recognize the name. "Permanent residences in the south of France," she said, "for council members and their families."

Swimney slapped a hand on the table.

"Of course," he said, looking annoyed that he hadn't thought of it. "But Dvora Lansky died more than twenty years ago. Whatever she had would be long gone."

Maribel shook her head.

"Like I said, they're permanent: lifetime and beyond," she said. "If the person dies, no one inherits. There are hundreds of these council-owned places, some haven't been opened since the last time the owner locked the door. If they left dirty laundry on the floor, it's still there. They're basically museums to the people who lived in them."

Andra studied the steam rising from her coffee cup, no longer caring about the drink.

"And I suppose you can find hers through council records," she said. "But even if you do, how do we get in? It's locked from whenever she last left, right?"

"It is, but you already have the key," Swimney said, eyes twinkling. "I'll show you where it is when we get there."

"We're going?" Andra said.

"ASAP," Swimney said, pulling up airline departure information on his tablet as he marched out of the room.

Maribel didn't look happy.

"Your grandmother had secrets beyond anything the council knew about," she said.

Great, Andra thought. *More family secrets*. "Meaning what?" she said.

Maribel stood up.

"Meaning I don't think I want you poking around there without me. You've already cost me my son. Any more bungling and I'll lose my grand—"

"Wait—'I cost you your son'... you really think that?" Andra interrupted, feeling as if she might explode.

"Of course. This is *all* on you. All you had to do was decline your proxy selection, exactly like I said. Was it really so hard to do? Are you really *that dense* that you didn't think a non-Cinüe showing up at a Sugar Dandruff vote might, just *might*, put your family in jeopardy?"

"Oh, so you have the nerve to criticize me after what you—"

"Don't give me that," Maribel said. "You flat-out ignored me, and it cost your brother his life! He knew you'd cause trouble—that's exactly why he went there, sick as he was, using all the Cinüe tech he could muster to get himself there in his condition: just to make sure he could wheedle his meddling baby sister out of whatever mess she stirred up. And look what it got him!"

Andra felt as if her soul had turned to ice.

"If you'd just declined that selection, like I told you to, Jackson's still alive," Maribel said, slamming her expresso cup on the table. "It's as simple as that."

Andra wished she had something handy to slam of her own.

"Simple?" she said. "You covering up what Jackson was up to, probably even helping him get the Cinüe tech to make it happen—you call that simple? Maybe if you told me what was going on..."

She wanted to rage, and grieve...to release it all. But she knew she couldn't, not now, not with Cera's life at stake.

"Look, never mind," she said. "You want to be with us at Lonacco Trove? Fine. Meet us at the airport in Paris. But don't be late. We're not waiting around."

Maribel scoffed.

"I don't *want* to be there with you at all," she said. "But I won't have you rummaging my mother's place, not without me supervising. And I definitely won't have you mucking up whatever chance we have at saving my granddaughter."

Maribel ended the call. The abrupt conclusion felt like a hovering cloud. Furious, Andra grabbed the phone and fired it into the couch cushions. Then she remembered it wasn't hers and was relieved to find it still worked. Swimney reentered the room like it might have land mines hidden in the carpet.

“If it makes you feel any better,” he said, measuring his words, “we won’t need your mother with us to enter Lonacco. Though there is the possibility that the place might jog her memories a bit, maybe lead to something we’d otherwise miss.”

Andra plopped herself on the couch, in the same spot where she’d just retrieved the phone.

“Mother will be a nightmare, at least for me,” she said. “But I can deal with that because this isn’t about me. It’s about Cera. Trust me, if Mother can help us out in any way, I’m more than willing to put up with her.”

She finally sipped her coffee, didn't like the taste, put it down near-full.

“And if her version of ‘help’ conflicts with our needs?” Swimney said.

Andra sighed.

“Then we do what needs to be done anyway,” she said.

SEVENTEEN

Capsule

They flew to Paris the next day, joining Maribel at a Gare de Lyon patisserie before boarding the 10:32 duplex train to Cannes. Andra didn't say one word to her mother, who mimicked the indifference. Swimney seemed relieved, interrupting the silence only to give them an update on the Maybe Objective—a topic he found listed in several of the council's pending action reports.

"I'm still trying to find out exactly what it is," he said.

Something bad, that's what it is, Andra thought. She wished she could somehow find Cera, curl up at home, and forget the whole thing. *Except I don't have Cera and I don't have a home*, she thought, sullen. Her diminishing days had kept her on the road; with Cristina no longer a friend, their living arrangement at Cristina's townhome was also finished. Wade's place, an Atlanta apartment that she never knew he had until the baby was born, was such an obvious focus for council eyeballs that it wasn't an option. Same with her mother's house... which was also out of the question for an entire laundry list of reasons. That left using her own place. *Oh yeah... guess I should have gotten one of those.* As the train picked up speed she couldn't help think of it as another council conspirator, carrying her away from the stability she so wanted.

Their first look at the coast came three long hours later, a panoramic view of Mediterranean homes and whitecapped waters from the train's second level. The backdrop made the subsequent couple of hours go by much faster.

"And here I thought everything the council owned was a hellhole," Andra said to Swimney as the coach doors slid open in Cannes.

The attorney tugged at his grey suit, smoothing it as he followed her and her mother onto the platform. "The council hold's some of the world's most precious real estate," he said. "You just happened to visit two of their least pleasant locations."

They rented a sedan and drove south along the Cote d'Azur. Maribel kept her nose in a celebrity biography she'd been reading since midway through the flight. Andra, eager to catch the view—and avoid conversation—let Swimney drive. Heavy traffic didn't seem so bad when backdropped with palatial homes, stunning ocean views, and sports cars glistening in their stone-lined driveways.

After a silent, frosty hour Swimney pulled onto a two-lane road lined with trees. Their engine growled, even in fourth gear, as they made their way up a shaded, shrouded hill. The road curved and the trees vanished, giving way to several expensive-looking bungalows built into the side of the hill, with swaying palm trees and a full ocean panorama splayed before them. Each bungalow had a stone exterior with a red tile roof, stone pavers running between as walkways, and seasonal flowers for landscaping. The crescent driveway was long enough to pull three freight trucks inside, one after another.

"Not as old a place as I imagined," Andra said.

"Actually, it is," Swimney said, parking their car along the curb at the far end of the crescent, "but the council updates the exterior every few years so the buildings don't draw attention."

The weather was sunny, warm, Mediterranean... everything it was supposed to be. As they gawked at the view, and the bungalows, Andra considered the significance of what she was about to try. Knowing you can enter your late grandmother's residence was one thing; actually being there, on the verge of doing so, was a more emotional experience. She felt uneasy, wondering whether going inside was a violation of Dvora Lansky's privacy... especially with her mother acting like some sort of chaperone.

Maybe Mother's right. Maybe we shouldn't be doing this. But there's no choice.

Swimney glanced at his phone, double-checking the address they were looking for, then led them along one of the paverstone walkways. The shade between buildings felt good, and Andra smelled a sweet fragrance she didn't recognize.

"This is it," Swimney said, pointing to a patio on their left.

"No," Maribel said, speaking for the first time in hours. "It's the one on the right side."

Andra stared. "You remember this place?"

Her mother nodded. "From when I was a child," she said. "Didn't mean anything then, of course. It was just another place we went. But it's coming back to me now. Yes... definitely the place on the right."

Swimney checked his phone again.

"She's correct," he said. "I read the address wrong."

Andra waited for her mother to make a snippy remark, but none came.

Tense, they filed onto an entry patio edged in lavender and sided with trellised vines. A small, glass table occupied a cutout on the patio's left side, while the opposite side was a pathway leading to the front door. The area smelled damp and water droplets twinkled atop the pansy petals, hints of recent sprinkler activity.

Andra followed her mother to the front door. Stained in dark birch, the door looked hand-carved with swirls at the four corners, intersecting rectangles at the center top and bottom, and a series of ovals in the middle that gave the impression of an owl's head.

"Each door in the complex has a different animal," Maribel said. "As a girl I always loved looking at the owl while my mom unlocked the door."

She reached for the handle, a sculpted brass column with a flat trigger at the top.

"Locked," she said. "And it's not opening for me. But then again, it never did. Only for Mom."

Swimney stepped forward for a closer look.

"That's because it's a, Cinüe lock," he said. "But there's a bypass."

He dashed from the patio to the car, returning with a small medical kit.

"We'll need to make a pinprick in your thumb," he said to Maribel, then looked at Andra. "Yours too."

The tension doubled.

"Poke *her*, not me," Maribel said. "It's about time she lose a little blood out of all this."

Swimney intervened before Andra could say anything, insisting he needed samples from both of them for the door handle to identify them as direct descendants.

"Why not cheek cells?" Andra said. "Or skin cells, or anything that doesn't require needles?"

"Look, I didn't design the thing," Swimney said. "It's arcane tech, whatever that is, so you'll have to ask the council why other cells don't work."

Maribel scowled, but extended her hand to Swimney while turning away. A few seconds later the needle-prick was over and she had a small blood spot atop her thumb.

"Now squeeze the handle," Swimney said.

"I am," she said. "Nothing's happening. It's still locked."

He nodded. “And it always will be, for you. Third generation is the first with access.”

“Oh great,” Maribel said. “So why stick me at all?”

“We needed to establish your blood first, then Andra’s. After that she’ll have access without you.”

Andra couldn't help feeling a tiny bit satisfied—enough so that she didn't even wince as she received her pinprick.

“Now you grab the door,” Swimney said.

She squeezed the handle and pushed the latch with her thumb.

“Hmmm... still locked,” she said.

Maribel gave a vindictive laugh.

“Huh,” Swimney said. “It should work, says so in every Cinüe reference book I've ever checked. Try squeezing a little harder.”

She tried every variation she could imagine: harder, softer, inner part of the latch, outer part, middle part. She did the hokey-pokey, just to be funny. She even caressed it.

“Maybe they have a built-in default against council troublemakers,” Maribel said, still looking pleased.

Andra sighed.

“Looks like we're going to have to break in,” she said.

“We can't,” Swimney said. “These places are sealed. Even the windows don't shatter, more arcane tech. If that lock doesn't open, we're not getting in.”

They stood back, uncertain of their next move.

"Chimney," Maribel pointed out. "You can lower a camera, take a look around."

"The chimney is a facade," Swimney said. "Cinüe homes use some sort of wall material that vents fireplace smoke as if there were no walls whatsoever. They only install the chimneys to avoid suspicion."

"How about the crawl space?" Andra said, spotting an access screen at the base of the home. "The house can't be fortified on its belly too, can it?"

No one knew, but Swimney was skeptical.

"Well then we've made a very long trip for nothing," Maribel said. "We're slinking around an old house that hasn't been opened since..."

Her head spun, toward the door. She pushed Andra aside, grabbed the handle, and squeezed, several times.

"Gad," she said.

"Mother, we already know it doesn't open for you. Accept it and move on."

Maribel stepped to one side while tugging Andra closer.

"You'll try it again," Maribel said. "But this time you'll look at the owl's eyes while you push the latch."

"Mother—"

"Do what I tell you... for a change."

Andra sighed. *Another order from all-knowing Mother*. She reached for the handle, looked at the carved ovals forming the owl-shape's eyes, and squeezed the latch.

The door lock clicked then slid from the jamb, squeaking and groaning from age.

"*Brava*!" Swimney said, wearing a broad grin. "Just like when you visited as a girl, apparently!"

Andra stepped back, shocked. Her mother issued a "told-you-so" frown. Both stared at the unlocked door, nervous for different reasons.

"It'll be like entering a time capsule," Maribel said.

"I don't need a time capsule," Andra said. "I need a way to save my daughter, and the clock's ticking. Let's go."

She pushed the door handle, softly at first then with more force as it refused to budge. Finally she heard a "snick" as if a vacuum seal had broken, and the door inched open.

Stagnant air, mixed with hints of old skin and moth-balled fabric, billowed onto the patio. Andra wrinkled her nose and turned her head, waiting for the fresh air to mix with the old. Then she peeked into the home's darkened interior.

"I can't see a thing," she said, feeling for a light switch. "Think the power's still on?"

Her answer came when she found a slender chain dangling from the ceiling. She pulled it and the home's interior sprang into view.

Maribel gasped.

"It's exactly the way I remember it," she said.

Andra stepped inside the entry hall, which was painted pale green and had checkered throw rugs on the floor. An ornate wooden buffet lined the side wall, with an oval mirror centered above it and candle sconces to either side. Floorboards squeaked as Andra walked, leaving the eerie feeling that the house was stretching its muscles after a long hibernation.

Another “snick” sent her heartbeat racing.

“Gotta’ keep the door shut,” Swimney said, from behind her. “The council probably wants to have a look in here too.”

She nodded in agreement, then continued. The hall's end was the parlor's beginning. It had floppy orange carpet, dark wood shutters on the windows, and a box-shaped television with a pair of tinfoil-wrapped antennae on top. Two marble end tables were topped by lamps with amber, columnar shades as tall as a ten-year-old child. A grandfather clock loomed from the far corner, it's lower shelves stuffed with red-spined encyclopedias.

“Same davenport,” Maribel said, pointing to a sofa with orange flowered fabric, the room's centerpiece. “Nothing’s changed. Everything’s still here.”

Andra noticed her mother’s voice seemed less hardened. She patted her hand against the matching love seat, expecting to see dust puff out, but it was clean. The whole room was clean. She ran her finger along a small coffee table, which had the same marble top as the end tables. It was cold and smooth—not a speck of dust. The clock had the correct time of day. The carpet was smashed down in several areas, as if someone often walked through even though they had just entered.

“What's that?” she asked her mother, pointing to a chair-sized piece of furniture. It looked like a wooden moving box with creme-colored fabric across the front.

"Record player," Maribel said. "Mono, of course. I never used it, never had records. But she did, from time to time. Orchestra records, some of them pretty old."

Her mother was right: the place felt like a time machine, old from a design standpoint yet fresh, as if it hadn't aged a day. Andra couldn't help but feel as if her grandmother might simply walk out and greet them. That sense wasn't a cure-all for the lingering tension and bitterness, but it was definitely making her feel rejoined with her younger, innocent years... and her mother seemed to be feeling the same way.

Maribel took Swimney with her to survey the kitchen, where they were fascinated by spotted laminate countertops, a small, yellow oven, and a matching refrigerator. A built-in, comma-shaped booth offered an eating spot if the adjacent dining room—another green-walled, orange carpeted wonder—seemed too formal.

The room suddenly brightened around them, and for a change the light didn't seem incandescent. They returned to the parlor and found Maribel opening the shutters, exposing a phenomenal, full ocean view.

"I remember everything now," she said. "Come on, I'll give you a quick tour."

She led them up a hallway. Both bedrooms had his-and-her beds with thin duvet covers, elaborate wood headboards, and matching dressers. An antique rocking chair in the master bedroom kept Andra entertained as she studied the room for anything unusual.

Swimney checked the bathroom and seemed to enjoy calling out its features. A footed bathtub and wash basin sink, both with separate knobs and faucets for the hot and cold water, seemed especially captivating. The pull-chain toilet was the only thing that showed its age; the water had yellowed and much of it had evaporated, leaving a calcium ring around the bowl.

"At least it still flushes," Swimney said, testing it.

"None of this helps us get into Stanshmoor," Andra said. "We'll need a search—and a major one. If we have to we'll strip the carpet, open the walls. Whatever it takes."

Maribel scowled.

"The upper kitchen cupboards are off-limits," she said.

"Mother, this is for Cera and we need—"

"Off limits," Maribel repeated. "Open to me only. Believe me, if I find something that can help my granddaughter, you'll get it."

Swimney nodded his okay to Andra, so she went along with the plan... but not without a few mutters about too many family secrets. They opened more shutters for additional light, hauled their luggage from the car, and started in. Reconvening a couple hours later, they saw dusk filling their windows.

"We'd do just as well checking for a key under the front doormat," Andra said. "I don't think my grandmother would put things in the obvious places we're looking. Mother, is there anything else you remember about this place? Maybe a basement, or an attic?"

"I was barely eight when I came here," she said. "If there was anything special, she didn't show me."

She looked around the room, soaking it in.

"It's wonderful," she said with an adoring tone. "Maybe because it's from a time before Mom and I... when there were no issues. Just a mom and her daughter. Before I started making judgements. Before everything became so..."

Her voice trailed off. Andra didn't pursue it, despite the parallels, but she understood the thrill of being here. Who wouldn't enjoy the chance to return to a childhood play spot, to the time when there was only a parent, and a place, and a happy bond?

Except my child won't have that chance—not unless I find a back door into Stanshmoor.

They paused for dinner—leftover patisserie food from their drive that they reheated in the little oven—and later, sleep. Andra used her late-night hours to think, and pump, and search the kitchen.

Cera will drink the milk, she told herself, placing a fresh bottle in the refrigerator. *I'll get her home safely, and she will drink it*. She finally crashed onto her bed, in the master bedroom, around 3 a.m. Excited shouts woke her in what seemed an instant later. Frustrated, she threw on a fresh t-shirt and jeans.

"We found her notebook," Swimney said, leafing through a diary-sized book as Andra entered the parlor. "Look: she's got hand-drawn maps inside."

Andra's groggy head cleared fast, especially when she noticed it was after 10 a.m. and the short sleep hadn't been so short after all. She joined her mother next to Swimney, her heartbeat racing as he showed it to her. The cover was simple enough, leather-bound with fleur-de-lis fabric extending to the edges and the handwritten title "My Words" at the top.

"Where'd she have it hidden?" Andra said.

Maribel smirked.

"Under a TV channel guide on top of the end table," Swimney said, pointing to one of the corner tables with the lamps. "None of us ever noticed."

"Crack detectives, us," Andra said, looking at the pages as Swimney leafed through.

"Not hidden means she wanted it found," Maribel added.

"Or she liked having it handy and didn't plan on dying," Andra said. "The book's got a lot of diagrams showing the hallways outside the council chamber. Would've come in handy last year."

Swimney flipped pages like a pirate digging through a freshly unearthed chest, barely staying on one before turning to the next.

"Hey—not so fast, it's old," Andra said.

He didn't seem to hear her. "Council banks, guest houses, a cemetery... some of these places have never been documented," he mumbled, eyes wide. "This is worth more than... wait, here it is. This is it! This is what we're here for."

She looked at the yellowed page beneath his pointing finger. Sure enough, her grandmother had drawn maps of Stanshmoor.

"There are three ways to get in," she said.

"Or to get out," her mother added, with a disapproving tone.

All three routes involved long, narrow passageways with steep drops and multiple security features, most of them indicated with single words such as "laser," stinger," and "pellets."

"Seems they have six more wall-mounted tongues for you," Swimney said.

"Never mind that, what we want is over here," Andra said, managing to turn the page before Swimney did. The scribbled words "From Below" topped a charcoal image showing a thicket of crosshatched lines. Underneath, Andra's grandmother had scrawled a few more words: "Through a hole dug anywhere. Only me. (Or heirs.)"

Andra grabbed the book from Swimney. The exterior felt like sun-hardened mud, pliant yet on the verge of total collapse. Flipping pages, by contrast, was like dragging a finger across a stubbled cheek.

"I wish she had more information," she said, deep in thought.

No one answered.

"Still, she added, "I think there's a chance..."

Glancing up after the continuing silence, she noticed her mother and Swimney staring at her.

"What?" she said.

Again they stared. Her mother looked shaken.

"What?" Andra repeated.

Her mother's jaw hung open.

"How are you doing that?" Maribel said.

"Doing what?" she said, then she noticed something unusual. "Wait, my voice... it's different."

Maribel studied her.

"Yeah," she said. "It's your grandmother's."

Andra gaped as she spoke some more, experimenting. The words sounded lighter, more feminine, but also with a trace of graininess and the hint of an eastern European accent.

"For the love of... we're in her house," Maribel said. "You doing that voice is disrespectful... and creepy. Knock it off!"

Andra wished she knew how. Frightened, she set the book down, stood up, and walked a few paces away before turning to face them.

"I have no idea how I'm doing it," she said. "Or how to get my regular voice back."

Her mother and Swimney did a double-take.

"There—you're yourself again," Swimney said. "Same voice as always. What changed?"

"I stood up?"

She considered sitting while talking gibberish, just to test whether anything would change.

"Wait—Mother, grab the book and say something."

Maribel complained but tried the idea anyway.

"See, no difference," she said, and it was true.

Andra scowled but Swimney jumped to his feet, excited.

"Hand it to Andra," he said, eyes gleaming.

Maribel passed the book to her daughter.

"I wonder if I need to sit with it, like I did before, to get it working," Andra said.

Their reaction told her she didn't.

"It happened again?" she said, stunned. "I sound like Grandma? But then why didn't it happen with Mother, unless... you think it's the same as with the front door?"

Swimney ran a finger along the book's top, but left it in her hands.

"Third generation heirs only," he said. "Again, a typical Cinüe approach."

They passed the book between them for the next several minutes, checking their theory. Only Andra's voice changed, and only when she was holding any part of the book—pages or cover, with one finger touching or many. Whenever she had contact—any contact—her voice changed.

"Hmmm... but why," she wondered aloud.

Swimney sat his chin in his hand for a moment, pondering.

"You have her blood, her notes, and her voice," he said, thinking aloud more than holding a conversation. "That's got to add up to... access."

"To Stanshmoor?" Andra said.

"There's a chance," Swimney said.

She didn't need time to think it over.

"If there's any chance at all, I'm taking it," she said. "I'm leaving for Stanshmoor."

"How?" Maribel said. "With a few old drawings and some fancy ventriloquism? That's what you're going to use to bust into the world's most secure prison?"

"No," she said, "because I don't need to bust in."

Swimney gave her a knowing look, but Maribel wasn't following.

"So what it is you need to do instead?" she said.

Andra exhaled a deep breath.

"Dig a hole," she said. "I'll need to dig a great big hole."

EIGHTEEN

Tendrils

They began shoveling at the base of a hillside near the back of the property. The terrain and surrounding shrubs masked the noise, which Andra found reassuring since she didn't want to explain herself to nearby residents—especially if the neighbors were Cinüe, as she suspected.

No one approached them, a surprise since rocks, roots, and muscles unaccustomed to digging meant the job was taking a long time. When lunchtime rolled around their effort still looked more like an elaborate pockmark than a hole.

"I don't care what that notebook says," Maribel mumbled as they broke for a sandwich. "It's hard to believe *this* would be your grandmother's method."

Even Andra had her doubts. By day's end they were blistered, sunburned, and worn out... but the hole was ready.

"Six feet deep, three wide," Swimney said, retracting his tape measure.

"Most graves are," Maribel said.

Andra laid her shovel near the edge, knowing she would become genius or jester in the next few minutes. Her mother placed a hand on her shoulder.

"You're exhausted," she said. "Wait until morning."

Andra closed her eyes. Her arms had spent the day shoveling, yet still felt shackled.

"You know I can't wait, Mother," she whispered.

Maribel stared at the hole.

"Your brother always said the same thing. He was always ready to make whatever sacrifice the family needed. Look where it got *him*."

Andra told herself to leave the comment alone, then ignored her own advice.

"I'm very aware of where it got him, Mother," she said, with as much restraint as she could muster. "I'll never *not* be aware of that. You don't need to remind me. Ever."

Maribel nodded.

"You're right," she said. "I'm just so crushed, so angry...with myself, though. Not you. Oh, yes, I wish you would have listened to me and declined your chance to be proxy, just like I wish Jackson would have listened to me and stayed at home, but... this is all on me."

Andra looked up, hoping for more, but didn't get it.

"Would you have gone to Stanshmoor?" she asked her mother. "If the council had kidnapped *me*, if it was *your* daughter who's life was at stake? You'd have gone, right?"

Her mother took a long time to answer. Longer than Andra liked.

"Now? Absolutely," Maribel finally said. "Then... I'm not sure. My selfishness messed a lot of things up for this family, Andra. It wasn't until later, when I discovered your grandmother was far more savvy than I gave her credit for, that's when I realized the mistake I'd made—that I could accomplish so much more from inside the council than from outside. Maybe that's why I pushed your brother and you so hard to become Diminishers—not that he needed much pushing."

Tears welled from the corners of her eyes.

"So would I do what you're doing? Yes—a thousand times, yes," she said. "For what it's worth, I tried steering your brother away from the council. Told him I'd proxy for him at the council's diminishing vote, when I found out he'd come up with a way to attend. To save him, you know? But he wouldn't listen."

The rare personal insight came as a surprise to Andra, one that didn't quite make sense.

"But Jackson died so he could give Wade and me a chance to escape—none of you could have known we'd need that kind of help beforehand," she said.

This time it was Maribel who closed her eyes.

"I knew the moment I found out you were going," she said. "You weren't going to vote the way they wanted, and of course Jackson would try to help you get away in the aftermath, so I knew my being there was the only thing that would save him. But would he listen? No."

Andra felt her frustration rising.

"So you just automatically assumed I'd let everyone down," she said.

Maribel smiled through her tears.

"I sure did... because that's what I'd have done at your age. As it turns out... well, you took a very different road. The high road, I suppose. Finding a way to satisfying both the vote and the need to make changes... that's a long way beyond anything that ever crossed my mind."

Andra folded her arms.

"Whatever," she said.

She appreciated her mother's compliment but this wasn't a conversation she wanted to have, not now. Not when she had a prisoner to free, and a daughter to save. Her mother's part of the family history would have to wait. She finished dinner, pumped, and packed a few tools and snacks in a lightweight day pack. The all-important notebook went alongside a small flashlight in her front pocket, where both were within easy reach.

"If this works I'll try following you through," Swimney said as they gathered at the hole's edge, backlit by twilight.

"If this works," Andra said, "it won't let you through. Only the heir, remember?"

He nodded, then shook her hand. She laughed at his distant approach, then gave him a hug. Maribel watched, her expression leaden.

"I'll be back by breakfast," Andra said. "Hopefully with guests."

Maribel forced a grin, then helped Swimney take Andra's hands and lower her inside the hole. Her butt scraped and slid along the packed dirt. By the time her feet touched the bottom she had to tilt her head upward to see the others. The tight space made her voice echo as she called up to them, and the only light shone in from above. She pulled her arms to her side and switched on her flashlight, which was clipped to her belt. The beam made a bright spot along the dusty granules in front of her, with just enough reflection to make out the shadowed soil around her.

"This is me, using my own voice, saying I'm off to Notorious' cell at Stanshmoor prison," she said, then grabbed the notebook and held it to her chest. "And *this*... this is me saying I'm off to Notorious' cell in my grandmother's voice."

The twilight above her head vanished, and the ground beneath her feet opened. She braced herself for some sort of free-fall drop, but nothing happened. Instead the earth itself seemed to move, as if she were a stationary point and someone was sliding the planet upward at immense speed. The rock textures blurred, then changed color several times, and the hole went from cold to freezing to blistering hot. As the blurring slowed everything shifted again, the planet changing directions, the blur returning first with a side-to-side motion, then diagonal.

Dizzy, Andra closed her eyes. Her head cleared in an instant; she felt no different from any other time she was standing still. Upon opening her eyes the dizziness returned, especially when she noticed her direction—or was it the Earth's?—had again shifted, the blur now running head to foot. Queasiness hit fast, so she re-shut her eyes.

After several minutes the torrid hole chilled, froze, then warmed a second time, only without the intense heat. She decided to risk a peek. The blurring slowed, then stopped. She lurched from the visual cue, even though her body hadn't moved whatsoever.

Looking up, she saw the top of the hole had returned, only this time the Cote d'Azur's soothing, twilight sky was gone, replaced by dense, yellow light. *The cell at Stanshmoor,* she guessed. Her fingers ached. Andra realized she was still gripping the notebook like a life preserver, clinging to it for fear of what might happen if she let go. She loosened the notebook from each hand, stretching her stiffened fingers, then tucked it in her front pocket. Reaching up, she grabbed the top of the hole with two hands and did a pull-up, lifting herself high enough to peer over the sides.

She felt like a point on a grid. The yellow field, familiar from her first visit, sat just left of the hole. To her right there was only manic fuzz, like a television's static screen with one key exception: black, crosshatched lines ran through the fuzz, matching the lines Andra's grandmother had drawn in the notebook.

The hole itself rested within a linear, gray strip extending as far as Andra could see, forward, back, or up. The strip looked like a long shadow, or maybe a shaft of shade plummeting from high above.

Maybe it's a border between cells, she guessed, without really knowing.

The silence was so crisp, so overwhelming, that she cringed at the sound of her own breathing, feeling every bit the intrusion she was. Was this part of the prison's security system? Did the council know she was here?

Andra pulled herself from the hole. The stone flooring within the gray strip had obvious, nook-and-cranny imperfections yet seemed polished, as if thousands of people had trampled through the area. She stepped gingerly, summoning her diminisher training, finding it deficient. Each step echoed down the gray corridor like the sole of a tap shoe. Her own arm and leg movements rustled her clothes, a shuffling so magnified it sounded like wind. She could hear her eyelids blink, her underpants glide, her blood flow.

She wondered whether her grandmother had once come to this same, awful place, then cracked open the notebook, looked at the crosshatch drawing, and decided she had.

"Okay, now what do I do?" she said, looking for an entry point to either side.

The notebook didn't offer any further detail. She studied the yellow field and decided against touching it. *If that's the god-human's cell, I've been there and I know what he wants,* she figured. The crosshatches, on the other hand...

There was no way to tell whose cell it was. She tried walking along its edge, searching for some indication of who lay imprisoned within. But there were no clues, only the boisterous, vibrating echoes of her own incursion. Frustrated, she stopped walking.

The ruckus faded, or at least most of it did. She placed the book back inside her pocket, spent more time studying the crosshatches, then decided to test them. Pulling a quarter from her other pocket, she flipped it in the air, caught it heads-up, then pitched it into the fuzzy, crosshatched field.

The quarter cut through the fuzz, stopped, then shifted direction, straight for the nearest crosshatched line. As it hit the line Andra heard the kind of vibrating rip that an old schoolbus makes when hitting its brakes. The quarter then shot downward along the vertical black line, like it was inside a waterway... *or an artery*, Andra thought, immediately regretting the grim image. The coin darted line to line, gaining speed as it went, then dropped below Andra's position and disappeared altogether.

That's when Andra understood: she wasn't on the ground. *The gray strip is a raised walkway, like a catwalk extending across a giant factory.* She double-checked the notebook, found no further clues, and stood there, stumped.

Then she thought about Cera. An instant later, she stepped into the fuzz.

A fiery explosion ignited the moment she made contact with it, blasting her backward, headlong down the gray corridor. She hit the floor with a sound that made her footsteps seem like falling dust, then remained motionless as she tallied her injuries: no burns, a mystery given the explosion, and no apparent concussion; the scrapes and bruises were no fun, but they weren't bad. She knew she hadn't broken anything because the sound of a broken bone, not to mention the blood flow changes around such an event, would have been obvious in the again-silent corridor.

"I didn't use the book," she realized, scolding herself.

Rising to her feet, she clutched the notebook and said, "I'm entering now."

She stepped inside the fuzz, fearing another explosion. Instead her body hovered for a moment, then shot toward one of the black, crosshatched lines. As soon as she hit the line everything went black—even her flashlight. A million pounds dropped atop her body... or at least, that's what it felt like, as if unseen Lilliputians had punched a gravity-increase button.

Andra sunk like a stone, only line-to-line. She could breathe, but inhaling and exhaling was now a concerted, forced activity. The gray walkway was somewhere well above her, yet she continued sinking to the bottom of... whatever this was. *A pit, maybe? The pit of—*

She stifled her own thought, too afraid to follow it through.

The weight, and the drop, felt excruciating. She wondered how much more of either she could take. Everything felt smashed—nose, chin, nipples, knees, hips, toes. Maybe she had dropped for minutes, maybe for hours, time no longer held meaning.

Then she hit bottom. The crushing smack she expected turned out to be more of a splat, into some sort of undulating, sticky goo. She sunk and coughed, her oxygen cut off, unable to roll her body or lift her head. Something surged beneath her, flexing like an immense muscle. She rose up, still blinded by sheer blackness, barely able to suck a couple of thin, raspy breaths.

Another surge struck. She rose, fell, rose again. The goo seemed more than pliant, it seemed... coiled.

"L-l-l-ift me."

The voice, like the one she heard within the warm, yellow cell during her first visit, came from both everywhere and nowhere. Whether that meant it was imagined or tangible, she couldn't say. All she knew was the voice sounded dry, dense, flattened, maybe even smashed.

Like it came from someone who's been down here for a long time.

Notorious?

The words repeated, strained but forceful, maybe even angry. This time they weren't as clear, but she understood nonetheless.

Lift me. She tried answering but couldn't get enough air to push the sounds through her throat. Another try made little difference. She was trapped, in agony, unable to help herself much less anyone else. Why hadn't her grandmother included any of this horror in her notes? And was this really where Stiletto spent her conjugal visit? Was that even possible?

The goo, or maybe the coiled muscles, surged again, lifting her. Something slimy wrapped around her waist, and her chest, then squeezed. Andra would have screamed but she couldn't. Every bit of air within her was now expelled. Through the pain she felt something trickling down her cheek... many somethings, she realized, like oozing, spidery tendrils. They reached her lips, passing between them even though they were smashed together by whatever was causing the intense gravity.

The trickling resumed, across her tongue, down her throat, then beyond, into her chest. Horrified, she wriggled and gagged, both to no avail. Images passed through her mind, many of them the diminishing victims she saw while sleeping every night. Childhood friends played tag, high school boyfriends flirted, roller coasters looped through amusement parks... the images went on, and on, familiar from yesteryear.

I'm dying, she realized. I'm actually—

The tendrils within her chest flexed, pushing her insides in a variety of directions, hard. Air flooded her lungs. The goo coiled around her waist then did the same; the air expelled. The actions repeated, harsh yet effective.

I'm breathing.

"L-l-l-ift me."

Now she had air. She could answer... barely.

"Only for... my... baby," she managed, much of it strained, maybe even garbled.

The muscles flexed, nearly crushing her, and the tendrils stopped their effort to help her breathe.

Message received, Andra thought. It's not "lift me," it's "lift me or else."

The ghastly respiration restarted. She knew it would. Given the demand, it had to.

"No!" she uttered, best she could. "Only... for... my baby."

She felt the goo surge and swirl, then heard a bubbling, steaming sound. Three glowing red slits appeared, faint but startling in the darkness, emptiness suddenly wrinkled. The slits rose then dropped several times, struggling against the same forces that pulled Andra to the pit's bottom. Eventually they lifted high enough for her to see a deep, orange hexagram centered along each slit.

This time fear, not muscled goo, stole her breath.

Eyes, she knew. *They're eyes.*

Each was triple the size of her head and packed with flaming embers. They stared at her, and over her, and through her. Somehow they seemed to make clear: she was nothing.

"Aaaaa-greed," the voice said.

Wait—did the thing just agree to free Cera?

Even under all the weight, and the coils, and scrutiny of the horrific eyes, Andra shuddered. Suddenly, she didn't want to do it. Her daughter meant more to her than anything, but she didn't mean more than anything to the world. Freeing this... this... "Other," as it was described during her first visit... it didn't seem right. Was

Notorious a devil? Was it... Satan, or at a minimum the basis for the Satanic stories? Much as she hated to side with an organization that would go about diminishing human beings, there was a chance the council knew exactly what it was doing when it sealed this thing at the bottom of Stanshmoor. Releasing it, even in exchange for her daughter's freedom, didn't make sense.

Except the god-human told me to do it.

But why? That makes no sense either!

Andra gagged, feeling the slimy tendrils withdrawing from her chest. The coils around her waist surged, then relaxed. The eyes grew larger, anticipating. She could feel their heat. Between that, the horrific weight, and the fact she couldn't breathe anymore, she knew this was it: do or die.

—Freeing Him frees all.—

The words from her earlier Stanshmoor visit circled to her mind's forefront, past the frenzied images, across the horrific pain, overriding the sight of those ghastly eyes.

—Freeing Him frees all.—

Something she had to accept... what, on faith?

Wait—I can't do anything anyway, not without a hole. My grandmother's notebook says that's how I have to start up.

Then she remembered: she was in a hole. Not just any hole either. Probably the biggest, deepest pit ever dug. If the notebook's transportation trick worked with her modest hole, it would certainly work here—assuming she could grab the book. Smashed flat onto her chest by the unseen, gravity-on-overdrive force, she wasn't so sure.

She inched her right hand beneath her stomach, angling it into her jacket pocket, and managed to grip the notebook. Grimacing, she pulled. Moving her other hand toward the book was harder, but waning oxygen motivated her struggle. She stretched her left fingers until she felt the book's cover between the tips.

Please, let this be the right decision.

Throat tight, lungs burning, she sucked in what air she could force into her lungs and uttered words as best she could.

"Get us... out... of here," she wheezed.

A wail erupted from the book. Andra, still embedded in goo, felt a thunderous shudder beneath her body, and an ear-jarring, bone-wrenching groan belched forth from far below. Another shudder jostled her about, this one stronger than the first.

Then she was rising, or maybe it was the coiled, muscled form below that was rising, or both, she couldn't be certain. All she knew was her head was rushing, her ears popping, her sinuses bubbling, all from a rapid ascent. Darkness thinned, as did the super-gravity that had forced her down. She found herself approaching the fuzz, and the walkway, and the cross-hatched arteries that had dragged her down in the first place.

As she rose above the gray path everything went black, as if someone had shut the lid on a jar. *Part of Stanshmoor security*? More likely they had simply reached the cell's ceiling, she decided. Her head wasn't hitting anything but apparently whatever force the notebook created *had*, halting their motion. *That's it, then. We're trapped.*

A deafening, terrifying grinding noise tore through her ears. Andra squeezed the notebook, to make sure she didn't drop it but also to be certain whatever Cinüe magic it contained was still active. The heavy shuddering returned, so violent that Andra was certain no earthquake scale could offer sufficient readings.

It's one Cinüe system straining against the other, she realized.

She felt air under her body as she rose and fell, slamming into unseen objects until a massive, metallic roar sounded and everything gave way, lurching upward once again.

Did we actually break out?

She reached for her flashlight, flicked it on, and saw movement: the oily, darkened walls were sliding down, similar to the sliding motion she saw inside the Lonacco Trove hole. Below her feet, far below, she spotted the gray path... along with three narrow, glowing slits with hexagram eyeballs, moving up with her.

The frightening reality hit her: *the notebook's mojo worked, and now we're heading up through Stanshmoor's levels... together.*

She found herself hoping Stanshmoor's security would hold them in place, that maybe it would keep them—keep *it*—locked up. The grinding became even louder, reaching a roar. Overhead, the darkness cracked as if smashed by the notebook's unseen force, sending fuzz and crosshatching falling in snowflake-like patterns.

Explosions ripped through the area, too many for Andra to count. They burst over the pit like fireworks, reeking of sulphur, blood, and horrible odors she couldn't identify. Crosshatching rained down and fuzz ran along her cheeks like electrified cotton balls, but she continued rising.

The darkness, crosshatching and fuzz suddenly transformed into a golden, warm yellow. The glow was so bright that she couldn't see the hexagram eyeballs below her anymore. Everything quieted, except for her still-ringing ears.

It's the god-human's cell, Andra realized. *The council must have surrounded the pit with his cell. Are we going to break through that too? By freeing one prisoner, am I freeing both?*

Again, her movement stopped, and the deafening, grinding noise returned. She clung to the notebook, correctly anticipating explosions as the notebook's unseen force mashed against the yellow barrier. Golden chunks fell like broken glass, only this glass spread soothing, massaging warmth as it shattered.

Another explosion, this one the loudest yet, shattered the last of the golden cells. Andra felt herself moving upward again, beyond the yellow, into... silver? *No, wait, it's steel, and some sort of bracing designed to hold—*

She watched as the steel—*or maybe it's titanium?*—split like pierced tinfoil, without offering much resistance. Klaxons sounded, lasers flashed, cannons boomed, bombs exploded. None of it seemed much more than noise. Andra saw Stanshmoor's guards firing their powder rifles from the compromised entry hallway, but whatever force the notebook created didn't appear slowed or harmed. She braced herself, seeing they were about to burrow into the rock above the hallway.

Then she noticed someone running across a catwalk... someone hooded.

Cobalt!

His dark robes spun like a starlet's dress as he whirled, looking at Andra.

"It won't work!" he yelled, his voice barely audible over the din. "You can move them, but only I can free them—and none of this will stop the Maybe Objective!"

Andra did a double-take. Wade was there too, dodging the guards.

He's still alive! And he escaped the guards I saw in the necrospondence!

She shouted to him, loud as she could, but he didn't hear her. Then her ascent reached the rock above the tunnel, showering sparks onto the catwalk. Wade looked up.

Andra shouted again. He shouted back, pointing up.

Yeah, I know I'm about to crash. But no, he was still pointing, ramped up about something. The grinding noise erupted again, only much louder than before, as the notebook's mojo burst the tunnel's ceiling apart. *If we passed through titanium without any problem, then why would simple rock...*

"Because it's not just rock," she said aloud, excited. "It's another cell!

The debris showered around her. Looking down she saw Wade dodging the falling chunks and hoped he could find shelter. The tunnel, and in turn Stanshmoor prison, now resembled the bottom end of a landslide.

Another lurch—she was into the upper cell now. Grinding gave way to blasting as the cell ruptured. Everything turned olive green, and she heard—and felt—the tremendous rumble of pipe organs. Then Andra saw a multi-colored blur. She held her breath, hoping beyond hope. The blur zoomed past, showering glistening sparks like a meteorite, each spark turning to tiny diamonds as they hit falling debris.

"Cera?" Andra shouted. "Cera! Oh my god, Cera! I'm here, Cera, I'm up *here*!"

She nearly let go of the notebook... but she knew if she stopped the escape before the cell was destroyed, Wade wouldn't have a pathway to get to Cera. So she watched, separated from Cera as she continued rising, smashing the olive green cell's topmost barriers, breaching soil and sod. Her breath caught as she lost site of the blur, and Wade... the only things that mattered, the only reasons she was there.

Everything moved quickly: Stanshmoor falling away, earth flowing around her as it had earlier. Heat and cold, nickel and lava, liquid and air, it all simply flowed, peacefully. If the ghastly eye slits were still below, Andra couldn't see them.

God either, for that matter. No sign of the god-human. There was just her, and movement, and exhaustion. Packed, earthen walls slowed, halted, solidified. Blue sky reappeared.

"Andra?"

Her mother's voice, calling from above. Andra extended her arms so Swimney and Maribel could help her up. Joy, tears, and questions hit her from all sides, even from within, but she had nothing left. She felt herself collapsing, felt Swimney's hands catching her... and then felt nothing at all.

NINETEEN

Chisels

Greasy tendrils slunk down Andra's throat. She felt them wiggle and curl inside her chest, ticklish, disgusting. They pushed into her lungs, choking her until learning her breathing rhythm, as before. For several moments they became part of her, helping hands taking the strain off her chest muscles, handling the autonomic breathing movements for her.

Then they slowed.

She gasped, desperate for air, but the tendrils wouldn't budge. She clutched her chest, head swooning, heart palpitating. Still the air wouldn't come, and the tendrils were in motion again, pressing against sensitive tissue, shoving harder, trying to punch holes into her lungs and remove her only chance at—

Andra screamed.

But how did I have enough air to scream?

She looked around, saw she was sitting up in bed, recognized her grandmother's master bedroom at

Lonacco Trove. Her t-shirt and jeans were on the floor, swapped for a soft, cotton nightshirt. She took a deep breath. Her lungs felt fine, but the rest of what she'd just experienced—dreamed?—refused to fade. The bed felt soft and the room seemed real, but she kept studying them regardless, waiting for some new revelation. A sudden cough gave her pause. She waited, expecting to feel something wiggling within her chest in response.

"Hard, isn't it," she heard her mother say. "That Cinüe arcane stuff blends everything. Makes you wonder what's real and what isn't. Pretty sure both answers are right."

Maribel Barger sat in the antique rocking chair but kept it motionless.

"The notebook..." Andra started, looking around.

"Safe," her mother said. "With me."

She held it up. The corners looked wrinkled and the cover creased, but that seemed minimal given all it had just endured.

"What about Cera, and Wade?" Andra said. "Are they out?"

Maribel looked devastated.

"No one's heard a thing dear."

Andra sat up. "That can't be right. I just tore that place to bits and... my only condition for going along with this was... are you sure?"

Her mother nodded.

Andra jumped up, raced to the parlor, looked out the bay windows. Outside, the Atlantic chopped and churned in all its sunlit glory, seabirds diving, parasailors veering, catamarans leaping.

"Nothing's changed," Maribel said, entering behind Andra.

"Yeah, I can see that."

Andra ran for the front door, flung it open, set out for the hillside behind the building at full pace, nightwear be damned.

"It's gone," she uttered, upon finding fresh, refilled Earth where the hole had been. "Why would they fill it? Why the hell would they refill the hole?"

She put her head in her hands, holding it, caressing her temples, trying to find... *myself*, she figured. *Right now, I need myself.*

And Cera. I need her too, and Wade. And after that, I need the craziness to go away. Just let me have my family. After all I've just done...

"We couldn't chance leaving it open," she heard her mother saying, and there was more, strategy and logic and whatever, but Andra wasn't listening.

She kept her head secure between her hands, same way she'd gripped the notebook, clinging for dear life, and a chance, and a road home. Her mother had her by the shoulders, turning her, steering her, trying to walk her back.

"I just don't understand," Andra said, lifting her head. "I freed them! Why is everything the same?"

Maribel stopped pushing her. *Maybe for the first time ever*, Andra thought.

"Your question makes no sense, dear," her mother said. "What is it you think should be different?"

"Everything. It should all be different."

Maribel made a palms-up motion.

"Mother, I just freed a god and a devil!" Andra said, exasperated. "Whatever these undiminished humans are, they're loose in the world because of me. Yet here it all is—no different from before."

She felt tears, not from weakness, sadness, or exhaustion. *From frustration*, she knew. From her growing sense that freeing two immense powers still hadn't been enough to overturn the council's hold. What was it David Stanford Swimney said before she'd set out for Stanshmoor? *Think of the implications if the council actually has enough power to hold God prisoner. Just think about that.*

She hadn't thought about it beyond an incarceration-technology level. But maybe that wasn't what concerned Swimney.

He's worried about pecking order, she realized. *If whoever's behind the council can lock up a god, they must have a higher perch on the cosmic food chain.*

"Just because you can't see a difference doesn't mean it isn't there," Maribel said. "We've had good and evil aplenty with those two locked up, and we still have it. The difference is, they're out there now, Andra. They're a part of things again. Over the long haul that's going to make a difference. But if you were expecting a cosmic boxing match in the night sky with frogs raining down upon us, that's not how it works."

Andra looked away, unsure of what she'd expected.

"Why do you say that?" she said.

Maribel sighed.

"Because I learned from someone who knew, that's why. Learned too much, really."

"Knowing more isn't a bad thing," Andra said.

"No... unless it's so overwhelming it drives you away, like it did with me. You want to know why I didn't want you in your grandmother's home? In her upper kitchen cabinet? You want to know the big secrets I'm protecting? Well here it is: it's the glacial forces. The continental creep. The big-picture mechanisms that a thumbnail-loving race like ours can't process... stuff that screws with your mind whenever a well-meaning individual, or relative, or worse, your own mother, decides to go ahead and let you in on it."

She took a breath, to refocus.

"Bottom line," she said, continuing, "is timeless beings don't brawl, dear. They mold, they craft, they chisel the cosmos. They create, and done right, creation is a meticulous process with only brief dramatic moments."

Andra shook her head.

"Then why bother to keep a god-human in prison?" she said. "What's the benefit?"

Maribel put an arm around her daughter.

"Fewer chefs in the kitchen," she said.

They stood there, together, and Andra noticed something she never expected: she enjoyed it.

"This is for later... for the future," Maribel said, placing a weathered envelope in Andra's hand.

"What is it?"

"It's a little bit of what was in the upper kitchen cabinet. Paperwork with names you've never seen. Names of... of your father. Your grandfather. Of the most important men in our lives."

Andra ran her fingers across the envelope's creases.

"You took it further than me," she said.

Her mother nodded. "Back then, not wanting the formality of a marriage meant sacrificing the relationship. The paper was viewed as the cement, moreso than the love."

"But a relationship can't truly develop with some piece of paper in the way, mandating its legitimacy."

Maribel smiled.

"Preaching to the choir, dear," she said. "Times are changing though. People are starting to understand. You might be able to pull it off."

"So far," Andra said. "Wade gets it... mostly. But it's still hard at times."

"That won't stop you?"

"No."

Her mother shrugged.

"Guess it didn't stop any of us," she said.

Screeching tires and a slammed car door interrupted the discussion. Andra pulled her mother toward her grandmother's home, expecting trouble, then hesitated when she saw David Stanford Swimney dashing between the buildings, cell phone in hand.

"It's Wade," he said. "No video, but I've got him on the line right now!"

Andra dashed forward and grabbed the phone.

"Where are you?" she said. "Have you found—?"

"I've got her, Annie," he said, his mild drawl disarming her panic. "Thanks to you busting the place up, I've got Cera. Though I gotta' tell you, she's not—"

"She's not what?"

Andra heard shouts and explosions over the phone.

"They're on me hard!" Wade said. "You someplace safe?"

"The safest," she said. "You need bread crumbs?"

"Uh uh. Be there in ten."

The connection clicked off.

"You're sure this place is a fortress, right?" she said to Swimney, passing the phone back to him.

"As close to one as we'll get," he said. "How's Wade going to find us?"

"He was the council's messenger, remember? Tracking people at their present address is pretty much what he does."

They hustled into Dvora Lansky's home, assessing it in a different manner this time.

"The bay windows will never hold if we're attacked," Andra said. "And what about the weather stripping under the front door, or the ventilation system? Someone could gas us through those."

Maribel walked to the windows.

"Not so much as a vibration," she said, pounding her fist against the glass. "Mom claimed they weren't windows. More like viewing screens made to look like windows."

Swimney found a ladder and went to examine the vents while Maribel checked their food supply.

"In case we're under siege for awhile," she said.

"The attic could be a problem too," Andra said. "There are air vents up there, right? Those could make for good access points. Oh, and the plumbing. Aren't there cities where snakes come in through the toilets? We'll need to secure the pipes."

Maribel looked sideways for a beat before placing her hands on Andra's shoulders.

"Go wait for Wade, dear. Mr. Swimney and I will get the place ready."

Andra started to object, then stopped; letting them handle things while she waited for Wade didn't seem like such a bad idea. She threw on her t-shirt and jeans then dashed outside, longing for the days when a shave ice was enough to make everything seem better.

No way he's coming in through the front, she decided, looking around the Lonacco complex.

Moments later she was at the rear hillside, studying the filled-in hole, wishing she could use it for an emergency exit. But digging it out would take a couple hours, and Wade had made it clear they wouldn't have that kind of time.

The more she thought about that, the more it bothered her. Wouldn't her grandmother—

A baritone purr sounded from the hill, rumbling her chest. She ran toward it, recognizing the sound of Wade's dark equine. The animal rounded the hill with its head extended at a forward angle, elongated eyes focused on the destination. Andalusian curls, goateed chin, and silver mane all swirled in the seaside breeze.

Wade sat atop the equine's back, his legs tucked deep into pouch-like ruffles that extended into the animal's sides. Andra was more concerned with the red spots—blood?—along Wade's shoulders. Then she spotted the small figure bundled against his chest.

"Cera?" Andra exclaimed as Wade brought the dark equine to a stop.

"No time!" he shouted, leaping off. "They're coming in hot, Annie—and they sent the Mechen Klav."

Oh God, she thought.

"How many?" she said, leading him and Cera between buildings as the equine whirled and departed, its clawed, toe-like hooves making small clicks every time it took a step.

"All of them."

TWENTY

Vacant

Andra stopped in her tracks.

"Are you sure?"

Wade nudged her forward.

"That's how serious they are about this. They want Cera back, they're really worried... and they're acting desperate."

As they ran, Andra thought back to the aftermath of the Diminishing Act vote. That was the only time she had seen the full Mechen Klav assembled, in the council chamber caverns below Uluru, in Australia. She guessed they had to be several hundred strong.

Maybe more.

Fireworks sounded above their heads. The Cote d'Azur's cerulean sky rippled with green specks that streaked, then spread, like algae storming a pond.

"That's the Klav, moving in on our position," Wade said. "The green'll drip down. We touch it, we're done. How much farther?"

Andra pointed to her grandmother's patio. Maribel already had the door wide open, and they could see Swimney in the hallway, beckoning them to hurry. They rushed inside and slammed the entry shut.

Locks and seals audibly snicked into place.

"We're good," Andra said.

She and Wade took deep breaths, eyeballed one another, then rushed forward and embraced, Cera between them, still bundled against her father's chest. The girl's face appeared above the bundle, cheeks like rainbows, wearing a huge grin.

Andra thought her heart might melt. She hugged the two of them again, smiling, tears pouring down her face.

"Is she okay?" Andra said, as soon as she felt she could speak without breaking up. "And you, Wade, are you okay?"

He shrugged, lifted the girl from the carrying pouch on his chest, passed her to Andra.

Even with the world falling apart outside, Andra couldn't remember ever feeling so happy. Cera glowed and grinned, but didn't otherwise react. Maribel leaned in, brows lowered, studying her granddaughter.

"Why isn't she making any sounds?" Maribel said.

"Mother, she's overwhelmed," Andra said. "I was only in Stanshmoor a short time and look how shaken I was when I got back. Cera was there for weeks."

Wade stuck a toothpick between his teeth and began chewing, lips pursed, expression grim.

"Actually... somethin's not quite right with her," he said. "She smiles, and recognizes, but that's it. Otherwise she seems... I don't know, blank maybe. As if she's here, but not quite conscious of it."

Andra felt her joy vaporize. She studied Cera, hoping for signs Wade was wrong. He wasn't. The baby smiled, and seemed content, but that was it. Her eyes held no depth, no emotion, no latent curiosity.

"She's vacant," Andra mumbled, horrified. "Do you think they drugged her? Or... worse?"

She checked for scars and blemishes, but found none. *Maybe Cinüe techniques don't require needles or scalpels?*

Then she remembered Cobalt's comment at Stanshmoor: "You can move them, but only I can free them."

She closed her eyes, forcing back tears.

"We have Cera's body, but they still have her... I don't know, her consciousness maybe," she mumbled. "More arcane tech—somehow they must be able to separate the two, jail them in different locations."

She gave Wade a forlorn look, but couldn't force more words. *The council still has our daughter. Our beloved Cera is still a prisoner.*

"That means they *still* have the god-human, and that devil thing too," Maribel said, her words pointed. "You freed them physically, but the council still holds the essence of who they are."

"Yes Mother, I get it, I need to go back," she said, exasperated. "I screwed up again. Is that what you want me to say? Then yes, it's very apparent that I promised to free two god-like beings and probably didn't get it done. I didn't even get Cera out."

She wished the hole was out back, so she could crawl into it.

"Darlin,' there was no way for either of us to know—" Wade started.

"Don't call me darling," she said.

The lighting dimmed. They looked toward the bay windows and saw green algae streaked across the glass, spreading, blotting their view.

"Everything's covered out there," Maribel said, peering through one of the few remaining window portions they could see through. "Land, road, homes. Even our car."

Just like that, the Stanshmoor prison dilemma gave way to the reality that they were under attack.

"The vents are safe," Swimney told everyone, racing from the hall. "No exterior access points. It's as if the system teleports fresh air from other locations rather than drawing it in from directly outside. From what I can tell the electrical and water systems work the same way."

Wade paced the parlor, scrutinizing.

"What about the attic?" he said.

"There is none," Swimney said. "And no authentic vents of any kind on the roof. They're all facades."

"Crawl space?" Wade said.

"None."

"Basement?"

"The place is a bunker," Swimney said, lighting a cigar then extinguishing it when he caught sight of the baby.

"A bunker with twenty-year-old food," Maribel said.

Wade nodded. "Even if they don't manage to bust in, we're not going to be able to hold out for more than a few days."

Swimney seemed taken aback.

"The Mechen Klav enforce Council Law, and it's against Council Law for them to enter," he said.

Wade pulled his jacket off, patted his shirt pocket, removed a toothpick.

"It's not going to be illegal for much longer," he said, stuffing the pick between his teeth, gnawing. "They're voting on an emergency rules change right now."

"Not a chance," Swimney said. "That would be a complete disregard for laws and procedures established generations ago."

"I'm tellin' ya, everyone workin' the prison was talkin' about it. Rules are about to change. It's part of the whole Maybe Objective thing. Whatever it is, they're determined to make sure nothin' stops it—and right now they view Cera as threat number one."

Andra weighed Swimney's law versus Wade's prison rumors and didn't like what her intuition was telling her. She hugged her daughter even tighter.

"You think she's that high of a priority?" she asked Wade.

He nodded. "You saw Stanshmoor. They had her in a cell designed for a god. We've made the only new, undiminished human and they want her contained no matter—"

Andra's cell phone rang.

They stared at it, startled. The display read 'Unknown Caller.'

"They've never been able to track this phone," Andra said.

She watched it ringing, figuring she'd let the call go to voicemail... then changed her mind.

"Ann it's me," an airy voice said.

"Cristina?"

Andra couldn't believe Cristina actually had the nerve to call after betraying their friendship.

"Girl, listen: they're about to come at you with arcane tech," Cristina said. "Dvora's place won't protect you. You need to find a way out, fast."

A commotion erupted from Cristina's end of the phone: buzzing, crashing sounds, and shouts.

"Gotta' go," Cristina said. "I'm sorry for what happened—really, I am. Run while there's still time."

The call dropped. Andra relayed the message.

"So much for this place being a bunker," Maribel said.

"She's probably just trying to flush us out," Andra said. "It's not like we can trust her."

Swimney began tossing paperwork into his briefcase.

"We can trust her," he said.

"Why do you say that?" Andra said.

“Because, he said, “she’s the one who was supplying us the names of the pregnant Cinüe.”

Andra gave him a look, but Swimney wasn’t the least bit apologetic.

“You were on your way to Stanshmoor when you asked me about it,” he said. “Much as I was confident they wouldn’t harm you, I couldn’t risk the chance they might take a shot at extracting the name of our source.”

Andra, though irritated, let it drop.

“So the Mechen Klav is just the beginning,” she said. “The council’s coming at us with everything they've got.”

Maribel's face paled.

“If they use everything they've got then Wade’s right,” she said. “We're not going to be able to hold out for long.”

Andra, watching her mother talk, had the sudden impression that the woman looked old. Her facial crags appeared deeper, her crow's feet extended longer, her jowl lines rippled further than before. *But not from age, or stress,* Andra decided. *From buried knowledge.*

“What aren't you telling us, Mother?” Andra said.

Maribel gave the same warning glance she made when ordering them away from the kitchen cabinets.

“All you need to know is that I've been there,” she said, with a heavy edge to her voice. “I've been to Edenshire. Not to the prison, like you, to the rest of it—and it’s extensive, and mindblowing. If they bring things from that place to use on us here...”

Andra shook her head. All these years and she was just now hearing that her mother had, somehow, at some time, visited a place that was off-limits to human beings.

"What kinds of things?" she said. "Weapons, animals, what?"

Maribel looked lifeless, and seemed deep in thought.

"Unexplainable things," she said, her voice a near-monotone. "Like those stars you said they used when they grabbed Cera. Things we can't defend against."

They sat in silence, the parlor now dark, their view and access to the outside world choked off.

"You've been there too, right?" Andra said softly, to Wade.

"Only for a few minutes, here and again. A few crazy minutes, droppin' packages. Abberdeen, he's brave for an equine but we turned tail soon as we could. That place is... too different."

She put her arm around his shoulder. "Worse than the deliveries to Asantha Cooray?"

He looked her in the eyes.

"No, not worse. Just different."

"How different?"

He paused, thinking it over.

"So different you question what's real and what isn't."

A rumble shook the house, not violent but startling. When it subsided they heard a buzzing noise outside, around the entire house. The sound was too soft for power tools but louder than a bee swarm, and seemed to be getting closer. Andra looked at Cera, heart racing. The thought of losing her daughter again...

"We need a hole, like the one you filled up out back," she blurted. "Then I can use the notebook to get us pretty much anywhere."

They didn't get a chance to discuss the matter. A pink circle formed on the wall near the bay windows and the buzzing went from outside the house to inside their heads. Andra felt as if her brain were hollow and insects were flitting about, painless yet dizzying. Her tongue swelled, and she tasted a series of flavors... liver, seafood, then castor oil, all of it building to a horrid bile taste.

Everyone held their heads, slapped their ears, gagged at the horrific flavors. Only Cera seemed unaffected, her vacant grin unceasing. The pink spot darkened. The buzzing, and the taste, got worse. Then it faded, and the sensations eased.

As the symptoms disappeared, the spot did too. Andra did her best to shake the effects quickly, eager to make sure Cera hadn't been hurt.

"You see," Maribel managed, still trying to recover. "The stuff they have seeps through, no matter where you're holed up. And they'll keep at it until they drive us out."

They regained composure quickly, except for Swimney, who was incensed.

"Using that weapon is a violation of the 482 Treaty," he said, furious. "Whoever authorized it should be apprehended and prosecuted!"

Wade shook his head.

"You're not gettin' the full picture here," he said. "The laws ain't in effect when it comes to us, not so long as we got Cera."

Swimney huffed.

"Without the laws we've got nothing," he said, as agitated as Andra had ever seen him. "We're back to wild nature, and I won't stand for it!"

He looked at Andra.

"I'm going out there."

"David, we need you here, with us," she said.

"I *will* be with you—as your attorney. If the laws are changing behind closed doors, someone needs to stand up against it... and stand up for your rights, in a court of law."

Maribel scoffed.

"They'll just stick you in a cell... or worse," she said.

He curled his lower lip, pulled a cigar from his jacket, and lit it, careful not to make eye contact with the baby.

"Then that's what they'll do," he said, puffing.

"No, she's right," Andra said. "You'll be giving yourself up for nothing. If the council's doing whatever it pleases then laws are words on paper, no more."

Swimney pulled his cigar from his mouth, eyeballing her.

"No more?" he said. "The law is *everything*. It's the difference between us and the animals, and the reason we're not still in the Stone Age."

He jammed the cigar into his mouth for a quick puff, then pulled it back out.

"I've helped interpret some of the very laws they're throwing out the window, and I won't let those people get away with what they're doing," he said. "Not without fighting back in the only forum I'm any good at fighting in."

Andra could tell he was upset with her for trivializing Council Law...but she also knew that his plan might cost him his life.

"There's no way to get outside," she countered weakly. "The algae will get you."

"Not on the patio—that's part of your grandmother's house so it's secure," he said. "I'll step outside, you'll lock the door behind me, then I'll stand there and wait. Mechen Klav officers will spot me soon enough, I can assure you."

The rest of them glanced at one another, none of them happy with his idea.

"You'd better be good before a judge," Andra said.

"It won't matter, Ms. Barger," he said, snuffing his cigar against the window. "Clearly, my clients have the strongest harassment case ever."

He gathered his briefcase, slid into his gray suit coat, and stepped to the door.

"Have one," he said, passing Andra a cigar. "Someday we'll smoke it together, to celebrate."

She took it, ran it along her nostrils, wrinkled her nose.

"You sure I can't change your mind?" she said.

"Ms. Barger," he said, "your attorney is on this for you. And he *will* succeed."

Swimney unlatched the door locks, slipped outside, and pulled the door shut behind him in one continuous motion. Andra thought it ironic that the smoke cloud which accompanied him everywhere remained inside. As Wade reset the locks they heard a commotion out front. Then all went quiet.

"Open up!" they heard Swimney call, after several moments passed. "Quick, open up before they get here!"

Maribel stepped toward the door but Wade held her back.

"Sorry Darlin,' door stays shut," he said.

"Oh come on, you don't think—"

Another pink spot appeared on the wall before Maribel could finish but this time they spotted it sooner, when it was still a small, growing dot.

"Into the master bedroom!" Andra shouted, wrapping Cera against her chest.

They swung the door shut behind them, nestling into a walk-in closet. The buzzing and taste changes were still bad, but not nearly so severe. Andra looked at the dark closet as the effects subsided, reminded again of her time in the hole.

The hole.

Ever since seeing it filled, a niggling thought had slowly worked its way forward.

"My grandmother wouldn't have dug a hole," she said, locking on to what was irritating her subconscious.

"What are you talking about?" Maribel said.

"Grandmother wasn't out digging six-foot-deep holes every time she wanted to use that notebook, and there aren't any caves nearby. She must have had another way."

Wade chewed his toothpick.

"The place doesn't have a basement or a crawl space, Swimney already checked it out," he said.

Andra wasn't willing to give up.

"Maybe... maybe it didn't need one," she said, pointing to the room's only window.

The building shuddered again, and they heard the sound of something drilling into every corner in the home.

"Annie, doll, if you've got an idea we need it fast," Wade said.

She gave him a nasty look for calling her 'doll,' though in this case her heart wasn't in it.

"The complex was built into the hillside, which is why there aren't any windows on the back side," she said.

Maribel's head whipped.

"So this whole room's in a hole," she said.

"Yeah," Andra said. "Or, maybe. Depending upon how you look at it."

"Doesn't matter how we look at it," Wade said. "Only how the notebook looks at it."

Another shudder. A crack formed along the exterior wall, and in the ceiling above them.

"Wade, get whatever you need," Andra said, fingering the notebook. "We're leaving."

Wade returned from the living room a few seconds later, shutting the bedroom door behind him.

"Here, pass me Cera," Wade said.

Andra started wiggling out of the shoulder harness of the baby carrier she was wearing, then changed her mind.

"Uh uh," she said. "This time she's with me. And Wade?"

She gave him an apologetic look.

"Just for today, you can call me doll... and darling. It better be pure southern charm, though. None of that macho variety."

Wade gave her a "who, me?" look.

More shudders, buzzing, and horrid tastes hit them; an explosion, a chorus of deafening church bells, and several crashes erupted from the living room. Andra, dizzy, heard multiple boot steps swarming the entry hall and a series of chaotic shouts. She blocked them out, hoping she still had time, focusing on the notebook, on its rough texture against her fingers. A dozen destinations passed through her mind, all of them remote and, for the time being, safe.

She ignored every one of them.

"Get everyone in this room to... get us to Cobalt's home," she gambled, speaking over the din, holding the book in front of Cera.

The bedroom door burst open, slamming it into the wall, exposing a hallway filled with Mechen Klav officers... then everything blurred. The buzzing and bad tastes faded. The walls moved downwards, as if they were in a sideless elevator. Cera giggled, apparently thinking it was a fun ride. Looking to either side, Andra was relieved to find she and Cera weren't alone. Wade and her mother were next to her. They looked confused, but no matter. They were with her... and knowing so felt good.

The blurring slowed, forming patterned wallpaper, white wainscoting, and a massive, wall-mounted, flat screen television. Andra took a deep breath—they all did—and put a finger to her lips so they wouldn't say anything. Looking around, she saw they were inside a large family room with plush carpet, recliners, an elegant bar, and a watercolor art collection. A carpeted staircase at the far end of the room had a golf bag leading against it and spiraled toward an open door one flight up.

A basement. Cobalt's got a snazzy basement.

She gave Cera a reassuring pat, then realized the fact she could see her surroundings was a warning sign.

The basement lights are on. Someone's close by.

She motioned for the others to stay quiet but saw Wade already had her mother headed for the shadows behind the bar. Andra passed Cera to Wade, unslung the baby carrier, then crept to the staircase.

The door above slammed shut.

He knows I'm here. But how?

Andra raced up but the knob was locked from the outside. Wade was already next to her, a surprise since she hadn't heard him mount the steps.

"Your mother has Cera," he said, kicking at the door. "If we get outside I can call Abberdeen and get us out of here."

"Okay, you head outside," she said as the door gave way. "I'm after Cobalt."

Wade looked confused.

"I brought us here to search for information on how to free Cera's consciousness," she explained, "but since he's home I'll get it straight from the snake's head."

They burst into an entry foyer. A massive flower bouquet loomed from an ornate table, and family photos lined the curved walls.

"There—front doors," Andra said, pointing at a pair of hefty, carved doors to their left.

Wade made a whistling shape with his mouth but no sound came forth. Maribel did, however, with Cera slung to her chest.

"All of us, doll," Wade said to Andra.

She shook her head.

"My turn to take the field. You get them somewhere safe."

Wade paused, thinking about it, but didn't seem to make his decision until he looked at Cera.

"Back soon," he said, opening the doors.

A massive green field with streams and grazing cows filled the pastoral expanse before them. If there was another home nearby, they couldn't see it from the doorstep. Wade led the others outside. Andra's heart sank as she watched them go, especially Cera. Maribel's eyes begged Andra for a change of heart. Andra had a feeling her own eyes were begging for the same thing; her heart certainly was.

She shut the doors, unable to look any longer. A rumbling purr and the sound of air whooshing against the windows told her Abberdeen had arrived and was carrying the others away. Tucking herself into shadows, she strode through the foyer, into what she assumed would be a living room.

It was a library. Two stories high, the room carried the rich fragrance of ancient paper. Many of the books had crusted, leather spines. A table at the room's center housed a card catalogue, a computer workstation... and a discarded hood with cobalt stripes.

Andra resisted the urge to step from the shadows and grab it. Her patience paid off when she noticed she wasn't the room's only moving shadow. Another slender figure worked bookcase-to-bookcase, then stopped.

“He's not here,” a woman's voice said. “But I've called for help. You'll be surrounded by Mechen Klav any second now.”

The shadow stepped out from between the bookcases, transforming into a tall woman wearing a slitted, velvet dress that framed a pair of long legs and a set of high heels that looked just as long.

Stiletto... the leggy lady who somehow survived a conjugal visit with Notorious, at the prison cell.

Andra stepped from her shadows, facing the woman.

"How did you make it out of that cell?" Andra said.

The woman appeared surprised, but unbothered. "How did *you*?" she said.

She knows who I am.

Andra wasn't sure of her next move. The library probably had a treasure trove of Cinüe information, but she didn't have time to look and Cobalt had apparently fled. She nodded at the woman, turned, and took off through the hall. At the entry foyer she grabbed the double-doorknobs and stepped outside... then hesitated.

Looking over her shoulder at the family photos, she saw the same leggy woman posed with two kids, with pets, with an older couple that might have been her parents, and with combinations of all.

But no husband—no male whatsoever for that matter—and no other apparent significant other.

Maybe Cobalt was just a friend of hers? But no, she had specifically asked the notebook to take her to Cobalt's home. And the photos all centered around Stiletto.

Meaning Stiletto, the leggy woman... is Cobalt?

"You put it together, huh?" the woman said, stepping into her foyer, the hood with the cobalt stripe in her left hand. "My little Cinüe voice-change trick fooled the Old Boys Club, that's for sure."

Andra stepped back inside.

"Your Mechen Klav seem to be running late," she said.

Cobalt shrugged. "Didn't call 'em. Don't need 'em."

"You sure?" Andra said.

The comment spurred a silken laugh. "I handle the council, and what was in the pit," Cobalt said. "You think I'm going to worry about *you*?"

Andra nodded. "I notice you said, 'what *was* in the pit.' Funny how it's not there anymore."

Cobalt stepped forward, walked a half moon pattern around Andra, then walked back the other way.

"You think your little jail break accomplished anything?" she said. "Those things are still in there—the only part of them that counts, anyway. The part that thinks, and loves, and hates, and takes action. The core of who they are as beings, that's still there. The rest... the parts you freed... that's just the meat. But I guess you've figured that out by now."

Andra choked off the memory of Cera's vacant smile.

"Your prison's destroyed, your most valuable prisoners incomplete," Andra said. "Leave my family alone and I'll leave you alone."

Cobalt angled her head, as if amused. "Your child makes that impossible."

She walked another half-moon pattern. *Like a wolf sizing up its prey*, Andra thought. She stood her ground, hoping her diminisher training would offer an escape if she needed one.

"I don't see where you have any position of strength in this," Cobalt said.

"And you won't see it, not unless I want you too. By then it's too late."

Another silken laugh.

"Lot of bluster for just a few tastes of arcane tech," she said. "I *am* arcane tech."

The house disappeared. Stunned, Andra checked her surroundings. Nothing but the grass field, and the scattered cows under afternoon sunlight.

No shadows for blending. I'm completely exposed.

One thought gave her hope. *So is she.*

Cobalt paced another half moon, her pace unhampered by the sod-piercing stilettos. The methodical stride his five steps, then ten, then the grass blades shot up, obliterating Andra's vision. The grass hardened, then sharpened, slicing her hands, neck, and face as it grew. Then it was gone, the landscape barren dirt, the befuddled cows unharmed, searching for their lost meal. Andra stood her ground, bloodied skin be damned.

Cobalt walked the far end of her half moon pattern.

The loose dirt shot up, enveloping Andra in dust, pounding her with minuscule pebbles flying at impossible speed, sandblasting her skin like the most severe desert windstorm. The dirt vanished just as fast, the landscape turned to barren rock, the cows looking even more baffled than before.

Cobalt paced past.

Clouds fell from the sky, surrounding Andra. They stung her with their frozen water particles, tortured her with their abrasive, electrified atoms, froze her already tattered skin. Then the cloud, too, vanished. This time the cows galloped away, terrified.

"Curl your skin, bake your eyelashes, boil your eyes, dissolve your toenails... it's easy for me," Cobalt said. "I just don't see your power position in all this."

Andra watched, waiting... then grabbed the woman's arm at the moment her steady half moon brought her closest.

"How about I unleash my daughter," she said.

Cobalt yanked her arm back, eyes wide.

With fear, Andra recognized.

The woman recovered her composure in an instant, but it was too late. Andra knew what she had seen, even if she didn't fully understand it. Still, Cobalt might not know she didn't understand.

"No more tricks," Andra said. "Soul or no soul, my daughter's still a threat... in fact she might be more of a threat *without* her soul than she is with it."

The woman renewed her pacing but made a point of staying a few steps back, out of reach.

"That's all you have, more bluster?" Cobalt said. "Stanshmoor tells me your daughter's not demonstrating yet."

Andra smiled. "Good thing she's much more comfortable around her family."

Cobalt froze in her tracks. "I don't believe you," she said.

"I don't care."

Cobalt studied Andra, eyes-to-chest-to feet, back to eyes. Then she started into her half-moon pattern again.

"Talk all you want," Cobalt said. "Your words are as hollow as your heritage. Related by adoption—as if that makes you a true Cinüe. I don't know why the others are going along with it but as soon as the Maybe Objective's done I'll see to it that—"

Andra disappeared.

The illusion lasted only a couple seconds, and she didn't truly vanish, but stretching the pebbles' shadows up and out gave a split-second strobe impression that made it seem she'd disappeared. *Best trick in my diminisher arsenal,* she knew, *and it doesn't give me much more than a confused moment so I'll need to move fast.*

She sprung feet-first, colliding with Cobalt's jaw, knocking her down. The house returned, slowly filled with grass and an askew cow, then disappeared. The surroundings appeared and disappeared twice more, as if controlled by a wonky TV remote.

Cobalt cursed and crawled away but Andra was already on her, slamming her face-first against the floor, then against the ground as the environment continued flickering. She grabbed the woman's arm, twisting it back and up, causing an anguished yell.

But Cobalt flipped herself over and onto her feet in one move, and the fight was over. Andra barely saw the leg-kick, and couldn't avoid the knee to her gut. She doubled over but never hit ground, her chin slamming against something just as solid—*the woman's fist?*—as her vision, and consciousness, wavered.

Dazed, she made a weak, slashing grab with her hands and actually managed to grasp Cobalt's right hand, but not for long. Cobalt's eyes widened and she snatched the hand away, taking a step back as she did so.

Same way she did before, Andra thought. When Cobalt initially yanked her hand back, her eyes just as wide, Andra had assumed it was because of the threat to unleash Cera's power.

But maybe it wasn't.

Maybe... no! Really?

Could it be she didn't want me touching her hand?

She'd been down this path before. Was Cobalt playing her the same way Cooray had? She wondered how many evenings she had found herself in bed, awake, reliving that crazy, desperate moment when she'd chosen to lash out at Asantha Cooray using the only real weapon she had: diminishing gel. The whole thing was childish, really. She never expected to make contact with Cooray's spectral form, much less have the gel actually do its job.

Which had apparently been Cooray's plan all along.

Now here was Cobalt, doing the same thing. *But no*, she realized... *Asantha Cooray was never afraid, not like this.* Cobalt's eyes suddenly had the same terrified expression Julia had, and the other Cinüe victims. *The one where they realize their children could get hit with something irreversible.*

Energized, Andra stood up. Her entire body hurt, and blood dribbled down her face and arms. Cobalt wasn't looking her finest either, her velvet dress now dirt-smeared, her cheek bruised from Andra slamming it against the floor.

The house reappeared, Cobalt still unable to control her surroundings. Andra stumbled inside the entry foyer and stopped. Though dizzy, she looked at the walls and found what she was looking for: the photos. Grabbing two of them, she flipped them over and unraveled the jagged mounting wire, cursing as it snagged the pearl cap on her diminishing gel ring, spilling it everywhere. Stretching the slick, shiny wire between her two hands, she waited.

The house disappeared. Cobalt was in front of her, upright, the bruises somehow enhancing the already confident appearance.

"Asantha will tear me apart when I tell her I've killed you," Cobalt said, "but it might just be worth it."

Andra wanted to leap up and entwine Cobalt with the wire, but didn't have the strength. Twice she tried, lifting herself up, groaning in pain, collapsing down again.

"Cinüe heir, my ass," Cobalt said.

The house reappeared around Andra, and this time it stayed. Cobalt's high heels clunked against the wooden steps as she approached, entered the foyer, then stopped in her tracks.

Andra wasn't there.

The split-second strobe lasted just long enough for Andra to reach out from a shadow and wrap the picture wire around Cobalt's left wrist. Cobalt spun with a furious yell, the tiny hairs on her arms transforming into spark-showering barbs. Andra matched her twist and yanked the wire taut, ignoring the fiery sparks as she inched the woman's two wrists closer, hoping to bind them.

Cobalt's eyelashes became tiny spines and serrated, exterior teeth appeared around her lips. She grabbed onto the wire and thrashed violently, tossing Andra side-to-side with enough force to make the slick wire slice into both of their palms. Their clothes caught fire from the sparks, but Andra managed to snake more wire around Cobalt's other wrist.

One final twist and a strong kick to the stomach finished the job. Cobalt was on the floor, her wrists tied behind her back.

Andra dropped and rolled, snuffing the tiny flames. Cobalt's were already out. The woman stopped thrashing, sparks and spines fading, her controlled attitude regained.

"Does this make you feel strong?" Cobalt said, vindictive. "Do you really think you've accomplished anything significant here?"

Andra took a breath, then nudged the pearl flip-cap on her ring and coated her finger with a dollop of glittering gel. "I'll accomplish something the moment I apply this to your palm," she said.

Cobalt's eyes reacted as if the diminishing gel were poison. She bit her lower lip. "That's what you thought when Asantha Cooray manipulated you into diminishing her... into completing the Maybe Objective," she said. "Haven't you learned your lesson?"

The words stung far more than the cuts and burns.

"Maybe you're the one being manipulated this time," Andra said. "All of this could be Asantha Cooray's way of making sure your god-human baby gets diminished. What if we're both her pawns?"

Cobalt's lack of reaction seemed a reaction in itself, as if she was trying too hard to not concede a valid idea. Her eyes flicked away, if only briefly, but long enough to convey concern for Andra's point.

"That's why you shouldn't do it," Cobalt said, her voice suddenly weak.

"Probably not," Andra said, waggling her finger, flashing the gel. "But I've seen what you were with, down in that pit. If ever there was a pregnancy to diminish, it's yours."

"We won't get to that point," Cobalt said, "because if that happens I won't take you to the only person who can free the souls you need. Three captive souls, right? An easy exchange for my palm remaining clean."

Andra eyed her, impressed that that she'd locked onto the very deal Andra was planning to offer before administering the gel.

"Why would I trust you?" she said.

Cobalt issued her velvet smile.

"Because I'm not the one making the deal."

The house vanished, replaced with endless nothing: no color, no light, no dark, no sound. Andra gagged, and coughed, her lungs filling with warm, gooey, oily liquid.

Oh no.

No!

Horrified, she felt the liquid tightening around her, the same sensation she had experienced in the pit beneath Uluru. She squirmed, trying to remain calm but failing as her lungs struggled to retain their remaining air. Cobalt was still with her, enduring the same misery, her wrists still bound. Beyond Cobalt, though, Andra saw translucent shapes, coiled and sponge-like outlines she had seen before: a whale-sized brain with muscle, bone, and other parts. That, and the liquid, told her exactly who Cobalt had taken her to see.

Asantha Cooray.

TWENTY-ONE

Designs

Andra coughed carbon dioxide, instinctively inhaled, and felt another gulp of Asantha Cooray's thick, stale liquid pour into her mouth. It glided past her throat, hitting her lungs with a clogging, burning sensation. She tasted castor oil and felt as if her chest was on fire as she inhaled more of the liquid. Her body thrashed, her eyes bulged.

She drowned.

Only she didn't lose consciousness, didn't lose the agony. Somehow her body breathed the horrific liquid and she remained aware, seeing things beyond anything her typical sight allowed. As she spasmed, then stiffened, she felt her mind broaden. Suddenly she was everywhere, and nowhere, all at once.

Asantha Cooray is the one holding Cera's consciousness? She's the one who is higher up the cosmic food chain than... than God? It didn't seem possible.

"This deal is the best way?" she heard.

Asantha Cooray's voice boomed just as it had the last time Andra had joined her: a gritty, empty voice, the vocalized form of the clearness. Andra was about to answer when Cobalt spoke up, and she realized Asantha hadn't been talking to her.

"The best under the terms you've given me," Cobalt said. "But the Barger child is still an issue."

Andra felt a surge of impatience from within and without.

"No, the child would have been an issue in any other era," Asantha Cooray said. "But once Andra applied the gel to my palm and you became the first to succeed in the pit, everything finally lined up. That makes her infant a footnote. Myself, and your child, we are now the only priority."

Cobalt shrugged. "Then yes... this deal works best."

Andra felt the liquid tighten around her, more than before. The idea that Asantha Cooray had spent millions of years like this, manipulating, persisting, all to further some mysterious 'Maybe Objective'... it was difficult to wrap her head around.

"Fine—I'll free the three souls," Asantha Cooray said. "In exchange, Andra agrees not to diminish this unborn child and her death sentence for diminishing Cinüe is commuted."

There was a pause, then a strange gurgling-breath sound.

"And Ms. Barger," Asantha Cooray added. "You'll keep your baby out of our way. Now, and always."

Andra was pretty sure the words were spoken as an order, separate from the agreement, but before she could say anything three glowing specks the size of gnats appeared from the clear gel and shot into her palm.

"Release them when you return," Asantha Cooray said. "They will find their own way from there."

One of these specks is Cera's consciousness?

She marveled at how tiny they were compared to the vastness around them, wondering how to tell them apart, but the only questions she managed had nothing to do with them.

"Why is this woman's unborn child so important to you?" she called, somehow speaking loud and clear even though her broadened form had no throat, mouth, chest, or head. "What's the connection between your diminished baby and the devil-human that Cobalt's carrying?"

Andra felt wind, which didn't seem possible, not in this place. Had Asantha Cooray just sighed? Was she feeling the exasperation of a timeless being?

"As always, you are but a pup in an elderly universe," Asantha Cooray said. "Never once wondering how diminishing gel works... never once considering it might not be the gel I needed from you, but the swipe and the gel combined."

Andra didn't see the significance. "I remember you saying you needed me because I'm the only human diminisher. But that doesn't—"

"Your uniqueness comes from cells and soul, not your humanity."

"Aren't they... one and the same?"

Andra felt more wind, but different this time; amusement rather than exasperation, perhaps. *Asantha Cooray thinks I said something funny?*

"Only half of them are one and the same. Your humanity, that half comes from your mother and father. The rest of you... the part that the diminishing gel so nicely pulled forth from your skin cells and applied to me during your swipe... is not you whatsoever."

What? There's a part of me that's not me? Andra felt the universe bend, as if her shock had issued ripples through the cosmos.

"What is it then?" she said, hesitant, uncertain she wanted the answer but knowing she needed to hear it.

Asantha Cooray's translucent outlines, especially the whale-sized brain, grew closer, tighter.

"What else *could* it be?" the gritty, empty voice boomed from the clearness. "It's me."

Stunned, Andra replayed the response in her mind, convinced she must have misunderstood. "What does that even mean?" she said.

A third wind puff roiled the cosmos.

"It means you've served your purpose," Asantha Cooray said. "The women of your family carry my essence; reinfusion every other generation maintains me. You are who you are because of me, I persist because of you. For others, human and Cinüe alike, the gel diminishes. For me it replenishes, pulling cell genetics from your palm, transferring them, securing my continued existence. Your grandmother, her grandmother, and every other generation in turn; dozens upon dozens of women, carefully harvested to secure my longevity."

Her translucent form grew larger, the edges thickening, as she spoke.

"I... I would have heard about this before if that were true," Andra said, her voice shaking. "My mother would have told me... or my grandmother. My brother, even."

Asantha Cooray sounded an amused chord. "Of course they would have, if not for certain... safeguards."

Andra felt her gut sink. *Is my entire family truly this captive? Don't we have any self-determination whatsoever?*

"Everything is preplanned, pup," Asantha Cooray continued. "It's why I keep the males who come in contact with the women in your family close at hand—as I've done with your mailman. It's why your family's relationships with those males don't last. And of course, it's why you and the other women in your family don't *want* them to last."

Andra's mind reeled, swirling the universe. Was Asantha Cooray suggesting the reason she loved Wade but didn't want to marry him was due to inherent genetic design? Was she saying that was the same reason she didn't know her father or grandfather? Was she implying that they were all murdered... and that Wade was therefore doomed to the same outcome?

"Not everything's preplanned," she stammered, desperate for any retort she could cling to, any means to demonstrate she still held some semblance of control. "Cera... you didn't preplan *her*. You didn't know about Wade and I. No one knew."

She expected a whoosh, a surge, some sort of angered reaction. Instead, there was only indifference.

"Orchestrating event-level procreation is beyond you," Asantha Cooray said. "You and the mailman have produced someone special, but what the Maybe Objective will now produce... that will be divine."

Cobalt's silhouette suddenly loomed next to Asantha Cooray, a victorious gleam beaming forth from where the woman's eyes should have been. "My baby and the refreshed Asantha Cooray... they'll join, and once they do they'll have enough combined strength to free Edenshire," she said, her tone vindictive. "Centuries of diminishing, all of the effort to sustain Asantha Cooray by storing her genetics in your family's women... it's all about to pay off."

Andra suddenly understood why Asantha Cooray had never come after her and Wade following the Diminishing Act vote, or after they had unveiled their child to the panicked council. *Because I've served my purpose. In her grand scheme, I'm no longer important.* Except she knew that wasn't entirely true. After the diminishing vote, Asantha Cooray had flat-out told her a human diminisher was unique, as was a human council proxy, and that both were necessary to achieve her goals.

"Why did you adopt my grandmother?" Andra said, staring daggers at Asantha Cooray. "Why am I a member of your family?"

The translucent outlines thickened further. "Machinations, pup," Asantha Cooray said. "Dvora's adoption enabled your diminisher training and the eventual proxy position, which basically places *me* on the council. True, you're only half me, but thanks to some changes your great grandfather made to the diminishing formula that percentage increases as generations progress. In time, I won't just guide the council, I'll *be* the council."

Which will give her both spiritual and functional control over Cinüe culture, Andra realized... an appalling thought mitigated by one realization. *She still needs me*, Andra knew. *Or rather, she still needs me to give her a diminished child.*

"But why would my great grandfather, a human, help the Cinüe cause?" she said.

Asantha Cooray hesitated before answering. "Hudson Lansky and I had certain... arrangements."

Andra had no idea what that meant but she understood the significance. "His changes to the diminisher formula required a human diminisher, rather than a Cinüe," she said, voicing her guess.

"A simple difference... and Hudson insisted upon me favoring his future family," Asantha Cooray said. "Parameters easily accomplished by using the Barger women."

Using. Andra felt whatever meaning her life still held slipping away. All she had left was Cera... and Wade, if she could overcome the designs working against them.

"This discussion is done," Asantha Cooray said, her booming voice thrusting Cobalt away, into the cosmic background. "Our deal is complete. Do keep your unusual baby away from us. If you don't, then my blue-hooded friend here will do it for you... again."

Andra didn't miss the emphasis on 'again.' *So it was Cobalt who engineered Cera's kidnapping.* She turned and saw Cobalt in the distance, looking at her with that confident, velvet smile, and knew that despite giving up the freed souls she felt the arrangement had very much gone in her favor. But why? If Cobalt hadn't kidnapped Cera, Andra never would have gone after Cobalt. None of it would have happened. Where was the victory?

In the agreement, she decided. *They wanted an agreement with me ensuring that I will not diminish Cobalt's unborn child. They must have figured that sooner or later I'd have found out about the pregnancy and come after her.*

She thought about it.

They were right.

TWENTY-TWO

Milk

Nothingness changed to a furnished room. *My grandmother's parlor*, Andra knew, but she hardly noticed. For the second time—first after the Sugar Dandruff Council vote, and now—she felt a victim of Asantha Cooray's machinations. The Maybe Objective was practically a done deal. Humanity's run as a dominant population was likely coming to an end. Rescuing three souls, including that of a god-human and her own daughter, meant nothing. Asantha Cooray had wanted protection against diminishing for Cobalt's future child, and that's exactly what she had achieved.

Andra felt herself gathering together, her atoms re-uniting. Then agony struck. Her lungs felt heavy, cemented, motionless. Her chest burned. She belched thick liquid, spewing it over herself and the room, her lungs gasping between spews, suddenly desperate for oxygen. Blood flowed, neurons re-fired.

Thirty minutes later she was breathing normally and regaining mental clarity. The parlor was a mess, not all of it her own. The green algae was no longer on the bay windows but the place had been ransacked, and she saw Mechen Klav officers stationed in the hallway. They didn't seem bothered by her sudden presence. There was no sign of Cobalt but Andra heard a familiar voice on the patio, shuffling paperwork and ordering the officers off the premises.

"David?" she said, her voice weak and her eyes squinting.

"Ah, perfect, you're back," David Stanford Swimney said, entering the hallway. "I was just informing these gentlemen that their entry into this home is a violation of Council Law, punishable by trial. Seems they had no warrant for such a search, and in fact the council did not advocate their actions. A full investigation is now underway."

She started to say something but he held up his hand.

"The law," he said, "works."

He looked so pleased that even weary, she couldn't help but feel good for him.

"What's that glowing in your hand?" he asked.

She lifted her closed fist.

"This," she said, "is a promise fulfilled."

She opened her hand and the three yellow pinpoints soared out. The first became multicolored, then zoomed away; the second dove down, disappearing into the earth. But the third swirled, glittering and vibrant.

"What's it doing?" Swimney said.

Andra had no idea.

Swimney leaned forward, scrutinizing the glowing, yellow dot. "Do you know which of the three it is?" he said.

"Yeah, I think maybe I do," she said. "Cera's consciousness was multi-colored; I could feel it. The other one headed for the depths as soon as it was free, so I think we know who that was. Which means this one... I'm pretty sure this one's the god-human. This is the consciousness of the one we needed free, most of all."

They watched the pinpoint hover, the intensity of its glow varying, pulsar-like. If there was a pattern to the pulses, Andra couldn't see it. Still, several moments later it remained, unmoving.

"Maybe it's waiting for something?" Swimney said. "Do you think we need to make an offering? Or kneel, or something like that?"

Andra smiled, seeing him cower in reverence before a thumbtack-sized speck of light.

"After what that it's been through, I'm thinking it might have something more practical in mind," she said. "Maybe it wants to—"

The dot pulsed again, so bright this time that Andra had to shut her eyes from the glare. A memory suddenly popped into her head, of picture wire, a snag, a cap flipping open, and an ensuing, gooey mess.

She tried reopening her eyes but as she did the dot brightened again. The same memory flashed, crisp and vibrant, as if this was a reminder rather than a simple, stored rehash. *But what am I supposed to...*

Andra gasped, then burst into joyous laughter, understanding the significance. The gleaming, yellow pinpoint flared to sunlight-brightness, then poofed away. Smiling ear-to-ear, Andra felt as if she might explode from delight. All she could think of was the picture wire, remembering it's slick, shiny surface... not from a protective coating, she now understood, but from the goo the wire had fallen into.

"Cobalt grabbed it," she said, ebullient. "She wrapped her hands around the damn wire!"

Swimney, gaping and baffled by everything he had just witnessed, begged her to explain but his cell started ringing before she could answer. He looked at the display.

"It's Wade," he said, passing it to her. "Might be important."

She nodded, grinning.

"It is," she said, joyous tears forming as she remembered the multicolored pinpoint. "He's calling to say Cera's back."

She walked to the refrigerator, found nearly a dozen milk bottles tucked inside, and removed the most recent.

Cera will drink the milk, she knew. *She's coming home safely, and she will, finally, drink the milk.*

ABOUT THE AUTHOR

Dan Cray sold his first story at age sixteen and won *Time* magazine's national essay contest two years later. His fiction includes two award-winning short stories and the paranormal thrillers *Piercing Maybe* and *Mother Tongue*. In nonfiction, he wrote *Soaring Stones: A Kite-Powered Approach To Building Egypt's Pyramids* and spent twenty-three years covering science for *Time*, where he reported sixty cover stories and shared a National Headliner Award. He holds a UCLA English degree and lives in Los Angeles with his wife and son.

Visit him at www.dancraybooks.com

www.ingramcontent.com/pod-product-compliance
Lightning Source LLC
Chambersburg PA
CBHW030517310726
48979CB00010B/1709/J

* 9 7 8 1 9 4 0 3 1 7 1 3 7 *